VAMPIRE HUNTER D

C1

Other Vampire Hunter D books published by
Dark Horse Books and Digital Manga Publishing

VAMPIRE HUNTER D

VOLUME 16
TYRANT'S STARS
PARTS ONE AND TWO

Written by
HIDEYUKI KIKUCHI

Illustrations by
YOSHITAKA AMANO

English translation by
KEVIN LEAHY

Dark Horse Books®   Digital Manga Publishing
Milwaukie   Los Angeles

VAMPIRE HUNTER D VOLUME 16: TYRANT'S STARS PARTS ONE AND TWO
© Hideyuki Kikuchi 2011. Originally published in Japan in 2000 by ASAHI SONORAMA Co.
English translation copyright © 2011 by Dark Horse Books and Digital Manga Publishing.

Cover art by Yoshitaka Amano
English translation by Kevin Leahy
Book design by Krystal Hennes

Published by
Dark Horse Books
A division of Dark Horse Comics, Inc.
10956 SE Main Street
Milwaukie, OR 97222
DarkHorse.com

Digital Manga Publishing
1487 West 178th Street, Suite 300
Gardena, CA 90248
DMPBooks.com

Library of Congress Cataloging-in-Publication Data

Kikuchi, Hideyuki, 1949-
[D--Bokun no hoshi. English]
Tyrant's stars. Parts one and two / written by Hideyuki Kikuchi ; illustrated by Yoshitaka Amano ; english translation by Kevin Leahy. -- 1st Dark Horse Books ed.
p. cm. -- (Vampire Hunter D ; v. 16)
"Originally published in Japan in 2000 by Asahi Sonorama, Tokyo"--T.p. verso.
ISBN 978-1-59582-572-8
I. Amano, Yoshitaka. II. Leahy, Kevin. III. Title.
PL832.I37D23513 2011
895.6'36--dc22
2010040396

First Dark Horse Books Edition: April 2011
10 9 8 7 6 5 4 3 2 1
Printed at Lake Book Manufacturing, Inc., Melrose Park, IL, U.S.A.

VAMPIRE HUNTER D

Tyrant's Stars

PART ONE

The Coming of an Evil Star

I

Eyes shut, he sat on his throne listening to the echoes of battle ringing out on the floor below. He shouldn't have been hearing these sounds. The clang of sword on sword as iron met steel, the crunch of severed flesh and bone, and then the noises that took their place—the thud of combatants hitting the floor without so much as a final cry. He could even see the sparks from when blade struck blade. All the defensive systems of his castle had been rendered ineffective and his warriors had been slain, and all that remained were the last fifteen stalwart individuals who now faced his fearsome foe in the chamber beneath him.

There was no light in his room. Naturally, there were no windows either. Though there were those who, despite having eyes that could see in complete darkness, used candles, lamps, and other sources of light just as humans did, he had forgone all of that. As a result, there was nothing in this chamber except the chair on which he sat, a table, and a coffin. He had no need of the darkness outside. So long as he remained in the room, an inky blackness equally dark and dense would surround him forever.

How long had it been since he'd decided not to leave?

A white glow shone behind his eyelids: someone's face. He heard an agonized cry. The groan that rang out was the death rattle of the fifteenth of his retainers, stabbed through the heart.

It was too early. Such speed was terrifying—amazing, even impossible. His foe was truly capable. There was a feverish aching deep in his chest. Power called to power—but though he endeavored to recall the person's name, he fared poorly. That had all been forgotten long ago, the instant he took a seat in this room. And ever since, he'd been at peace.

Inaudible footsteps were climbing the stairs. Unable to slow the racing of his heart, he opened his eyes. Dust filled his field of view, but the world soon became visible.

His foe was on the other side of the door. The dimensional vortex, phase-switching device, hypnocircuits, and other defenses that had been imprinted into the two-inch-thick door would no doubt do their deadly best to eliminate the intruder. But he got the feeling none of them would do any good. His brain could no longer form any picture from the sounds he heard. Between the door and that attacker, a breathtaking life-or-death conflict had to be taking place.

A minute passed.

There was a flash at one edge of the door—at the side where the lock was. It carved the lock right out of the door as if it were slicing through water.

The door was opening without a sound . . . and he was directly across from it. The fine crack of light grew broader, and when it'd taken on an oblong shape, he saw the shadowy figure that stood on the other side. In the intruder's right hand was the sword he'd lowered. Oddly enough, not a single drop of blood clung to its blade. He wore a wide-brimmed traveler's hat and a long black coat. The instant the Nobleman glimpsed the face below that hat, he let a gasp of surprise escape in spite of himself. He had to clear his throat with a cough before he could even speak.

"I'd heard there was a Hunter of unearthly beauty out there, but

I never thought I'd lay eyes on him myself. I am Count Braujou. And you are?"

"D."

His reply was more a concept than a name.

"That's what I'd also heard."

First his eyelids and now his lips—both had stirred up storms of swirling dust, but through it Count Braujou stared at the gorgeous embodiment of death who stood there, silent and stock still.

"I didn't think there was anyone left in the world who'd hire you to destroy me. The outside world should've long since forgotten about my manse, my servants, and me. Why, when I stepped into this room for the last time, it must've been—"

"Five thousand and one years ago," said the assassin who'd identified himself as D, supplying the answer. He spoke without a whit of murderous intent. Count Braujou couldn't help but voice his surprise.

"Hmm, has it been that long? So, is it the farmers of this region who've come to find an old fossil of a Noble like me an obstruction? I don't suppose a Hunter like yourself is too free with information, but if you could, I'd like you to tell me who sent you."

"It was the Capital," D said.

"The Capital? But these are the southernmost reaches of the southern Frontier—not the kind of place likely to draw the least bit of attention from the Capital."

"For human beings, five millennia is time enough for a great many things to change," said D. "The Capital has set about actively developing the Frontier regions. On the surface, it appears that they're out to eliminate the abhorrent influence of the Nobility who remain on the Frontier—and give the farmers some peace of mind— but their actual aim is the things hidden in places like this."

The count smiled thinly.

"The wisdom and treasures of the Nobility? So, the lowly humans would pick through the dregs of those they called monsters? I can see where a fossil like me might be a hindrance."

He made a bow to D where he stood by the door.

"Thank you for sharing this with me. I greatly appreciate it. And to show my gratitude, I shall shake off five millennia of rust and battle you with all my heart and soul."

Putting his hands on the armrests, the count slowly rose to his feet. From head to foot he was shrouded in gray detritus—dust that had collected on him over the span of five thousand years. Since taking his place in his chair, he hadn't moved a single step. The dust actually felt rather nice as it slid off his skin.

Putting his hands on his hips, the count stretched. Not only from his waist, but also from his spine and shoulder blades, there were snaps and pops. Warming himself up, he swung his arms from side to side, bending and stretching them.

"It seems I'm not as rusty as I thought. I suppose this place will serve."

Looking around, he found the entire chamber filled with gray ash. The eddying dust constantly filled his field of view.

All this time, D watched him silently. You might say it was an incredible folly on his part. Who in their right mind would give a motionless Noble the chance to move again?

The count reached for the spear that was leaning against his chair. Once he'd grabbed it and given it a single swing, the dust fell from it, and his imposing black weapon was awakened from five thousand years of sleep. Twenty feet long, the great spear had a tip that ran a third of that length, and although it seemed like it would be a highly impractical toy or decoration, such would be the case only if this weapon were in the hands of an ordinary person. Having risen from his throne, the Nobleman stood exactly ten feet tall—it was over six and a half feet from the floor to the seat of his chair. Yet the way he pointed his weapon at D's chest without another test swing or any rousing battle cry seemed terribly naive, and the count was entirely devoid of killing lust. Just like D.

"Most kind of you to wait. Have at you!" he said, and then the entire situation changed.

D's body warped as if he were behind a heat shimmer—the murderous intent radiating from the tip of the Nobleman's spear was transforming the air. A normal adversary would've fainted dead away just by seeing it directed at him.

In response, D slowly raised his longsword.

Just then, the count said, "My word—who knew that D was such a man?" This time his voice shook with infinite terror as the words spilled from the corner of his mouth. But whatever he'd felt, it would never be made known.

D kicked off the floor. Only those Nobles who'd fallen to his blade knew how amazing and horrifying it was to have it come down at their heads. A millisecond opening—and then a glittering waterwheel spun beneath that shooting star and the trail it left behind. Was it sparks that were sent flying, or the blade?

With the most mellifluous of sounds, D's sword bounced back, and the hem of his black garb spread like the wings of some mystic bird as he made a great bound to the left. As the Hunter landed, so gently he didn't stir up even a mote of dust, the head of the spinning spear whistled toward his feet. The figure in black narrowly evaded it with a leap, but the shaft of the weapon buzzed at his torso from an impossible angle, only to meet his sword with a thud.

The swipe D made with his blade in midair was fearsome; a heartbeat later, the spear's apparently steel shaft had been severed a foot and a half from the end and was sailing through the air. D's left hand rose, and a black glint screamed through the air to pierce the base of the giant's throat with unerring accuracy.

Though he staggered for an instant without making a sound, Count Braujou swiftly grabbed the murderous implement with his left hand and tossed it away, groaning, "What have we here?"

It was the severed end of the spear. Lopping it off, D had caught it with his left hand and hurled it like a throwing knife. And that was why he'd sliced it off at an angle.

However, even as black blood gushed from the wound, the giant wasn't the least bit rattled as he stood with his long spear at the ready.

D was equally composed. The right ankle of his boot was split diagonally, with fresh blood seeping out, showing that the count's attack earlier hadn't been without effect. Yet the Hunter remained perfectly still with his sword held straight at eye level, like an exquisite ice sculpture standing in the inky blackness.

The darkness solidified. The temperature in the room was rapidly falling, thanks to the killing lust that billowed at D from the giant.

What would D do to counter it?

The young man in black simply stood there. In fact, the killing lust disappeared as soon as it touched him—it was unclear whether he absorbed it or deflected it. However, his form distorted mysteriously, and from it there was just one flash—his blade alone remaining immutable, poised to take action against the fearsome spearman.

There was no point in asking which of them moved. Harsh sparks were scattered in a chamber lacquered over with five millennia of pitch blackness.

But before this fleeting light vanished in the air, a voice told the Hunter, "Wait. The life I abandoned five millennia ago isn't dear to me. I have remained here like the dead for just such a moment as this. D—we will settle this. But may I ask that before I fulfill this promise to you, you allow me to fulfill an earlier pledge?"

The murderous intent had already evaporated, and the two figures—one with sword extended, the other with long spear sweeping to one side—looked as if they had dissolved into one.

"A star just shot by," D said.

His head only came up to the solar plexus of the giant. But from a room with no windows, his eyes had apparently glimpsed something in space.

"Is that the reason?" the giant said. "Valcua has returned."

There was a faraway sound to his voice, and a distant look in his eyes. The eyes gave off a red glow.

"And he's bound to see to it that those who drove him into space are charred to the bone. He'll be merciless with their innocent descendants.

But I must prevent him from doing so. You see, it's in keeping with a pledge I made in days long past to one of their ancestors."

The tangled silhouettes separated. At the very moment the count lowered his long spear, there was the click of hilt against scabbard by D's shoulder. His blade had been sheathed. Turning a defenseless back to his foe, D walked toward the door.

"You have my thanks," the count said, although it was unclear if his words reached the Hunter. "The last time I raise my spear, it shall be against you."

As D exited the darkened chamber, his left hand rose casually, and from it a hoarse voice said, "I really have to hand it to you this time. You saw it. I did, too. Yep, we saw the same thing he did. A wicked star fell in the northern reaches. I can still see the long long tail that streamed behind it. Oh—here it comes! An impact only we'd sense. But it's neither its death nor the end. Five . . ."

D kept walking. Not pausing for even a second, he began to descend the staircase.

"Four . . ."

In the midst of the darkness, the giant heaved a long sigh.

"Three . . ."

In one tiny village in a western Frontier sector, a family of three awoke.

"Two . . ."

D halted in the middle of the staircase.

"One . . ."

The star was swallowed by a land of great forests and tundra.

"Zero."

It was quiet. A silence gripped the world as if time itself had stopped.

Then, when the hoarse voice finally told him, "There it goes," the gorgeous young man in black who'd been like a sculpture of death finally began walking again.

"Half a northern Frontier sector has been laid to waste!" the hoarse voice continued.

The Hunter's eyes as well might have beheld that vision of death.

II

It was two days later that the survey party from the Northern Frontier Administration Bureau set out for the area where the meteorite had landed.

"This is just . . ." The young geologist was going to say horrible, but the spectacle before his eyes had finally robbed him of his speech.

It was a sight that no one could ignore. The roar that assailed their ears was that of a muddy torrent that snaked by in a thick ocher flow just a few yards from where the men had frozen on their mounts. And there wasn't just muddy water. Titanic trees floated by—the places where they'd snapped in two showing plain as day—and the dull thuds that rang out from time to time were the sound of these countless boles banging into one another. As if tethered to the trees, the remains of enormous armored beasts and other unidentifiable monsters also flowed past—as did human corpses.

"The ice on the tundra's melted."

"It'll still take two days to reach where it came down. And yet here we are, running into a river like this? The damn thing's gotta be dozens of yards across!"

Another of them pulled out a map and a photo and compared them to the scene before them. The river was easily in excess of five hundred yards wide, and while the spray from the water didn't create it, a fog hung over the opposite shore that kept them from making out anything on that side. There wasn't any trace of the great stands of trees depicted on their map. For that matter, it didn't show this river, either.

"There's bound to be more of this. I say screw it!"

"Shut up, Dan. Back in the Capital, folks are sitting on pins and needles waiting for word from us, you know. I don't care if it's a river or the sea; if it's in our way, we're crossing it. Start getting ready for a fording right away."

Nearly twenty men dismounted in unison and began to take their gear down off their horses' backs.

"We're all set with the ropes!" someone shouted twenty or thirty minutes later. Another twenty minutes after that, explosions rang out overhead.

Rocket launchers shot ropes to the unseen opposite shore, and special metal-alloy drill tips on the ends of the ropes bore down dozens of yards into the earth to secure them. When the current was strong, there was no other way to cross with their horses except to hold onto these ropes.

Resigned to their pitiful lot, the group members looked up to the sky as one.

"What in the world's that?"

"Choppers, I think."

"Whose?"

These shouted remarks had been drawn by five aircraft flying purposefully across the cloudy, ash-gray sky.

"I don't think any of the villages around here own anything like that—which can only mean . . ."

The rest of that sentence had already formed in the heart of every man present.

"They're bandits!"

"Those bastards—they're fucking ghouls! They'll loot the place dry!" another man cursed, the words rising with the sound of his teeth grinding.

But this statement became a cry of astonishment.

All five helicopters had been thrown off course simultaneously and dropped behind that silky veil that wasn't quite spray or mist. Rotor struck rotor, throwing free chunks that impacted on still other aircraft—and no sooner had this happened than the sky was filled with fiery lotus blossoms. Black smoke spread in the air and flames consumed hundreds of pieces of debris as all the crimson blooms scattered their petals. Once they'd vanished into the depths of the fog, only the smoke snaked into the sky, and then that too disappeared.

"What the hell happened?"

"Turbulence?"

"The wind ain't blowing all that hard—the meteorite's gotta be to blame. A cursed star is what it is!"

"Damn! If we get too close, we're liable to drown. We'd do well to turn back, boss."

"Shut your pie hole, Josh. You're gonna be the first to go across."

"Shit. I wish I'd kept quiet."

Ultimately it took half the day for the whole group to cross the stream, dodging oncoming trees and corpses floating in the current. Not only was it more than five hundred yards wide, but they had to get their horses and baggage across, too. The dense fog hid any scenery more than three feet away behind endless white, so the leader ordered the men to form a circle and to be sure to keep tabs on the people to either side of them.

"The ground's mush."

"Yeah. And it's warm."

"You think maybe there was a volcano or something in the area?"

"Nope. That wasn't it. It's still warm on account of the friction when the meteorite struck."

"You've gotta be kidding me! That was two days ago. This should've long since cooled."

"Which tells us something—the meteorite itself is still boiling hot. Just look. We're still two days' journey from where it fell, yet every last tree's been uprooted. The ice hereabouts runs a foot thick, but it's been turned into this river and the fog. Every village we've passed up till now was knocked flat by a quake or swallowed by cracks in the earth. Hills crumbled, swamps boiled away, and there's not a bird or a beast to be seen. I don't care how big a meteorite we're talking about. There's no way it could do all this. On top of that, the communiqué from the Capital said astronomers watching the shooting star reported that it was just a little deal, less than eight inches in diameter. There's no way in hell it could've caused a disaster of this proportion."

"Why didn't you say anything about that before, boss?" several men asked.

Their leader replied impassively, "Oh, that's simple. Because if I'd let that slip, there's not a man among you who would've come along!"

"Well, you're right about that, but still—"

Just then, the old huntsman who'd been by the campfire with his eyes shut tight put his finger to his lips and shushed them.

"What is it, Pops?" the leader asked.

"Something's coming from the north. And it's headed this way at a hell of a speed," he said.

"What is it?"

"I don't know. Hey, put that fire out. Everyone, don't make a sound, now."

The whole group grew tense. Aside from the old huntsman, they were all farmers who'd just signed on for the per diem and the reputation that came from having taken part in a survey party. But farmers were only used to dealing with the sort of supernatural creatures and monsters that ravaged their fields. Scattering an extinguishing powder on their campfire, they grabbed their respective weapons and took cover behind their baggage—all without a single extraneous action.

A minute passed. After another thirty seconds, red points of light appeared in the depths of the fog.

"Here they come," the old huntsman said, cocking the old-fashioned rifle he carried.

The points of light swiftly grew from the size of a fingertip to that of a fist, and by this time the things had become visible as black silhouettes in the fog. From the bottom of cylinders about six and a half feet tall, a number of thin pipes wriggled like tentacles. A red point of light glowed from a spot about halfway up each cylinder. There were more than a dozen of these things.

The leader looked at the huntsman. When it came to combat, he was a veteran.

The old huntsman ignored him. His instincts had been triggered by the approaching foe. The same instincts that time and again had pulled him back from the jaws of death into the land of the living told him not to mess with this. They weren't telling him to run—just not to mess with it.

But before the huntsman could take any action, hostilities were declared.

"Draw them in before you open fire," the leader ordered his group.

The silhouettes glided closer. They'd heard him.

"Fire!"

The shout was followed by ear-shattering reports, while the old huntsman leaned his rifle up against his pack and grabbed the right lapel of his fire-beast vest. Telling himself to calm down, the old man focused his attention on his own fingertip, which soon found something hard and thin.

Up ahead, screams split the night air. A tentacle had just snared one member of the party. Legs thrashing, he was hoisted up overhead. Along the way, he raised his rifle and fired. There was the sound of something hard being struck, and his slug changed direction.

The cylinders were now plainly visible. Entirely silver, they were supported by two of the tentacles, which seemed to be tied to them by iron rings. The other six tentacles were apparently meant for combat, and they seized another member of the party who'd taken cover under his baggage by the ankle and effortlessly pulled him out again.

Screams rang out here and there. The crack of rifles followed, and soon there was silence.

The men hadn't abandoned resistance voluntarily. As they were struggling in midair, a tentacle had been put against the back of each man's head, and from the end of it a slim needle had penetrated the skull. Although it didn't look as if the needles had pierced very deeply, this attack had a horrifying effect on the party members. There was a slight pain in their heads—as if something were flowing out from them to nowhere in particular. And that was the last thing the men felt before they lost consciousness—and their lives. By the time their limp bodies were thrown to the ground, they'd already stopped breathing.

Scanning wildly all the while, the cylinders passed over the dead, and then they finally spotted the old huntsman crouched down behind his baggage. A tentacle stretched from one of the approaching cylinders and touched the base of his neck. It soon came away again, and as if they'd lost all interest, the cylinders disappeared without another moment's hesitation into the mist from which they'd come—into the depths of the steam.

After the tentacles, which acted as sensors, had registered whether the person they came into contact with was living or dead, a long, needlelike suction device drew out what was essentially the core of his life force. A human's life force flowed through his body from the chakra. As an individual reached higher mental and physical levels, the chakra shifted to a loftier position in the back of the head, linking human beings to the power of the universe. This is why when people had ascended to an existence that was more than human, they'd been depicted in ancient artwork as saints with glowing halos behind their heads. This was undoubtedly the reason the cylinders chose to extract the life force from the back of the head.

The shore lay under the stillness of death. While the sound of the river hadn't died out, it still felt that way. This was probably due to the blanket of pitiful corpses. When an hour had passed since the butchers had left, there was movement in this dead world. It came at the moment when dawn tinged the eastern sky blue, its light spreading across the cruel ground like faint wings. It was the corpse of the old huntsman. His body had been like a mummy's, with its pulse stopped, brain waves gone, and every trace of vitality missing; but now it was returning to life. The blood pumped fiercely through his body, his heart beat strongly, and he opened his eyes. Then, closing his eyes for a few seconds to reflect back on what had happened an hour ago, he—strangely enough—reached for the very same spot on the back of his head where the cylinders had drained the life from his compatriots and pulled out a long thin needle. A foot in length, the needle was stark-white beast bone—and he'd learned where to jab it from his father, who in turn had learned the trick from his grandfather.

If you're in the forest or out on the tundra and can't move, and you don't think you've got enough food to last till help comes, press here. When you do, you'll become a corpse. Aside from the very smallest of arteries, which will carry blood to your brain to keep it from dying, you'll be a dead body in all other respects. And no one will be able to detect that pulse. Depending on how you push the needle in, you can make it last a half hour or an hour, a year, or even a decade if you like.

His father had told him he'd survive all that time without anything to eat or drink, and that he had to make sure there were no wild beasts around before using the needle on the appropriate spot.

Your grandfather's grandfather said that a long, long time ago, these things with bodies like cylinders and snaking tentacles appeared and started killing folks like crazy. Our ancestor was the only one to survive because at the time he happened to be doing these experiments with needles.

The old huntsman mouthed something softly: words of thanks to his father and his ancestors.

Looking out across the gruesome tableau, he muttered, "I'm gonna have to get these boys buried."

And with that he reached for the rifle leaning up against his pack. Once it was back in his hands, he was transformed into a professional on the hunt. By the time the stock came to rest against his shoulder, he already had the hammer cocked. The two-pound rifle meant for killing armored fire dragons was trained unwaveringly on the muddy flow; the huntsman's ears had detected a change in the water's roar.

III

The old huntsman's eye caught an arm reaching for shore from the filthy torrent. Appearing to struggle against being washed downstream, a second arm appeared, and a moment later the whole body popped up. While it couldn't exactly be described as effortless, the figure managed to collapse on land after being pushed just a foot or two further by the water.

The old huntsman called out to the wheezing form, "That you, boss?"

The mud-covered figure jumped up, but his tension passed as soon as he saw the old man.

"Pops!" he said, letting out a deep breath. "I'm glad you made it. The fact that those damned things didn't go into the water saved my skin. I suppose everyone else . . ."

The old huntsman nodded. "They all bought it. You're lucky to be alive—oh, but you're a veteran fish trapper, aren't you?"

Though the leader tried to smile, he couldn't.

For generations, his family had made a living hunting the fish that lived in the ponds and lakes near his village. Up to ten feet long, these fish were voracious carnivores, but there wasn't one of them that the leader's family couldn't land with ease. The leader was better than anyone at this sort of hunting because of the way he'd been raised—he could stop his breathing and remain underwater for more than an hour.

"When they grabbed Roscoe, I jumped into the water. I clung to some weeds—damn, I must've been scared, because I couldn't come out for over an hour. Anyway, I'm glad you survived, too. From here on out, having someone else along should be more reassuring than going it alone."

"You don't mean to tell me you intend to keep going?" the old huntsman said, his eyes growing wide. "Those things will be up ahead. Probably worse stuff, too."

As he got his breathing under control, the leader lay flat on his back on the ground again.

"I can't help it. See, that's the job. Back in the village, everyone's scared stiff, waiting for our return. I can't very well be the only one to come moping back. For starters, it'd mean all the rest of these guys died for nothing."

At this point, he finally realized something.

"Oh, I can't force you to go along with me, Pops. You're lucky to have survived. You don't just turn around and throw all that away. I'll continue on alone from here on out—Godspeed to you."

"At any rate, let's get everyone buried," the old man said, gazing at where light hung in the eastern sky. "Then we'll set out. Get as far inland as we can while we've got daylight. I'll go along with you."

After burying eight corpses and taking a short rest, they embarked at just past noon. But before they'd walked an hour, the pair found their surroundings had begun to take on a weirder aspect. With the gradual thinning of the fog they could see quite far into the distance, but all that greeted their eyes was a wasteland. Perhaps it would've been better to call it desolation. Black soil spread as far as the eye could see. There was no sign of any living creatures, and the pair was surrounded by such a vast expanse that the glowing red lights of those cylindrical things would've almost been a welcome sight. With provisions and weapons on their backs, the two men sank ankle deep into the miry ground, and steam hid the blue vault of the heavens—although it also occasionally filled the pair's field of view with rainbows, as if to atone for its sins.

Two hours passed, and then two became four. Just as they were about to enter their fifth hour, there was a change in their surroundings. The boots they pulled up out of the mud met the one thing the pair presently desired more than anything—solid ground.

"Huh?"

After glancing down at their feet, the pair looked across the earth stretching into the distance. It could've been described as a silvery land.

"What the hell is this?" the leader asked, sounding unnerved.

Here was a man who'd been chosen to lead a survey party in exploring the unknown, and he burned with such a sense of duty that he still pressed forward even after watching most of his men get killed. He certainly wasn't a coward. But his voice was quaking.

"Damned if I know," the huntsman said, shaking his head. "I don't know what it is, but it's sure as hell gonna be like this all the way to where that meteorite fell. We've gone and stepped into a whole other world."

"What kind of other world are we talking about here?"

"Good question."

"You mean like the world of the Nobility?"

"Probably."

Something about the huntsman's tone bothered the leader.

"Is it or isn't it? Spell it out for me, man!"

"It's just a hunch."

"Oh."

Halting, the old huntsman adjusted the pack strapped to his back. He soon started walking again.

"Nobles are Nobles—but this is some different kind of Noble, or so I think," the old man said.

"Different? You mean to tell me there are other kinds of Nobility?"

"I don't know. That's why I said it's just a hunch."

"Well, I trust your hunch," the leader said, looking all around with a chilled expression.

There was nothing but fog and silvery terrain. No hills, no trees, no tundra locked away under eternal ice. Even after twilight fell, the pair continued walking in the darkness—they were afraid to stop. From time to time the leader pulled out his map and survey records and checked their position, but he did so while they were still on the move. The further they advanced, the more a terror and despair that had nothing to do with their exhaustion spread through their hearts, heavy and dark.

We'll never make it back. We're gonna die out here.

Despite this, however, both pairs of eyes gleamed with a resolute determination to fight. Even if they were going to die, they had to see what lay out there. And without fail, they'd get word of what they discovered to those who waited.

In the middle of the night, they took a rest. The leader had collapsed. When he awoke, it was past noon. The fog and the featureless silver land stretched on forever. For quite some time, both men had held in their hearts a certain conviction: This land is man made. But who could've made something so incredible? Who'd packed it away in an eight-inch meteorite?

After having something to eat, they started walking again. And the old huntsman ended up telling a story about a giant he'd seen in the western Frontier sectors when he was young.

"You know, Pops, you're a good-enough shot to hit an angel worm from a mile away. You've got nerve enough to take on a Sanki dragon with no more than a machete, so no one can fault you there. You shouldn't be rotting away on some lousy little mountain bagging birds and beasts to sell their meat when you could go to the Capital and find a better job. So, why don't you?" the leader asked, and that's how the tale began.

"It was quite a ways back," the old man said, starting the story.

Like so many other young men with boundless confidence in their own strength, he'd wandered through various parts of the Frontier looking for an opportunity to make a name for himself. At the time, he heard about a legendary creature that would eat every beast on a mountain in a year's time and then move onto the next mountain to sate its appetite. That sparked a desire for honor and combat which burned like a flame in the young huntsman. When he headed up the same kind of mountain where he lived even now with no more than his trusty rifle, it wasn't out of rashness at all. Rather, it was merely a manifestation of his youthful fervor. For a whole month he moved among the colossal boles and weirdly shaped rock as if he were the lord of the mountain, but he'd abandoned the search and was on his way back down when he was swallowed by a thick fog. As soon as he decided to bivouac there, the fog grew even denser, and it showed no sign of clearing any time soon. Not even the wind blew.

On his third night camping there, the situation suddenly took a stranger turn. From the swirling white depths of the fog, a gigantic figure appeared, accompanied by a great rumbling in the earth.

"When I was a wee young'un, I'd seen the same thing in a picture book all about the Nobility. It was a giant beast that combined machinery with an artificial life form. More than a dozen feet high it stood, wearing rusty old armor and a helm, and carrying an iron club with its hairy arms. As for its face, I suppose you could say it looked like a crazy person. Its eyes were vacant, and drool ran down from the corner of its mouth like a waterfall. Black drool, at that. Even now I can still recall how it reeked of oil. There was just one thing that bothered me then, and still bothers me now. According to that picture book, that type of creature had supposedly been dubbed a failure, and they were freed from computer control and destroyed by the Nobility more than five thousand years ago."

The beast had headed straight toward the huntsman. Pure luck was the only way to describe the way the man managed to dodge the iron club the thing swung down at him—but the way he got off a shot with his rifle as he was rolling around on the ground was the work of a born sure shot. His bullet hit the giant beast right in the middle of the face, and the creature's upper body jerked back.

"Well, I thought I'd hit it dead bang. And that was the way it looked, too. But the thing didn't fall. It didn't even drop to one knee; it just spat up a wad of blood, which landed at my feet. But what I'd thought was a wad of blood turned out to be a bloodstained slug and one of that thing's fangs. Why, that freak . . ."

Seven hundred and fifty miles per hour—his bullet had flown nearly at the speed of sound, and the thing had stopped it with its fangs, giving a whole new meaning to the expression "biting the bullet."

The huntsman was so stunned that he didn't get another shot off until the creature charged him. Made in desperation, his second shot hit its chest protector and ricocheted off, while his third streaked through empty space, for the giant had unexpectedly leaped to one side.

In the fog to his right there was a great forest. From it echoed the sounds of enormous trees being snapped or uprooted by something that was approaching with tremendous speed. The giant beast only had time to loose a single howl of insanity. Because what bounded from the fog was a figure every bit as titanic as itself.

"His coat and cape were in tatters—but I could tell at a glance they'd both been crafted from the finest materials. I swear, I'll never understand why Nobles would ever use anything as flimsy as all that when they could've made the same thing from indestructible metal fibers."

The giant's weapon was a long spear. Carved with intricate designs, it was well over fifteen feet long, and the keenness of the point that ran almost half its length was just as imposing as his foe's iron club.

The giant beast struck first. Though the Nobility had created this creature for combat, those same Nobles had decided that the control DNA in this type alone hadn't functioned properly. The iron club it brought down appeared just as fast as the huntsman's bullets. But it rebounded, and then the giant beast, leaning forward from the attack, was knocked away. As it lurched, a gleam of light streaked at its neck.

After deflecting the club with its shaft, the long spear had turned around to cut through the opponent's neck; and then, in the giant's black-gloved hands, it spun in another great arc before halting.

"I watched the whole thing there from behind a tree, out of sight. Right off the bat, I knew it had to be a giant straight out of the legends. Dangling from the shoulders of that red cape of his were the corpses of greater elk and twin-headed bears. Maybe he didn't notice me—more likely he did and just didn't care. Toting the body of the giant beast like it was nothing, he headed back into the same fog he came from. I didn't go after him. Hell, I was scared. It had to be a Noble. But what kind of Noble can walk around free as you please in the light of the sun? The mere thought of what he really was makes my hair stand on end."

And yet, about five minutes after the sound of the giant's footfalls had faded completely, he chambered a new round in his rifle and went after the enormous figure. And then, high above the ground where the giant's footprints remained so clearly, he saw an enormous head glaring down at him. The instant he realized it was the severed head of the giant beast, he turned around without a word and climbed down the mountain that very day.

Fiendish Opening Moves

CHAPTER 2

I

"After that, I headed straight back to my hometown and holed up in the old mountain I'd known since childhood. Seeing that thing, I never wanted to wander around any other mountains ever again. As a huntsman, it scared me to death. Years later, when I heard that the skeletons of giants who'd lived thousands of years ago had been found on that same mountain and that they'd looked so fresh the villagers had been spooked enough to blow the whole cave up, I was beyond caring. If it was that gigantic beast, maybe I'd actually been wandering around that mountain thousands of years in the past that day, but that didn't matter either. See, by the time I'd got back home, I was an old man in a young man's body. And there's the answer to your question."

The party leader had listened intently to the tale, and he'd only gone about ten paces after this last confession before he asked, "If you're such a coward, why'd you want to sign on with this survey party?"

"Hell, I wanted to give it one last try. I figured maybe those cracks had closed up. Once you get old, you're not afraid of so many things anymore," the old man laughed softly.

Waiting until that laughter had faded, the leader said, "I guess I should tell you my story, too."

†

This was a good thirty years ago, when I was fifteen. As you know, my whole family's got diving in their blood. According to my great-grandfather, one of my ancestors got a water sprite to teach him how to breathe underwater, but I don't know about that. In our family, when you turn fifteen, you have to head off on your own and hone your skills at catching fish. My father did it, and so did my brothers, though two of my three brothers never came back.

I went to a cluster of lakes in the western part of the northern Frontier. There are nearly two hundred lakes and swamps there, and various legends hang over them like a miasma. Stories like how every year, on a certain day of a certain month, there's an enormous mouth that appears in the center of the lake and drinks it dry. Or how if you go out into a particular swamp in a boat on a moonlit night, you can look down into the water and see all the villagers who died there pouring each other drinks. Or the tale about how if the water gets even a little bit polluted, from that day forward, the houses by the shore will be pushed into the lake one by one by a water phantom. They're all little more than tall tales and silly legends.

The only one I believed came from the swampy region to the southeast—a little lake covering less than four square miles. In spite of its small size, it reached depths of more than three hundred feet, and it was also said to contain the ruins of an ancient shrine. According to local tradition, far beneath the bottom of the lake— down near the earth's core—ancient gods were imprisoned, but it was said that shifts in the crust had brought them up.

On a clear day, I went out in a boat and peered down into the water. And I saw stuff. There were broken columns and the remains of what looked to be buildings—and a beautiful woman lying in a glass box set in the center of the ruins.

Hell, fish are pretty much the same everywhere. Once you've got the knack, you can spear them all day long, whether they're vicious or not. When it came to honing my own skills, I figured I'd practice taking fish in a special environment. I posted a note on the edge of town saying I'd not only catch the fish in the lake ten at a time, but I'd also bring that sleeping beauty from the glass case up to the surface. I knew they'd be able to use the name and address I'd written on the message to send word back to my family, if necessary. Three days later, with folks from the village watching, I paddled my boat out to where I'd spotted the ruins and the woman and dove into the water. People from the village regarded the temple and the beautiful woman with a mixture of reverence, curiosity, and fear; and since the last of those was the strongest, I'd heard from the village children that up to that point everyone had just left them alone. So I had a hunch things might not go well for me when I went through with my plan.

Around three hundred feet down, the fish attacked. No matter how many times I saw them, they always gave me the creeps. And every time they got near me, I wondered if maybe they weren't fish at all. From way off I could see the big fifteen-foot suckers closing in on me, all the while gnashing rakelike teeth, and with harder-than-steel scales glittering with light from the surface. You wouldn't believe how clear the water was. I threw down with eight of them with no more than my knife and spear. Got hurt doing it, too. See how I'm missing the middle finger on my left hand? But once there was blood in the water, those stupid fish couldn't tell friend from foe. They started gobbling each other up. Zipping between them, I stabbed them through their hearts, which just made them see more blood. Inside of fifteen minutes I'd taken care of all eight of them.

The rest would be easy—or so I thought. Just dive down to six hundred feet, grab the woman in the glass under one arm, and head back to the surface. Not surprisingly, once I was down past six hundred feet, the water pressure had my head ringing, and I started going through my remaining oxygen a lot faster. Not worrying about that, I went over to that glass casket and tried to smash it with my knife, but it didn't work. See, it was no ordinary glass. Meaning I had no choice but to go with my last resort.

I had plastic explosive in my pants pocket—common enough stuff for taking care of especially large fish or for blowing a hole through ice blocking the surface of the frozen sea. As I packed it little by little along the place where the glass met the stone base, I stared at the woman in adoration. Her gleaming blond hair swayed like waves, and the breast of her white dress was decorated with a purple rose. Her eye shadow and lipstick were the same color. Such a beauty—there couldn't have been anyone like her on earth. Enchanted by the shape of her shut eyelids, trembling at the dainty lines of her nose, I didn't even realize that I'd gone through nearly all my air. My breath caught in my throat. I had less than five minutes of air remaining.

Though I was reluctant to leave the sleeper, I swam a good sixty feet away and pressed the detonator. Black smoke and sparks shot through the water, disappearing instantly. It looked like I hadn't even put a scratch in the glass. I thought that couldn't be right as I swam back over, putting my hand on the glass to try to open it. It opened from the inside.

The beautiful woman soon lay in the water—and then she suddenly grabbed my left wrist. The loathsome sensation of being crushed in the grip of a thousand snakes rolled all the way down to my balls. In that moment, I knew her for the Noble she was. As I struggled to free myself, the eyes she turned toward me were already open. Even now they haunt me. That hellish gaze invades my dreams. Had I met her eyes a second longer, I'm sure I'd have lost my mind.

I think it must've been the work of God that, without thinking, I swung at her with my other hand, still holding the spear. She covered her left eye, and from between what had to be the finest pair of hands on earth a stream of bright blood flowed. The next thing I knew, I was headed for the surface faster than I'd ever gone in my whole life. The woman must've given chase, because the thread of blood right beside me twisted and turned as it rose. If I'd looked back, it probably would've been the end of me. I felt something cold and hard brush the tips of my toes, and I have no doubt it was her fingers.

Once I'd gone a little higher I lost consciousness, and when I came around again, I found myself in the village hospital. As for the woman—a boater saw her turn around underwater the second I crawled back into my own boat. Apparently the water got cloudy with blood, and he soon lost sight of her.

The day I was discharged, I headed home. It was another three years before I started catching fish again. Even now, my mind sometimes wanders, and I expect a beauty with one bad eye to appear out of the watery blackness. So you probably understand my reason for coming out here. It's the same as yours, old-timer.

Night called once again on the silvery world of fog. Exhausted to the core of their beings, the pair lay down on the metallic ground and closed their eyes, swallowed in an instant by the pitch-black abyss.

On rising, both spotted the blue lights at the same time. They counted ten of them burning blearily in the depths of the fog. They weren't very large, but that might've been due to their distance—in which case, the lights must have been quite powerful.

"What in blazes is that?" the leader said, pulling his spear gun closer.

The old huntsman put a finger to his lips.

"Make like a stone," he ordered softly, lying down. That meant they were not to move, no matter what happened. People on the Frontier could even stop their breathing.

Fortunately, the lights drew no closer, and after drifting for a while they vanished in the same direction the pair was headed.

"We must be close, eh?"

"Let's move."

Although fatigue had pooled like sludge in the marrow of their bones, the pair started off again as if it didn't bother them. The scenery was so monotonous their psyches were driven toward madness, but they swiftly returned to normal.

In less than ten minutes, the fog cleared, and a bizarre tableau emblazoned itself on the pair's retinas. They guessed it was about six miles to the spot where countless blue lights flashed. The lights illuminated the outlines of buildings of various shapes. As their minds processed the number and size of those structures, the leader and the huntsman looked at each other.

"It's like the freaking Capital."

"No, it's bigger."

On hearing this reply from the aged huntsman, the leader turned a frightened expression toward his compatriot and said, "We're talking about an eight-inch-wide meteorite here. How the hell does that turn into the Capital?"

"Oh, a Noble could manage it," the old man replied. "And if it were a different kind of Noble, it'd be even easier for 'im. Is that where it fell?"

Checking his map and the observations from the Capital, the leader nodded.

"Let's go."

Presently the imposing structures towered before the pair. Their most daunting aspect wasn't the way their height challenged the heavens or the way their mass seemed to surpass that of a mountain chain. It was their shape. The long sides towered into the indigo void and out of sight, forming equilateral triangles; even the short ones seemed to be more than three miles long. But when the men took a step closer and looked up, the walls took on what were most definitely their true shapes—rows of rectangular buildings fifteen hundred feet tall, a thousand feet wide, and more than three thousand feet long. Then they were gone in the blink of an eye. It was more than a magic trick of the slightly drifting mist. It seemed from the strange way the light was being refracted that the area was being distorted four-dimensionally.

Beneath the pair's feet, great staircases spiraled down into the earth, broad highways disappeared into spaces between buildings that even a single person couldn't squeeze through, and massive columns that looked to be more than three hundred feet in diameter broke off after fifty or sixty feet. Yet for all this, the pair's eyes found nothing incongruous about their enormousness.

Balls of blue light drifted around the travelers, a number of them passing within inches of their bodies, and then they disappeared. As they advanced through the titanic metropolis that disregarded three-dimensional dynamics, the men—numbed by so many marvels—finally noticed that something was amiss. Their bodies itched all over. Apparently they'd been scratching at themselves for some time without realizing it, and on glancing down, they found their skin broken open, but despite the fact that the flesh below had been exposed, not a drop of blood ran out.

"What the hell is this?" the leader said, chilled.

"This Capital is overflowing with energy. Our bodies are getting attuned to it. If we press on like this, we might end up turning into something else entirely."

Staring at the old huntsman intently, the leader asked, "You mean to say if we turn back now, we won't change into anything?"

"Hell, I don't know."

"In that case, let's keep going."

A white glow lit the faces of the pair: lightning that had fallen from space. It was then swallowed by something beyond the cluster of enormous buildings, forming a blinding dome of light. There had to be something back there. After all, that was where the tiny star had fallen, where a colossal metropolis had been created, and from where the vast expanse of silvery terrain had spread.

II

As the pair pressed forward, their bodies underwent changes. Their skin flaked off like thin bits of paper dancing in the breeze, and the flesh that was left exposed became flecked with silver. By the time the two men reached the point of impact, they were no more than living corpses with a scant amount of flesh and innards left clinging to their bones.

Each of the blue lights that had massed there must have been easily fifty yards in diameter. Naturally, the pair couldn't see beyond the mountainous chain they formed.

"What's that?" the leader asked, his voice no longer a voice at all.

"I don't know," the huntsman responded in the same tone. The two of them were conversing with an unprecedented clarity.

The old man continued, "It's probably a mass of energy. It's filled with the life force of all our guys—the ones they killed."

"With this much collected life force—what in the world do you think they're trying to do?" The leader's tone was soft. Shifts in emotion no longer existed for the two men.

"I don't know. But even if everything in the area got wiped out when that meteorite fell, there couldn't have been that many living things out here. That energy is not from Earth."

"Then it—along with the meteorite—came from space?"

"No doubt about it. Either that, or it might've been whipped up inside that building."

The old man's words made the leader turn around. He was a bare skeleton. Having turned transparent, his bones allowed the other man to see through him to the expanse of silver and the building in the distance. Lightning made a stark connection between the heavens and the earth, but in reverse—from the ground up to the heavens. The pair of skeletons looked up to see the mountainous chain of lights rising into the air. They were soon swallowed by the darkness, disappearing into space devoid of even a single star.

The leader heard the huntsman mutter, "There's a light."

A few seconds later, the glow that formed in the blackness had spread its growing light, bleaching the heavens white. The silvery terrain reflected it, causing the pair of skeletons to dissolve into its shine. And then the sky was robbed of its light in an instant. The light converged into a single streak that came down to earth but created no new dome of light. The streak was swallowed up by a small, black depression on the ground. It was the very spot where the meteor had fallen and where all this had begun.

The leader looked up into the sky to his left, the bones in his neck creaking all the while. A red point of light was approaching. A dimensional missile, launched from an unknown location, carved a hole three miles wide in the air five hundred yards above the target point. The silvery terrain and colossal buildings rose up as if they were papier-mâché miniatures about to be devoured by the hole. It seemed someone knew what the meteorite was and intended to get rid of it. In the hands of the Nobility, time-space circuits could be altered to eliminate space and fuse it back together again in ten seconds flat. This was time enough to make the entire northern Frontier disappear.

However, the insane climb stopped abruptly. A heartbeat later, all the rubble that hung in the air rained down upon the earth . . . and then it was sucked up. By that little black depression.

"The hole!" the old huntsman heard the leader scream. He sounded a million miles away. "It's been turned inside out!"

The dimensional hole that had opened in space had begun to extend a black pathway, stretching into a threadlike tendril that connected it to the depression in the ground. As the pathway was absorbed, the hole was drawn down and pulled narrower until it became a single streak that was swallowed by the earth. How much energy had it taken to tear that hole in space?

Once it was gone, stillness lay over the depression that had swallowed it and the rest of the world. Lightning flashed in the distance. No one could say how much time had passed before a black form rose from the same spot. It was clearly a human head, followed by a neck. His golden hair fell in gentle waves that swayed around his ears and his nape. His shoulders emerged, then his chest. His pectorals were thick and powerful; they had to be part of an impressive physique. Put a sword in either hand, and he could probably hold his own against thousands of soldiers and horses. The boundary between his upper and lower body was held by a tight waist and sculpted abdominal muscles. From the hips down to the thighs he was the pinnacle of savage grace. If he were to kick off the ground, he could soar up to the very heavens; and if he were to step onto the crests of the waves, he'd undoubtedly be able to race across the sea itself. Such spirit, such bearing, such grace—he'd make anyone want to arm him with sword and spear and bow, give him a million troops, and send him off to war.

His eyelids gradually opened. His eyes were crimson. They seemed to cry, *Give me power! Do so, and I'll create mountains of corpses and rivers of blood as I exterminate every living creature on this world!*

The man howled. The heavens and earth rumbled. Lightning struck down at him. The wind groaned. Not even bothering to brush the golden locks out of his eyes, the man cried out a phrase. Repeating it time and again, he swung his right hand around. It was like a gesture someone might make while delivering a speech.

Perhaps the longsword that suddenly appeared in his fist was the reward for those gestures. A straight blade over three feet long and eight inches wide, it had the luster of black steel.

"This is the enchanted sword Glencalibur. Nothing can withstand its edge. Sacred Ancestor, I have returned after five millennia. And from this moment forward, Nobles and humans alike will fear the night. I swear it on the name of the Ultimate Noble driven off to the stars along with my entire domain by none other than the Sacred Ancestor—as sure as my name is Lawrence Valcua, third master of the house of Valcua."

The world melted into white—it was a massive bolt of lightning. In its stark luster, the naked man raised the enchanted sword Glencalibur high and smiled most impressively.

"First I have some respects to pay to the humans and Nobles who helped the Sacred Ancestor banish me to space. And now I'm off!"

The last thing he said was lost to the thunder. Lightning flashed

incessantly, and both the words and the form of the "Ultimate Noble," Lawrence Valcua, melded starkly with the white light that seemed to last an eternity.

A pitch-black vehicle raced across the plains, leaving grass and whitish steam swirling in its wake. With eight great wheels—four on each side—the massive frame of the fifty-foot-long and fifteen-foot-high horseless carriage was driven by the huffing of its steam turbine. Black curtains were now drawn across its windows all day—or while there was daylight, which spoke most eloquently about the nature of its occupant. Even without seeing the golden crest flanked on either side by proud lions with fangs bared, it was clear that this car belonged to Count Braujou.

After nine or ten days on the move since he'd left his castle in the southern Frontier, he was now in an agricultural region near the center of the western Frontier. What was it that he searched for day and night without respite? This same question concerned the mounted figure that looked down from the crest of a hill at the speeding black vehicle and its trail of white smoke. It was D.

"My, but we're in a hurry. You'd think his kid was under the gun," a hoarse voice said with amusement from the left hand D had wrapped around the reins.

"Where's he going?" D asked. It must have been a painful ordeal for him, a dhampir, to be out in the sunlight, but there wasn't a hint of anguish to his handsome features as they glowed like a corona around the moon.

"If you mean what towns lie up ahead, there's Shilgoddum, Warhalla, Somui—nothing special about any of them. All characterless hick villages. However," the hoarse voice said, pausing for a breath, "there's something that concerns me more than that. Why'd you stay your blade? You always slay your opponents. I can't imagine why you've turned your back on that principle this time. You're not the kind of softy he could dissuade with a tender little tale. You know, the way that pissant from the Capital stopped his bellyaching and froze with one sharp look from you must have been the funniest thing I've ever seen. Oof!"

D had given a sudden kick to his steed's abdomen. The cyborg horse, which had been equally tireless in its pursuit of the vehicle, once again galloped up the hill with terrific force.

About ten minutes later, the unmistakable roar of flowing water up ahead could be heard.

"Wow! I'll be damned. I knew the damage caused by that meteorite extended all the way here, but not that it'd made a whole new river."

Rather than a river, it would've been closer to the truth to describe it as an expanse of madly churning water. From what they could see at the top of the hill, it had to be at least six hundred feet wide at the narrowest point. And there was no sign of a bridge.

"Well, looks like we'll have to detour until we can find a shallow spot or a bridge. It's not like Braujou's ride could—what in the world?"

Not slowing in the least, the long black vehicle had gone to the water's edge and then plunged into the torrent without ever stopping.

"Damn! You mean to tell me that thing's got a submarine mode?" the hoarse voice exclaimed in disbelief.

Gazing calmly at the violent flow, the gorgeous young man in black soon saw the vehicle burst from the water near the opposite bank, flames licking from its rocket boosters as it hit the shore and raced inland. He wheeled his horse around, saying, "There's a place to cross to the west."

Though the crossing was too far away to be discerned with the naked eye, the young man saw it with no trouble.

"Well, if you knew where the landing was, why didn't you say so sooner? Or better yet, why didn't you go there? You're just letting him get more of a lead on you!"

Completely ignoring the din from his left hand, D galloped down the hill and into a dark forest of colossal trees. Racing over and around the snaking roots as if he were on flat ground, he reached the ferry landing in about ten minutes. Count Braujou's vehicle had been traveling across the plains to avoid meeting travelers, but the highway ran straight to a hastily improvised crossing point. The road had already been there; it was the passage that had been fashioned on short notice.

In front of the dangerous and disturbing bridge—which was just a collection of ropes strung across the river—seven or eight travelers had gathered. Oddly enough, all of them had their backs to the bridge and the violent torrent as they stared at a massive blue oak that towered by the side of the road. Each and every one of them looked appalled. D rode to a spot where he could see what they were looking at before halting his steed.

"What's this?" the hoarse voice said, conveying a surprise that was all too real.

Pinned against the trunk of the blue oak and drawing the eyes of curious travelers was a partially decayed corpse, its head hung low as if dejected by the way it had been left on exhibit. The corpse was no stranger to D.

"General Gaskell," the hoarse voice said in a strangely soft tone.

One had to wonder who could've done such a thing to the only Noble who'd crossed swords with D and still managed to flee upon defeat—a fiend beyond compare.

A sort of white thread wound about the body and the tree trunk, and around the heart of the deceased the clothing had been stained with black blood, dried in a bizarre pattern. However, any human who knew about the vital points of the Nobility would've cocked her head and wondered if that was really the cause of death. The brutally crushed head's right eye dangled over the chest by its optic nerve, the lips and nose had been turned inside out, and every last tooth was missing. A dry substance that appeared to be brains spilled from the ears, and the ends of broken ribs jutted out in all directions through the chest and sides. The whole body gave the impression of having been compacted; and on closer inspection, it became clear this was because after being torn out, the shattered limbs had been forced back into place and secured there. Gaskell hadn't merely been killed. He'd been butchered in the most brutal manner imaginable.

"The great, indestructible general . . . It must've taken an army to do this. Hell, even thousands of average warriors or lesser Nobility couldn't have destroyed someone like him . . . What kind of freak, with what kind of power, could do this?"

"He was dropped," D stated plainly.

"Dropped?" the hoarse voice inquired, its brow surely wrinkled. "You mean to tell me someone dropped this immortal Noble from above, and then finished him off while he was still reeling? He could've been dropped three thousand feet and he still would've completely recovered from the impact in two seconds."

"How about from thirty thousand feet?"

"What?"

"How about one hundred sixty thousand feet?"

"First thirty thousand, now one hundred sixty thousand—damn, you don't mean to tell me he got dropped from the stratosphere? Now I get it. Even the great General Gaskell would be ripped limb from limb by that, and it'd probably take him days to recover. But who could do something like that? From the look of him, he's been dead a good two days. What happened two days ago?"

By this point the curious people had apparently wearied of the thing that, upon closer inspection, was revealed to be just a corpse, and they'd all turned around. Those who were relatively unencumbered had started across the rope bridge.

D walked over to the tattered corpse. Naturally, the callous young man wasn't moved to bury him. However, as the lone figure gazed quietly up at his former enemy, his expression revealed more than just remorse for the deceased. After gazing at him for several seconds, he did something strange. He called out, "Gaskell."

It wasn't an emotional outpouring. He was just speaking to him. And the corpse answered, "Is that you, D?"

III

A lone traveler had come back to look for something he'd dropped, but when he saw the two of them he must've known dangerous business was afoot, because he forgot all about what he was looking for and hurried back toward the bridge.

"Who did this to you?" D inquired in a disinterested manner of the man who'd died two days earlier. The great general was indeed dead—he'd been destroyed. If not, he'd never have remained there in such horrible shape. Despite that fact, his parched and split lips moved.

"S-S-Speeny . . ."

"Just who's that?" the hoarse voice inquired.

"D . . . you must go . . . to the home of the Dyalhis family . . . Valcua . . . will come after them . . ."

"Dyalhis? Who the heck are they?"

"On the northern edge . . . of the village of Somui . . . Help them . . . though it probably won't do any good . . . He has seven servants . . . and it only took one of them . . . to destroy me."

"So, what's your connection to these Dyalhis folks anyway? Hey!" the hoarse voice said, as his question was drowned out by D's voice.

"Do you know Count Braujou?"

The crushed head seemed to nod.

"When Valcua was driven into space . . . five thousand years ago . . . on the Sacred Ancestor's orders . . . it was by him . . . and me . . . and Duchess Miranda . . . And at that time . . . we had help . . . from a certain human . . . Valcua made a declaration . . . Said he'd come back . . . and take vengeance . . . on us all . . . And we believed him . . . So we took an oath . . . When Valcua came back to Earth . . . we swore we'd protect Dyalhis's descendants . . . On learning that Valcua had returned . . . I headed as fast as I could . . . to where Dyalhis's descendants were . . . And look what became of me . . . D . . . Go . . . Go to them . . ."

General Gaskell may have intended to ask him to protect the descendants or to destroy Valcua, but he spoke no more, and something no eye could detect fled his body.

"Holy!" a voice called out in the distance. It belonged to one of the travelers from earlier, who'd been watching the whole affair with trepidation. Not only had he been terrified by the sight of a talking corpse, but on seeing the head and limbs suddenly drop off and the body vanish into the air like some kind of mist or haze, the traveler had collapsed on the spot.

"So, he survived for two days after his death?" the hoarse voice muttered. It sounded impressed. "Looks like he was pretty worried about Dyalhis's descendants. I'm warning you here and now: don't get any funny ideas, D."

D turned his gaze to the flowing water. "Count Braujou will also be there."

"Hmm," the hoarse voice said, and then it sighed with woe. "Once the sun goes down, that Speeny character will be on the move, too. Let's go."

The black horse and rider broke into a gallop that left the wind swirling in their wake. Easily bounding over the heads of travelers who turned to look when they heard the echoing hoofbeats, they landed spectacularly at one end of the rope that swayed in the slight breeze. Considering that the bridge was nothing more than five ropes zigzagging back and forth with eight-inch gaps between them, this was a display of ungodly equestrian skill. A number of people who were just finishing the crossing lost their footing, barely managing to catch hold of the rope handrails and cursing D as a damned fool. But the young man in black rode across the precarious bridge at full speed, the hem of his coat fluttering in the wind.

Crossing half the six hundred feet in the blink of an eye, he heard a woman's voice ring in his ears.

"You who spoke with Gaskell—who spoke with a corpse—I would have your name."

D galloped on as if he hadn't heard the youthful voice, so like the peals of a golden bell.

"The only people who can converse with corpses are Nobles. But that's not what you are. You're neither Noble nor human. That means you have no place in this world. You should die here and now!"

The bridge dipped down. In a heartbeat, D was in the water. Churning its legs desperately, his horse was swept along by the mighty torrent. The only thing that allowed D to remain on its back was his skillful mastery of the reins, which kept his mount pointed in the right direction. For every ten feet they were pulled, they moved three feet closer to the opposite shore.

The cyborg horse tilted backward. Looking behind him, D caught sight of a pair of pale hands stretching from the muddy water. The right one was holding his horse by the tail, while the left reached for its haunches. In the blink of an eye, it ripped the tail free. The hide over the mount's haunches peeled off, some meat still attached to it. Metal-alloy bones were laid bare, and torn cables made contact with the muddy water, sending sparks shooting out. A hand slipped into the opening. When it grabbed hold of the colored wires that acted as the animal's nerves, D's blade flashed into action. He struck at the hand, but it felt like slicing through water. Without a single mark on it, the woman's hand tore out the wires. Sparks flew more colorfully and violently than ever. The cyborg horse shuddered.

The white hands sank smoothly back into the water. At precisely the same moment, a pale woman stood up about fifteen feet ahead of the Hunter. With golden hair that hung down to her waist and a tight white dress that suited her elegant beauty, the woman stood atop the madly flowing water. All but the head of the cyborg horse had already vanished beneath the surface as the beast was pushed along with D still on its back. The woman on top of the water followed D at the same speed. Her left eye was covered.

"You're not frightened, are you?" the woman said, her voice quivering with malice and surprise. "Those who live outside the water fear it. I should like to hold a great man like you tight against my bosom, but it would seem you pose a serious impediment to our aims. Though I don't believe you are one of the other two Nobles whom Gaskell was left to await, I shall take it upon myself to dispose of you. Your handsome face and fine form shall sink into the muddy water. And as soon as my work is done, I shall find you and seal you away for all time in a crystal-clear lake."

"We'll see about that," a hoarse voice snickered, but it was unclear whether or not the water witch noticed.

"Your name—I should like to have it. I am known as Lucienne."

"D."

The pale beauty's one good eye snapped open wide. "You're D? But of course. I knew you must be from the very moment I saw you. Ah, and yet I still couldn't understand. You were far more beautiful than I'd imagined. I've heard about you hundreds, if not thousands, of times. Heard about the dhampir of a beauty rarely seen in this world, with a strength that makes both gods and demons grow pale."

The water witch—Lucienne—quivered with rapture.

"This is a pleasure, D. I'm so glad to meet you—so glad to kill you. I'll fill those exquisite lungs and stomach of yours with mud and let you rest forever beneath the water."

Her body sank seductively into the depths. With her lovely face alone breaking the surface, the woman twisted her lips into a wanton grin and glided straight toward D.

How would D respond? The uselessness of his blade had already been made clear.

When the distance between the two had closed to just six feet, Lucienne leaped up. As she broke the surface, the hem of her dress melded with the water, drawing a long ocher trail behind her. Her face glowed with the surpassing bliss of one seeking their love's embrace, but then there was another flash of light, and her expression warped into one of intense pain. A silvery gleam passed through her from the top of her head down, and her body split lengthwise. Loosing a scream that defied description, Lucienne broke apart in midair, forming innumerable droplets that rained back down on the muddy torrent.

As D allowed himself to be pushed along by the water that was now up to his chest, the left hand he had wrapped around the reins snickered with amusement. "She underestimated you. Lousy little water monster."

"I cut her, but she got away."

The laughter stopped.

"Oh. Then we'd better come up with another way to deal with her."

"I've got to cross this river first."

"Of course. If you don't hurry up, there's a good chance you'll miss out on the reward money for ol' Braujou. Heck, it's probably already too late."

D squeezed the reins. Half-dead, his horse gave a single whinny, and then began feebly paddling through the water once more with all its remaining strength.

Those Who Dwell in the Demon's Sphere

CHAPTER 3

I

In the village of Somui, the giant onions and hallucinogenic blue wheat had brought a hundred dalas. That would hold them a month. Around the middle of next month, they'd harvest twice what he had today, and that would be enough to tide them over until fall. Tapping the leather bag of coins in his coat pocket, Matthew Dyalhis hurried down the road that led to the edge of town. That's where he'd left his covered wagon.

Undoubtedly the fact that he'd pulled in twice as much as he'd expected had served to distract him from how harsh fate could be. No sooner had he spotted the black mass near the spot for parking wagons than it resolved into five separate figures. What made Matthew despair was that out of them, one of the faces was very familiar. The other four were considered ne'er-do-wells—he'd known them since he was little—but the familiar one was a good deal older.

"Hi, Dad," Matthew called out to him. Somehow he managed a smile. "Mom and Sue are worried about you. Hurry on home, would you?"

"Aren't you the cold one," his father—Baird—said, letting out a belch that reeked of alcohol. "You're not even gonna ask me to go back with you?"

"Do you plan on going home?" Matthew asked, slipping past his father to reach the wagon. To his right were Otto Flanagan and Mizz Quarona, to his left Ogen Shaway and Joppes Lallacksiski—but aside from Joppes, who'd been practicing martial arts since he was a kid, they weren't much of a threat to him. He'd taken the other three all at once before and whipped them, and the two or three times he'd squared off against Joppes, it'd been a good fight. He believed he would've won if no one had interfered. As a result, these four rarely gave Matthew any trouble. But one of these days, there would have to be a reckoning.

As he reached for the driver's seat, he heard, "C'mon, Matthew. Give your old man a little help here." His father's tone was pathetic—he always sounded that way when he asked for money.

Stopping, Matthew heaved a sigh. Though he thought about looking back, he decided against it and raised his foot to the step. There was a dull thud behind him. It was drowned out by a cry of pain. He now had no choice but to turn around.

Clutching his solar plexus, Baird was collapsing. Before he could do so, Joppes got his right arm around the man's waist. Ogen kicked Matthew's reeling father in the stomach. When he tumbled forward, Otto and Mizz started kicking the hell out of him.

"Please, just stop it!" Baird groaned, shielding his head.

"How are you supposed to pay us back, you old shit?"

"I don't care if you have to peddle your wife and daughter; you get us that money!"

With every word the two thugs spoke, there was the sound of them striking the man in the back or stomach.

"Okay, take his right arm—and bust it!" Joppes ordered.

Mizz, the biggest of the bunch, got on the man's back. Poking out between the two figures, Baird's arm was pushed up toward his head. He began to let out a long cry.

Matthew turned around. He knew perfectly well what this would mean. If it hadn't been his father, he would've kept going. First, he faced Otto: the thug quickly stepped over Matthew's father and fled. Taking time to kick Baird in the hip, Mizz lost his chance to get into a stance, and Matthew landed a kick to his side. No matter how big or heavy Mizz was, his bones and nerves were no tougher than an ordinary person's. When he let out a cry and landed on his ass, the end of Matthew's boot caught him squarely in the middle of his face. That one blow sent him toppling backward.

Not even bothering to watch Mizz's landing, Matthew spun around. Joppes and Ogen were both waving him away to show they had no intent of fighting.

Still tense, Matthew walked over to his father and asked, "You okay?"

He heard whimpering for a response. It made him both exceedingly angry and sad.

The boy looked up at Joppes. A curse on all of them rolled out of his mouth. He didn't know how much they were owed, but this was more than just collecting on a debt.

"Come and get it," he said, standing up straight again. But the instant he felt power filling him once more, his legs were pulled out from under him.

"What—"

He fell face first, putting his hands out like he was doing a push-up to save himself from the impact. Joppes's boot knocked his hands out from under him. Somehow managing to keep the kick that came at him from hitting him anywhere important, Matthew put his right hand against the ground, then swung it hard at Joppes and Ogen. Catching a face full of dirt, both stopped what they were doing.

Matthew got up. A sharp pain shot through his right side. Swinging his right arm around, he grabbed his attacker by the scruff of the neck. He had a good idea who it was.

"Gimme some money, Matthew," his father said. His breath stank of liquor.

"Sorry," Matthew replied, and then he turned to Joppes and asked, "You're all in cahoots, aren't you?"

Joppes shrugged his shoulders and laughed. "Yeah, I guess we are. It was your old man's idea. Said he wanted to get some serious cash."

"Matthew," the man said as pain encroached further into his son, "hurry up and hand it over. Are you gonna give it to me or not?"

Baird twisted his knife, and his son fell into a sorrowful unconsciousness.

The next thing Matthew knew, he was in the wagon and it was moving. He didn't know whether he'd climbed in himself of if they'd put him in it. Knowing the way, the cyborg horses had started back toward the farm. The leather bag of coins was gone. Though he was lucky the wound to his side hadn't extended to any of his internal organs, he hardly felt like celebrating.

His surroundings had already been annexed by the dominion of darkness, and the road that led straight to their farm on the outskirts of the village stretched like a white ribbon across the hilly terrain. The moon was out.

Fighting through his pain, Matthew put on his moonlight goggles. Magnifying the faint light of the moon to make the world seem as bright as day, such goggles were essential items for any traveler who might find himself on the road at night. Off to the left-hand side he could see a black depression. Though it was said to be a crater caused by a major earthquake about two centuries earlier, it was simply too vast—it must've been nearly a quarter of a million acres. Apparently local bandit groups used it to stash their loot, while a variety of avian creatures left partially devoured human remains there. Since it also hid marshes that gave off an eerie glow, fields where only poisonous weeds grew, and no dearth of strange creatures, Matthew thought it best to get past the great depression as quickly as possible and raised his whip toward that end.

"What's that?" he exclaimed, catching a speeding black object out of the corner of his eye. It was coming from the west at a good speed. A horseless carriage—a car, and quite a large one at that.

"Don't tell me that thing's headed for our house!"

Before he could turn his head, fear blew its frosty breath into his heart. No one owned anything like that car except the Nobility. And it was headed toward his very own house, at night.

Just then, his fearful gaze was replaced by one of shock. Without slowing at all, the carriage, which must have weighed five tons, had floated up into the air. Matthew stopped his wagon in spite of himself. His eyes remained riveted on the vehicle, now stopped thirty feet off the ground, as he pulled out the first-aid kit under the driver's seat. He had an intense desire to see what would happen next. But to do that, he'd need something for his pain.

Rubbing an antibiotic ointment on his wound, he'd just popped a painkiller into his mouth when a figure descended head first from the heavens and stopped thirty feet from the front of the car. It was a man with limbs so long and gangly they looked like a spider's. His tight brown shirt left the lines of his body perfectly clear.

Matthew strained his ears. He caught fragments of a man's voice.

"Come out here and . . . Count Brau . . . Didn't you . . . how General Gas . . . wound up?"

On seeing the car's roof open and a man appear from it, Matthew let out a gasp. It was a giant who had to be at least ten feet tall. The spear in his right hand was long and thick. It looked like one swipe from it would be enough to start a tornado.

"Put . . . car . . . this instant," the giant commanded, pointing toward the ground.

"Why don't . . . try . . . make me?"

That was obviously an attempt to provoke the giant. Matthew had noticed that a thread of hostility stretched between the two of them.

"I would . . . your name," the giant said.

"It's Speeny."

The boy heard that statement clearly.

And with those words, the spindly man extended both arms and sent white strands billowing from his fingertips toward the giant. It was a spider's web—or so Matthew believed, since the man bore such a resemblance to a spider, and the streaks of white were like thread.

The giant didn't wait for them to make contact. Not moving from his position, where he'd taken a stance like a stern temple guardian, he shifted his grip on his spear to the very center, holding it up vertically as he spun it madly. The wind groaned. A colossal windmill appeared—the bottom of which just missed his toes, while the top reached far above his head as it spun in a blur. When the drifting threads struck it, they disappeared.

"Oh!" Matthew cried out.

As Speeny's body was shaken by an unmistakable surprise, the count hurled his spear. It was a streak of black light that jabbed through the center of Speeny's torso and out his back. With a disturbingly inhuman scream, the spiderish man twitched from head to toe, and then he moved no more. His limbs bent, pulling in toward his torso.

All this had transpired in less than a minute. Though Matthew was in a completely safe place, the tension of the deadly battle left him paralyzed.

For a short while the count stood like a wrathful deity on the roof of his vehicle in midair, with the impaled corpse swaying in the air before him, but then he unexpectedly made a remark that caused Matthew's eyes to widen.

"That's quite . . . playing dead."

Suddenly, Speeny's arms and legs extended. His narrow eyes opened.

"Ah . . . should've expected . . . Count Brau . . . Well . . . this back!"

Reaching for the spear with both hands, he smoothly pulled it out again. The man threw it easily, and the count caught it in midair.

"It would . . . you didn't see . . . General Gas . . . The very least . . . is give you . . . same death . . ."

The moment Speeny finished talking, the long spear pierced his face, came out of the back of his head at an angle, and jabbed into the ground below him.

Matthew gasped. When the spear was hurled for the second time, the car had already begun to rise, shooting up into the starry sky with such ferocious speed the count couldn't leap off. On returning to his senses, Matthew turned his attention to the spiderlike man. It was unclear where he might've vanished to, and there was no trace of him anywhere.

Feeling as if he'd just awakened from a nightmare, Matthew returned home. With one look at the bloodstained boy, his mother and sister set to patching him up without even bothering to listen to the tale of the bizarre battle he'd witnessed.

Once she'd finished taking care of him, his mother told him, "The first aid you did closed the wound and stopped the bleeding. But just to be on the safe side, go in to Doc Freddy's and let him have a look at you tomorrow."

Matthew nodded, and then said he wanted to turn in.

Saying nothing, his mother simply stared at him.

"What is it?"

"You really mean to tell me those four were the only ones in your fight?" she asked.

"That's right."

"Well, the way they stabbed you was pretty haphazard. Seems kinda—I don't know—hesitant?"

Matthew simply shrugged.

"You know, every time I go into town, I ask around about your father. All I ever hear is that he's still at her place, and that he drinks constantly. Seems he's been over to Mr. Harnja's general store a number of times to borrow money. He always apologizes and promises to pay after the next harvest. I wouldn't put him above hitting up his own son, too. And if that didn't work—I suppose he'd even stab you."

"Mom," Matthew said reproachfully. He knew nothing he could say would do any good. Her eyes held the absolute determination of a woman who'd raised two children alone on the Frontier.

"It was him, wasn't it?"

Matthew nodded.

Clapping him lightly on the shoulder, his mother told him, "Take it easy for the next couple of days. Sue and I will handle the rest of the harvesting."

As his mother headed for the door to his room, Matthew called to her, "Mom—don't tell anyone what happened."

His mother never paused on her way out of his room. The door closed.

Letting out a sigh, Matthew lay down on his bed. Maybe the painkillers had kicked in, because he felt groggy. A sharp rap snapped him wide awake. He thought hazily about what could've made it. It was the sound of glass. He turned to the right.

Beyond a window framing darkness, a pale face swayed—a blond woman of unearthly beauty. It wasn't her lovely face that shook off his sleepiness, but rather the strength of the eerie aura that billowed from her, blasting him through the glass.

II

Shutting his eyes, Matthew slowly counted to five, and then opened them again. The face had vanished.

I'm so beat my brain must be playing tricks on me, he thought. Come to think of it, as pretty as she was, she only had one eye.

There was another rap. He had enough presence of mind to tell that this time it was a knock at his door.

"Come in," he called out, taking his gaze off the window.

Sue came in. She wore a long robe over her pajamas.

"You're still up?"

"I was worried," Sue replied.

There'd been something fleeting about the girl ever since she was born, and although there was nothing physically wrong with her, her parents had always thought she wouldn't be long for this world—a thought Matthew himself sometimes shared. She remained that way even now, but having reached nearly fourteen years of age, she inspired hope that she'd somehow manage to keep on living.

"My wound's gonna be fine. After a full day's rest tomorrow, I'll be back in the fields."

"I'm glad," Sue said. The smile her bloodless lips formed was heartbreakingly sweet. Matthew always fought the urge to grab her by those dainty shoulders and give her a big hug.

"What's the matter?" Matthew inquired gently, seeing that his younger sister was staring at a single point, unable to hide her anxiety.

Bringing one hand to her lips, Sue bit the knuckle of her forefinger.

"Hey!"

"Matt, have you had that dream again?"

"What dream?"

"The one from the other day!"

"The other day, you say? You mean when we all had the same dream—ten days ago?"

Sue nodded. "We dreamed about a falling star. The northern Frontier was in a terrible state. And ever since, I've had the scariest dreams every night."

"What sort of dreams?"

"You mean you haven't been having them, too, Matt?"

"What sort do you mean?"

"Scary ones," Sue mumbled, eyes closed and hands folded before her chest. "There are these shadowy figures approaching out of a fog—a whole bunch of them. When I counted them last night, there were eight. One of the shadows was huge—like a mountain standing behind them, with the others at the foot of it—and they seemed to spring from his feet."

"You sure you're not reading too much into this? They're just dreams. Hell, there are dream demons to be found hereabouts."

"I just know something," Sue said as if making an entreaty, her body quivering.

"Know what exactly?"

"That someone's out to get us. We're the ones they're after!"

"When you say we—you mean me and Mom, too?"

"Yes, and Dad."

"Well, then, let's let him handle it."

"Matthew!"

Waving one hand at his sister's pained visage, Matthew said, "I was just kidding. But there's no reason why someone like that would be after us. I bet all kinds of people had weird dreams when that meteorite fell in the northern Frontier. That's just how dreams are. Even supposing someone were after us, what would that have to do with that meteorite? You mean to say these are assassins from the stars? And you don't find that strange?"

"That's why I asked if you'd been having them too, Matt."

"Nope. Not at all."

"Well, I'm glad then. It must just be me."

Sue leaned back against the door. From her expression it was clear that the anxiety hadn't left her. But the quiet girl was relieved for the rest of her family.

Matthew was going to ask her about whether their mother had the dreams or not, but then thought better of it. Just let sleeping dogs lie, he thought.

Climbing off his bed, he went over to his younger sister and took her hand. "Go to bed already. Dreams end as soon as you wake up. And even if you don't wake up, a knight will come to your rescue on a white steed."

"I suppose you're right," Sue said, smiling. Her smile was truly heartbreaking. The bastard Fate had plenty of pain in store for her, and the girl undoubtedly knew that better than anyone.

"Sue," he called out to her, and her expression changed.

She had the kind of eyes that people always complimented, saying they looked like they were full of dreams. It wasn't her brother that they now reflected; it was a figure standing outside the window.

Not bothering to see if the reflection was that of a man or a woman, Matthew turned around. The glass revealed only darkness.

Shaking his sister by her shoulders to bring her back from her mannequin-like state, Matthew asked, "Was there someone there?"

"A woman," Sue replied, the words like a gasp. "A really beautiful, but really terrible, woman. She's one of them. She's out to get us. I couldn't see her face clearly in my dreams, but now I know it's her."

"Go back to your room. Lock your door and windows, and keep some amulet grass with you. You've got a bolt gun, right?"

"Don't worry. I'm not scared at all," Sue told him, her hand over her heart to vouchsafe the statement. If he had touched it, Matthew was sure he would have felt it hammering like a broken bell, but he hugged his little sister for being so intolerably dear, fragile as a piece of spun glass and yet tough at the same time.

Tucking a hatchet and some rough wooden stakes in his belt, he went outside. Thanks to a pair of starlight goggles, he could see fine. Stars filled the sky above his head. But Matthew couldn't look up at them—the starlight goggles took the light from those stars and amplified it, turning night to day. If he were to look at an ordinary light source with them, it would sear his retinas in an instant, blinding him. Though he checked around the main house, there was nothing out of the ordinary.

He headed toward the barn. Packed full of cultivators and automated planters, machinery for repairing farm implements, gunpowder, and all sorts of chemicals, the eighteen-hundred-square-foot structure was less than two minutes from the main house. All that stood between the two buildings was an old well.

When he reached the entrance to the barn, Matthew halted. Putting his hand against the door, he pushed. Since he'd oiled the hinges just the day before last, it opened smoothly.

The barn was choked with darkness. He drew his hatchet, and then adjusted his grip on it. In a flash he thought, Maybe somebody's hiding right behind the door, and then he had to check. He slipped into the gap behind the door. And then someone appeared.

"What the hell?" he cried out in a hushed tone, stopping his raised hatchet in midair.

"Easy there," said a terribly familiar voice.

"Mom—what are you doing out here at this hour?"

"I saw something strange. But there's no one in the barn."

Across her muscular and hardly motherly arms rested a sawed-off shotgun. She'd gone out into the perilous night without saying a word to her children.

That's just like her, Matthew thought, trying to hide the fire in his heart as he said, "Don't do stuff like this, Mom. When you don't come to me for something like this, it's like you don't think I'm capable of handling it myself."

The boy's mother looked at him with pride, but her face soon grew stern. When he got up to mischief or talked back to her, that face meant he had a slap coming, and if he'd caused trouble for anyone else, that got upgraded to a punch.

"Don't be stupid. It'll be years before you're ready for this," she said, giving her son a sharp look as the two of them stepped outside. Matthew closed the door.

"Well, I say we head back to—" he began to say, and then he noticed that his mother had frozen. He looked in the same direction.

Beside the well stood a woman in a white dress. It left the better part of her bosom prominently displayed, was cinched tight around her hips, and had a wide, bell-shaped skirt. It was the sort of fancy attire the Nobility wore to a ball.

"Adele Dyalhis and her son Matthew," the woman remarked as she stared at them with glowing eyes. Her eyes had a golden sparkle, and the moonlight played across her blond hair as if it were the Milky Way.

The woman stepped forward.

"Keep away from us," the mother said, leveling her shotgun. She had probably loaded it with the same triple-ought buckshot as always. At this range, it could easily blow something the size of a person's head to pieces. "We're just the caretakers. The family that lives here's off on a trip. Won't be back until next year. What did you want from them?"

"Their lives," the woman said, grinning. Her smile was as still as a wintry night, and it left the mother and son feeling just as chilled. "I have come here to give you new life. If you would be so kind as to dispose of that gun."

Her bright tone echoed alluringly through their heads. Matthew and his mother both closed their eyes. The woman's golden gaze was emblazoned on their retinas. The mother slowly lowered her gun. Matthew couldn't move his hands.

"Come to me," the woman said, beckoning them with her hand. Like marionettes on invisible strings stretching from her fingers, the mother and son walked with unsteady steps to the woman. First the woman looked at Matthew, and then she shifted her eyes to his mother.

"You poor thing," she said, but her sarcastic remark swayed with pity. "These countless wrinkles, sagging flesh, and hardened gaze—all are products of the curse called aging. You must've been stunning when you were young. Now you shall reclaim the beauty of your youth."

Extending her pale forefinger, she slid it from the mother's chest all the way down to her belly, and the front of her shirt split down the middle. Adele didn't have anything on underneath. The other woman's hand brushed along her full breasts.

"Oh, what a fine chest you have. I can tell how nice and full of blood it is. Human blood is hot. All of my kind yearn for it. And I intend to drain it from right here."

Her hand came away from Adele's breasts, creeping across the mother's skin like some exquisite insect until it'd climbed to the nape of her neck. A finger merely scratching the surface was enough to make the mother pant faintly.

"Do you see how blood traces blue lines through my pale skin? You'll do well to remember where they are."

And then the woman pressed her vermilion lips against the nape of Adele's neck. From the space between those luscious and monstrous lips and the graceful neck there came a retching sound. Matthew and his mother backed away, while the woman staggered about with both hands pressed to the left side of her chest. From between her fists, the bloodied end of a wooden stake jutted.

"Damn you . . . Who . . . ?"

As the woman tried to turn, she was caught by the hair and yanked toward the well. Making no show of resistance at all, her body was dragged down into it. As Matthew and his mother looked at each other, they heard a splash.

"That woman's a Noble, Matthew!"

"I know. But what happened to her? And who's responsible?"

Matthew gripped his hatchet, and his mother quickly scooped up the shotgun.

Something shiny had risen to the well's surface. It spilled over the rock edge and spread out at the pair's feet. Water. There was no time to be surprised by it, for an alluring female shape had risen from the depths that even now continued to flow over the edge. She had golden tresses that hung down to her waist, a white dress, and features so lovely they seemed to put the moonlight to shame. However, it wasn't the same beauty who had just been there. Her dress was so sheer, it let every maddening curve of her body be seen. What's more, she only had one good eye.

"Who—who the hell are you?"

As Matthew raised his hatchet high, the woman's lips formed the words, "You're Adele Dyalhis and Matthew Dyalhis, aren't you? My name is Lucienne. I've come here on orders from a certain esteemed personage."

The droplets that fell without end from her hair and her chin were jewels with all the luster of moonlight. The way she'd made her appearance and the might she'd displayed in dispatching the Noblewoman said it all: this was the same water witch who'd done battle with D by daylight at the great river, being struck twice with his blade before making her escape—Lucienne.

III

Even the eerie aura billowing at them must've carried molecules of water, because droplets formed on the faces of mother and son, and Adele had to wipe her eyes with the back of her hand.

"Take Sue and get outta here!" she shouted.

"No, Mom, you take her and run. I'll handle this on my own."

"This freak destroyed a Noble. There's no way you'd be able to do anything against her. Go!"

"The hell I will!"

Digging his feet into the now mucky earth, Matthew charged forward.

The woman touched back down on the ground. The thin little smile she donned was cold enough to make the boy feel as if his heart would freeze solid. Grunting, he swung his right arm down with all his might. He was aiming for the woman's head. Finding its mark, the blade sank into her, and then his hand—followed by his shoulder and the rest of his body—pushed through her. Matthew came out behind the woman covered with thousands of beads of moisture and feeling like he'd taken a tunnel through the water.

Twisting his body as he fell forward, he put both hands out to pick himself back up as he exclaimed, "I went right through her. She's made of water!"

"Out of the way!" Adele cried, not even waiting for Matthew to run before she pulled the trigger.

There was a boom like a rumble rising from the earth, and then Lucienne's head blew to pieces. Barely straightening herself up again after the weapon's kick sent her reeling backward, Adele turned the gun with a second shot in its left barrel toward the woman, who stood stock still.

From the base of Lucienne's neck, a transparent lump had risen. In no time, it took on eyes and a nose, a silvery hue coursed into it, and then golden hair flowing in the breeze completed the woman's lovely face. Lucienne grinned smugly.

Despite the blood-chilling horror climbing her spine, Adele fired the second shot. The gun made an unsatisfactory sound, and black smoke curled from its barrel. It had misfired.

The water witch laughed without making a sound.

"It wasn't natural conditions that made your powder wet. It was my power. Perhaps I should use it to turn you and your son into mere bags of skin to hold the water that is so dear to me."

Lucienne took a gliding, smooth step forward.

Matthew grabbed her around the waist. "You goddamned freak! Run for it, Mom!"

The arm he'd wrapped around the witch sank deep into her waist. Once Lucienne's right hand had gone through her solar plexus and out her back, it caught Matthew by the scruff of his neck and jerked him forward. Though Matthew's flailing hands went through her arms, the hand the woman clamped on his neck was as solid as iron.

"I'll start with your dutiful son."

As the woman said this, her left hand went down Matthew's throat.

Matthew coughed. Crystal-clear water spilling from his mouth and nose, the boy writhed. In the moonlight—on dry land—the young man was on his way to drowning.

"Stop it!"

Discarding her shotgun, Adele drew a knife from the leather sheath on her belt. With a blade eight inches long, the knife was one she always kept close while she slept, and such weapons were absolute necessities on the Frontier. Realizing that she was inviting the same fate as Matthew, the mother still knew neither fear nor hesitation. Raising her knife, she dashed into action.

But a strange thing happened right in front of her. Something white, like a sort of fog, enveloped Lucienne. Letting out a scream that sounded like her throat was being crushed, the water witch writhed. Her arm slipped out of Matthew's mouth and the boy's head passed through her body as he hit the ground on his back. As Lucienne squirmed, the eyes and nose left her face, her arms fused with her torso, and her legs melded together. Barely retaining the shape of a human body, the watery mass remained shrouded in the glowing fog as it bounded toward the well, then fell again as if the last of its strength had been spent. Perhaps freed from the bonds of the fog, the woman who'd turned into water rained down into that dark hole like a waterfall.

Neither Adele nor Matthew could make a move. The weirdness they'd witnessed was far beyond the bounds of what the psyches of even two iron-willed Frontier natives like these could bear.

The fog was changing. It took on the general shape of a person. Four limbs formed, and blond hair swayed. A Noblewoman in a white dress stood quietly before the pair.

"That was an arrogant thing for a servant of the Nobility to do. Did she think a lackey could actually best a master?"

Turning to the pair, her vermilion lips poised to form a smile, the woman noticed the cause of the mother and son's shock. The tip of a tree branch protruded from the left side of her chest. The woman's smile became a wry grin as she grabbed one end of the branch and pulled it forward. Though there was the sound of tearing flesh, her expression betrayed no discomfort. Unless she'd been stabbed through a vital point, she wouldn't feel any pain. However, wasn't the left side of the chest—and the heart within it—supposed to be the Nobility's one great weakness?

"I shall deal with that woman later."

Throwing the branch away, the woman slowly extended a hand toward the pair. Once again, her eyes took on that mysterious golden hue.

"Come to me," the woman said. But no sooner had she beckoned to them than something fell from the sky into a pile of hay five yards to her rear.

There was an impact that sounded like a hundred cracks of thunder, and the earth quaked. The mother and son were both knocked back fifteen feet, slamming against the barn door and leaving the barn itself leaning a bit to one side. Even the Noblewoman was left shaken, and she clung to the well to steady herself. Flames went up. Heat from the friction of the object's fall had set the hay ablaze.

How far did that thing fall? The unspoken question was visible in the eyes of Adele and Matthew as the pair lay flat on the ground. The beauty's expression also seemed to pose the same query.

The answer soon presented itself.

A huge figure stood up from the flames in a wine-red gown. He had a great, fifteen-foot-long spear in his right hand. Though he appeared from the flames, when he took one massive stride out of them, there wasn't anything burning on him. Still, the prospect may have bothered him, as the giant used his free hand to slap at his shoulders and hips before peering down at the three of them intently and saying, "It's been ages, hasn't it, Miranda?"

"I'll thank you to address me as duchess, Count Braujou," the Noblewoman replied with a smile, looking up toward the heavens. "Where are you arriving from?"

"One hundred fifty thousand feet up," Count Braujou said, pounding the back of his own neck. "Some rascal calling himself Speeny, or something like that, managed to string me up in the sky. I was able to cut myself free, of course, but I ultimately ended up being dropped. Ah, the humiliation!"

"I see you are, as always, the same carefree man, full of fight. Do you think you're up to keeping your oath? Shaking off the dust of five millennia is no easy task," the pale beauty—Duchess Miranda—said reproachfully.

Count Braujou gave her a personable grin in return. It was the sort of smile that suggested that on a deeper level, the two understood each other.

"So," the giant began, looking at the mother and son who stood, stunned, in front of the barn, but he quickly headed off to the left.

Sue had just appeared from the front door of the main house. She was wrapped in a blue robe. An atomic lamp swayed in her hand.

"Mom! Matthew!" the girl called out. On noticing their bizarre callers, she became a statue.

"Sue, get in the house!"

But despite her mother's shout, the girl's feet wouldn't budge. She was stupefied. A ten-foot giant towered in the yard, in front of a gorgeous woman in a white dress that glittered in the moonlight, while behind them flames from the burning haystack lit up the night. It would've been strange if she'd actually been able to do anything at that point.

"Don't you lay a hand on my kids!" Adele said, standing in front of Matthew to shield him—not that there was anything an unarmed human could do against the Nobility. "Just try something funny. Before you can sink those filthy fangs of yours into my children's veins, I'll tear you to pieces!"

"That sounds amusing," Miranda said, her lip curling up. White fangs peeked from the corners of her smile.

"Stop it," the giant said, laying a hand on the Noblewoman. Her shoulder was so dainty, it seemed as if this gesture alone would've been enough to destroy it, yet she gave it a slight toss that easily knocked the giant's hand away.

"Stop it," the giant repeated, taking her shoulder again. It wouldn't move an inch.

"Why are you against me? Doing this would be in the family's best interest. Even the servants of the Nobility couldn't do any harm to humans who've been turned into Nobles. Nor could other Nobles."

"There is something to what you say."

"In that case, I'll thank you not to interfere."

"No, wait. Regardless of our opinion, we must first find out their thoughts on this matter. Would you like this lovely woman to drink your blood?" the count said, his question directed to the family.

"Hell, no! Don't come any closer," Adele said firmly.

It was an odd situation. Two Nobles had turned up at their house when there weren't supposed to be any in the area at all. And they hadn't come to drink the family's blood. Something else was going on. These two had a secret.

At any rate, they were Nobility—bloodsucking monsters. Adele's family absolutely could not let their guard down around them.

Though her body was close to freezing, hot blood started to pump through it as her determination grew.

Gazing down at Adele from his lofty vantage point, Count Braujou remarked, "She appears firmly opposed to this. You'll have to abandon your plan, Duchess."

"Ah, but it would be to the greatest benefit of us all. Will you not be so good as to reconsider, human mother?" Miranda said, her eyes beginning once more to carry a golden glow. A gleam of the same color sparked in the depths of Adele's eyes, and her resolute will began to melt away.

"Hey!"

"Be silent," Miranda said. Her voice was laden with malice, though her demeanor was that of an amiable Noblewoman. "Even you must know in your heart that this is for the best. I merely ask that she change her mind. I'll thank you to keep your remarks to yourself, Count. Come."

Adele responded to her summons, her sizable breasts still bare to the moonlight. The sturdy farmer's wife was about to fall into the vampire's bloody trap.

When the distance separating life from death had closed to just six feet, there was a bang and a flash by Miranda's feet, and pale-blue atomic flames spread. The flames leaped to her dress, instantly transforming the duchess into a human torch.

"Mom!" Matthew and Sue shouted as they raced over to the reeling Adele.

"Oh, my," the giant said with admiration from his lofty vantage point. It was a compliment for the slip of a girl who'd lobbed an atomic lantern at Miranda to save her mother from peril. She also had the bolt gun she always carried when she went outside in hand as she stood in front of her mother and brother to shield them.

"This family certainly has pluck. Now, Miranda . . ."

Although the Nobleman hadn't sought her agreement, the human torch replied, "Indeed. They may even be able to weather my response."

Raising her blazing arms by her sides, she let out a sharp breath as she swung them down again. The flames vanished . . . along with the atomic lamp. Neither the skin of the pale beauty nor her dress showed the slightest hint of being charred.

"Come to me. No, on second thought, I will come to you."

Before the count could stop her, she started walking, but halted after the second step. Duchess Miranda turned to look. As did Count Braujou. But what did they hear, and what did they see?

About five seconds later, the human mother and son learned the answers to those questions. From the darkness beyond the main house—and the entrance to the farm—the sound of hoof beats was drawing nearer. Who in the world could it be? The looks on the faces of Miranda and Braujou were hardly those of fearless Nobles.

"Who is it?" the duchess asked, her voice trembling.

"Someone with power," Braujou replied.

"Who?" Adele murmured. And the light of the moon picked the answer out for her.

The beautiful darkness that had appeared from the depths of the night took the shape of a black horse and rider as they rode into the moonlight. As he passed by a haystack, flames painted his body red. He halted at a spot about ten feet from Miranda and the giant.

"I don't know whether to say you're late or just in the nick of time—but at any rate, here you are, D!"

Catching the fear the count's tone carried, Duchess Miranda swallowed hard in spite of herself.

The Noble Who Came from the Stars

CHAPTER 4

I

The eyes of three fearful faces were glued to the faces of three others who weren't quite human. Gathered around the kitchen table were D, Count Braujou, and Duchess Miranda—and across from them, Adele Dyalhis sat alone. In terms of sheer might, the group had her outgunned to a surreal degree, although these three weren't foes of her or her children.

Matthew and Sue stood side by side in the doorway leading to the living room, and just like their mother, they wore expressions that were a mixture of terror and courageousness—but the odd tinge of infatuation was due to the gorgeous Hunter, who stood closer than the others to the siblings.

Both of them knew his name. His legendary skill with a sword had been branded into their hearts and minds with the unrivaled fire of a child's imagination. However, more than that, there was something else that made their hearts beat faster—his great beauty. Even someone who looked as exquisite and alluring as Duchess Miranda in the moonlight couldn't begin to compare to him. He was in an entirely different class. Though the children weren't staring, even a brief glance at him made their minds melt, and the world began to distort around them. D's good looks were so intense that Matthew and Sue lost all knowledge of ugliness. Count Braujou seemed unmoved by his presence, but when D ordered the giant and the duchess—who was the very epitome of the Nobility—to discuss matters inside, the latter had frowned but complied, and the humans had to wonder if that complicity hadn't been due to the Hunter's beauty.

Their rapture was so great, the children nearly forgot the shocking and horrifying truths that Count Braujou and Miranda had shared with them by turns—as did Adele. With her pride and her sense of maternal duty to consider, she barely managed to keep her eyes off D's handsome features and maintain her right state of mind, but her tightly clenched hands kept the front of the robe she wore over a fresh shirt closed. When D had appeared, her chest had been completely exposed. Perhaps it was on account of her embarrassment that she was able to exhibit a normal reaction to the Nobles' tale.

The fearful truth that besieged her and her children in the middle of the night was the tale of a Noble who'd returned from the stars.

Five thousand years ago, the entire northern Frontier, as well as the eastern and western sectors, had been under the control of a single Noble: Lawrence Valcua.

"They called him the Ultimate Noble," Count Braujou said, and though his expression could usually be described as rather mild, at that moment he looked like the devil himself. "A Noble among Nobles, he was one of the Greater Nobility, and no one dared challenge his power, his fortune, or his rank—he'd truly attained everything befitting someone of that title."

Though many Nobles loathed serving in the Frontier sectors, he'd actively pursued such duties, converting a castle from a mysterious and ancient human culture in the northern extreme of the very worst part of the Frontier, creating fortifications to lay claim to half of the northern Frontier, and then making a grab for the domains of other Nobles in the east, west, and south. Naturally, fighting ensued, but those overseeing the east and west were routed in less than fifty years. Only a band of Nobility in the south offered him stubborn resistance.

"That was Miranda's husband, Duke Harness; the great General Gaskell; and I. Though it pains me to admit it, none of us had a chance alone. In addition to his physical strength, he had the ability to construct bizarre and devastating weapons, and he had retainers who were far more powerful than we were. I can't completely disregard the rumors that he was related to the Sacred Ancestor. After he was exiled, the person in charge of learning the principles behind the machines and armaments that remained became so engrossed he forgot to eat or sleep, until he finally went mad and ran into the sunlight. No one could imagine why Valcua created such things. All we do know is that he had an insane hatred toward every living person, human or Noble. And something served to reveal all the evil he'd kept hidden inside himself. You see, beneath his castle, they discovered the remains of five million humans and Nobles who'd been murdered in every manner imaginable."

"Your memory must be failing you, Count Braujou," Duchess Miranda said, her voice tapering off into what seemed to be laughter. "The corpses only numbered four million; the remaining million still lived. At least, they still lived as severed heads or disembodied hearts. A single tube from a store of life-preserving drugs in an unseen tank that was said to exist in the fourth dimension kept them from dying. Moreover, the drugs contained vast quantities of painkillers and nanomachines to prevent death or madness, and they also provided an 'alternate reality' that would make the psyche succumb to the most extreme isolation and despair. It was for this reason that Lawrence Valcua was dubbed the Ultimate Noble."

But even Valcua found himself challenged by the combined might of the three forces from the south, and the battle stretched on for a thousand years. The Frontier was transformed into a wasteland, bloody rains created rivers and lakes of gore, battles with hex technology corrupted the earth down to the very magma core, and only a "dream" Duchess Miranda gave it left the land capable of sustaining life.

"Ah, what a time that was! It was the anniversary of an ancient holiday. We'd already tapped the power of magma and the ley lines to give Valcua a black eye, but we never imagined he'd pay us back with a shooting star."

His missiles were small, metallic meteors summoned by remote control from an asteroid belt two hundred million miles from Earth. Moving at fifteen miles per second when they hit the atmosphere, the five hundred meteorites were greeted with fire from space cannons, but one of them managed to make it through the defensive net and strike the very center of the Frontier. For three hundred miles in all directions the ground rose up to the heavens, mountains vanished, and seas boiled away. The dead numbered thirty million.

This incident caused such fervor among the Nobility that an inquest was held to find out why the meteorite hadn't been detected beforehand. The conclusion they reached was a simple one. Composed largely of darkness and radiation, outer space was something the Nobility loved like it was their own parent. It had never occurred to them that the majestic void might betray them, so they hadn't seen any reason to keep an eye on the heavens. Who would dare to probe the secrets of their beloved parent's heart?

However, they began to scrutinize space much more closely, and just five days later, they discovered a meteor six thousand miles in diameter—actually, a planet—flying toward Earth. Based on its shape and speed, they discovered this was one of the planetoids that orbited Alpha Centauri, and there was no way to stop it on such short notice. Not only had the Ultimate Noble managed to wrest a celestial body from its orbit in another solar system, he was also able to use it in a plan to wipe out another planet.

The black arms of despair embraced the three Nobles.

That's when it happened.

"The Sacred Ancestor stepped forward. It was unclear how the planetoid had evaded the immutable laws of the universe to travel to within five million miles of Earth, but it suddenly changed direction and flew off into the depths of space. In a sense, we were still numb from having to accept our own imminent extinction, but then the Sacred Ancestor commanded us to take Lawrence Valcua alive."

The greatest mystery of Earth's near destruction five millennia earlier was that on the day in question, Valcua was back in his own castle having a banquet with lakes of alcohol and mountains of meat. Perhaps he had some means of escaping. However, when the three Nobles entered his castle without even a single soldier to accompany them, he was there to face them all alone in a great hall.

Nothing could match the ghastliness of a battle to the death between immortal Nobles, but Duke Harness was ultimately slain, and General Gaskell was wounded. Even the intrepid and resolute Count Braujou knew that his end was near, but just then a solitary human figure appeared through the same hole the three Nobles had used to make their entry, the pair of swords he carried forming a cross that he pressed toward Valcua's forehead.

"Like this, you see," the count said, reenacting the gesture with his fingers even as he averted his gaze. "That shape troubles us like no other. But realizing that makes it fade completely from a human's memory—and I see you've already forgotten it, haven't you? Before that simple sign, the Ultimate Noble would be no different from any Lesser Noble. The same would probably even be true for the Sacred Ancestor—at any rate, when it was pressed against Valcua's forehead, he fell back, whereupon Gaskell and I seized him with a most disagreeable ease and left the castle by the same way we'd gone in."

At this point, the count gazed quietly at Adele and her two children.

"That brave human was a man who'd been imprisoned in Valcua's castle as a test subject but had managed to escape. Finding him by the side of the road suffering from a stomachache, I'd given him some medicine. I don't know why I did that, but I suppose it may have been because I thought I was going to my destruction. He thanked me and said he'd be sure to return the favor. We simply laughed and said in that case, he should go with us to Valcua's castle. After that, we didn't give him another thought. But he didn't forget the promise he'd made.

"When it came time to part company with him at the edge of Valcua's domain, we wished to reward the man, so we asked him what he wanted. He thought for a little while, and then told us he had the ability to see the future. It rarely manifested itself, and because of this he was bound to end his days as a poor wandering scholar, but it was this same ability that had shown him the trick with the swords he'd used to repel Valcua earlier. Now, strangely enough, it had shown him another vision of a star falling to Earth. Undoubtedly that was to mean that after Valcua had been exiled to space, he'd return at some unknown date. If the two of us still lived when he did, the man asked that we protect his family or their descendants. We agreed to that. And when, just as he'd said, the Sacred Ancestor didn't drive a stake through Valcua's heart but rather sentenced him to exile in the vastness of space, we came to believe that the Ultimate Noble would indeed return.

"And now Lawrence Valcua has come back and our battle has begun again. You see, we must honor our oath to protect the descendants of the brave human who saved us by keeping his own word. That bastard Valcua left us with a threat. I won't forget this. Mark my words. I will return to wreak a bloody vengeance the likes of which the devil himself could scarcely imagine on the two of you, and Harness's family. And of course I won't overlook the descendants of that meddling little human."

Adele had turned to stone, but at this point she finally opened her mouth to ask, "Who was he?"

"He said his name was Winslow Dyalhis. And though it feels like it was just yesterday that I met him, I don't doubt he was your ancestor from five millennia ago."

II

Count Braujou's assessment was correct—if not, there would be no accounting for the weird events of that very night. Though the man was an ancestor of theirs from five thousand years earlier, it was an incredibly long time ago, and they couldn't recall ever hearing his name before. The Nobleman so tall he looked likely to go through the ceiling and the coldly amiable Noblewoman said that on account of their promise to that man, they would protect his family from the Ultimate Noble and his forces. Adele had the feeling that her family would have been far better off if none of the Nobles had come to save them.

Once the fantastic story had been told, Adele said, "I can't quite wrap my head around it."

Apparently the three visitors had expected such a reaction.

"That's hardly a surprise. However, it's all true. Take the spider man I fought in the stratosphere, or the water witch who pierced Duchess Miranda through the heart. I think it's safe to say there are other fiends besides them who are after your family. And they've already slain the great General Gaskell. I'm not surprised that you doubt the truth of this, but your children are also in danger."

The count's words jabbed Adele in her weak point. After some contemplation, she nodded and said, "I see. But what should we do?"

"To start, you have to get out of here."

"Leave our farm? But . . ."

"If you were to stay isolated with your children, it'd be akin to standing naked in the wilderness with arms spread wide to welcome the hungry wolves that prowl there."

"But this is . . ." Adele wanted to shout at them, *this is all I have to show for a decade of hard work*, but she choked it back.

Her husband had been there for the first three years. He'd been a hard worker and the strongest guy in the neighborhood. Tilling the soil, he'd planted so much that when the right season came, they had more milk whistle grass and giant apples than anyone else. In winter, her husband went out hunting. So good with a long spear that he'd never been beaten at the village carnival, he'd taken down a number of the subterranean bull beasts and needle fiends that even professional huntsmen steered clear of, much to the astonishment of butchers and fur traders who called on the village. Gazing at the sweat glistening on her husband's muscles as he worked the plow, Adele always had been reminded of his reliability.

One day ten years earlier, a bar had opened in the village. It was an establishment from up north, and their idiotic mayor had invited them to set up shop there in hopes of making their town more appealing. If it had provided only alcohol, that would've been one thing, but with it came gaudy costumes, coquettish voices, and youthful bodies that capitalized on the vulgar atmosphere. Her husband had gone into town to sell their crops, and after that he started to find more and more reasons to head out, until before long he stopped coming back. She didn't know how many of the bar's women he'd been involved with by now.

At first, the villagers and Adele's neighbors—who lived a couple of miles away—had blamed the women who worked in the bar, but before long the blame shifted to her husband. Adele didn't know how many times she or her children had gone to a woman's room that reeked of face powder and cheap perfume and asked if Baird would come home. That's fine by me, a heavily painted face had always sneered, but not by him. According to the villagers, her husband hung around the woman's room all day. On the few occasions when he did go outside, he begged his acquaintances for change so he could buy himself a drink.

Adele hadn't left him to his own devices. She'd shaken him awake in that woman's bed, knocked him senseless with the butt of a rifle, and hauled him home against his will. But it was no use. When she saw him hit Matthew with a whip when the boy followed him in tears, something had vanished from Adele's heart. She got the feeling it was the smile her husband had worn with Sue on his shoulders, or giving a huge, freshly picked apple to his son, or the sight of his powerful back as he'd washed away the sweat of a day's labor on the farm with a bath in a steel drum.

From that day, Adele decided she would raise her children on her own. She'd hired men to work there time and again. Every time she did, they always ended up trying to sneak into her bed at night, and she had to get rid of them. Eventually, she abandoned that idea altogether.

But she already had a good man around. Although there was no way the seven-year-old could take her husband's place, he grew up watching his mother in action. The weight of a hoe had made him stagger, but three years later he started doing the tougher work in the fields, and when three more years had passed, Adele realized she no longer had to do the hardest jobs. She remembered how she stood alone in the kitchen that night, staring down at her hands— big, tough hands. When she snapped a finger against the palm of one hand, it made a hard sound. Thinking of how these were the same hands that had once picked flowers to adorn the house every day, she was terribly embarrassed of their roughness. When a hand reached around her left side and gently took hers, she wasn't quite sure what was happening. It was the hand of a young man. Far softer than Adele's, it was still strong. That was the first time Adele realized her son was thirteen years old, almost full grown.

After that, Adele went out to work in the fields less and less, but Sue acquired a variety of skills in her place. When the two siblings came back from the fields, the table was laid with the kind of dishes that made their neighbors arrange to pass by at the right time to catch a whiff of them on the breeze, and the children's torn clothing would be patched up by the next morning and hanging out on the clothesline with the sweet smell of soap. Someday her kids were bound to leave, but Adele consoled herself knowing these serene days would continue for a while yet.

But now she found herself sitting across the table from three Nobles (technically, one was only half Noble), discussing the situation. And they were telling Adele and her children that the hard and impoverished days, days that still had merit, were now at an end. She wanted to slam her hands down on the table and tell them, *No! Why are you here? You bust in on a family and take it upon yourself to tell them it's all over. And what's the reason for all this? A promise you made one of their ancestors five thousand years ago! You tell them to get off their farm as soon as they can . . .*

"I see," Adele said once more, again getting the feeling she was losing something. "Pack your things, kids. It's gonna be a long trip."

Upon hearing these words, Matthew's and Sue's faces clouded. They wanted to scream and shout even more than Adele did. Nevertheless, the two of them responded, "Yes, ma'am." For they'd already learned that life was all about dealing with the cheap shots fate could deliver unexpectedly.

Matthew was about to turn and walk through the doorway when he looked back and asked, "Mom—what'll we do about Dad?"

"I don't think we can just abandon him. Come daybreak, we'll go get him. So, where is it we're headed, anyway?"

"The central Frontier," the count said.

"Central? I didn't think there was such a place," Matthew remarked, furrowing his brow.

Adele told him, "There was, a long time ago. Now it's been nibbled away by the sectors to the north, south, east, and west, and largely forgotten, but part of it still remains. But what's out there?"

The duchess provided the answer.

"The fortress we constructed," she said. "Expecting that this day would come, we spent two millennia building a stronghold of unparalleled security. You should be thankful. All this has been done for you."

"It's not like I asked you to," Adele said, and her flippant remark made the duchess raise her eyebrows. "The next time you say anything patronizing like that, we're striking out on our own. I'll thank you to keep that in mind. I wanna be perfectly clear that we still don't trust the lot of you."

"My, my," the pale beauty replied with a sigh that made her shoulders fall. "It would seem five thousand years is more than enough time for humanity to grow ungrateful. In that case, I have something to tell you as well. From the very beginning, I've been opposed to showing you any mercy. If your ancestor hadn't tried to meddle in our affairs, I believe my husband would still be alive. I'm only here to honor the ridiculous promise my husband's allies made. Valcua is after me, too. Ordinarily, I wouldn't have been the least bit concerned about what happened to you. I would've remained in my own domain preparing my castle for attack. If you want to run from us, be my guest. The sooner you do, the happier I shall be. But don't think we'll be coming to rescue you again."

The two women glared at each other with fire in their eyes. Matthew and Sue were frozen, and even Count Braujou wore a wry grin.

But just then, a voice said, "Someone's coming."

The count and Miranda, to say nothing of the three humans, couldn't hide their surprise. That voice hadn't come from where they thought it should. The young man in black was looking out into the darkness beyond the window, but even those with the superhuman senses of the Nobility hadn't noticed his movements. It was probably Matthew and Sue who were most astonished. They hadn't taken their eyes off D the whole time—actually, they couldn't take their eyes off him. Even though all their nerves were focused on their mother's conversation with the bizarre visitors, the Hunter's heavenly visage seemed to sparkle in their eyes. Yet at some point he'd moved. The look on Matthew's face was more amazement than terror.

"Four coming from the west. On horseback."

"Indeed," the duchess said with a grin, "and, the way they ride—they must be human. They've dismounted. They're less than twenty yards from the house. From their voices, they're just striplings."

"Four young men . . ."

Adele and Matthew looked at each other.

"What the hell do those jerks want?" Matthew said, wearing a bleak expression as he slammed his fist into his palm.

"Kill the lights," his mother told him. "They're out to settle a grudge. And since they've stopped their horses so far from the house at this hour—they're pretty serious about it."

"Hmm. It would appear you have other problems, as well. You seem to be a person prone to misunderstandings," the duchess said, looking out the opposite window. "Soon, I shall have to sleep. But before I do, I believe I'll have some fun with these humans. And just so you know, I'm doing this for your sakes. As a wife, it's my duty to keep my dear husband's promise."

Rising gracefully from her chair, she walked over to the door and slipped like smoke through the narrow opening.

Adele went pale, as if watching that unprecedented exit had sucked the soul out of her, but she quickly turned to Matthew and ordered him sternly, "Get going. We can't let that woman attack those boys."

Matthew hesitated. "But Mom, they're—"

"I don't care how rotten they are. They still deserve a better death than that. We can't let a Noble tear 'em to ribbons. If we let it come to that, all of us will regret it for the rest of our days. Your father taught you that much."

Saying nothing, Matthew clapped his hand on his mother's shoulder, and then he got up to grab one of the stake guns they kept in every room.

Suddenly shock hung in the air. Adele had turned around and discovered the other Noble and the Hunter had vanished.

"When the heck did they leave? Sue?"

Standing by the door, her daughter shook her head, frightened. "When you said, your father taught you that much, the two of them went out . . ."

Still not sure what was going on, Matthew ran to one of the weapons.

III

By the time Matthew came flying out of the house, the action was half over.

About twenty yards from their back door, the duchess stood haughtily glaring at both the Hunter and the giant. From each of her

pale and delicate hands dangled a pair of unconscious youths. The trio of inhuman beings gave off a fierce aura of the supernatural that made human flesh prickle, and Matthew had no choice but to stop.

All three turned toward him in unison.

"What may I do for you, my lovely child?" Miranda inquired coolly. The fangs that peeked from her lips glittered in the moonlight.

"Let go of them," Matthew said. Even he thought he sounded pretty feeble.

"They're your enemies. I can see that plainly."

"Yeah, but you shouldn't hurt them. I'll take care of them myself. And another thing—I'd appreciate it if you didn't call me child."

The pale temptress laughed aloud, leaving her throat exposed. "I've heard that humans enjoy playing the hero, and it seems that's indeed the case. You should thank me for disposing of your foes without you ever having to get your own hands dirty."

"I can't do that. Humans deserve to die in a human fashion. Please, let go of them," the boy said, his body taut with determination.

"Dear me," the duchess said with a mocking grin. "What if I were to say I didn't wish to do so?"

Her remark sent a shudder through Matthew. All of his resolve evaporated with the ease of a mist. It was natural for a human to succumb to a Noble's demeanor.

Miranda's smile changed again. This time it became a sneer.

"Kindly step back."

It was a gentle but firm command from a Noble. Matthew backed away. And then he heard it. He heard the miserable, thread-thin voice from the end of one of the duchess's arms croak, "Help . . . me . . ."

Strength flooded Matthew's entire body. Although he hated the young man who was pleading for his life, the loftiest ambition a foolish human might have took hold of him. Never abandon the weak.

"Let 'em go," Matthew said, leveling his stake gun.

"Do you actually believe a toy like that will destroy me? I came into this life another five millennia before that promise was made to your ancestor. I'm not about to meet my end by no more than a rough wooden stake."

Matthew had personally witnessed proof that her confident claims were no lie when she'd battled that other pale woman, Lucienne. Even a wooden stake was only effective if driven right through a Noble's heart. A stake through the abdomen or lungs, between the eyes or through the top of the head, would prove completely ineffective and could simply be pulled right back out. The only other place said to be effective was the throat, in keeping with lore passed down through the ages—that to destroy a vampire, you had to drive a stake through her heart, then cut off her head when you were done. Yet a stake through this woman's heart wouldn't do any good.

However, the boy was no longer scared or confused. The barrel of the weapon he'd raised didn't move a hair as he kept it aimed straight at the duchess's impressive bosom.

"Go ahead and shoot," the duchess said, striking her chest with her left hand. She hadn't let go of the two punks she held with it. She had monstrous strength—with every effortless movement of the duchess's hand, the boys were tossed wildly.

Still, Matthew hesitated. The fact that the enchantress before him had come to save his family kept crossing his mind.

"Aren't you going to fire?" the duchess asked, revealing her white fangs. "Well, I shall make it easier for you to shoot. Watch."

Her hand had been lowered, but now the duchess jerked it back up, pulling one of the two figures who flapped about like pathetic dolls nearer and pressing her vermilion lips close to the nape of his neck.

"Please, help me!" he sobbed, and the light from the atomic lamp Matthew held against his chest shone on a face like that of a dead man—the face of Joppes Lallacksiski.

The instant Matthew saw the pair of fangs begin to press against the nape of the man's neck, he pulled the trigger. Driven by pressurized gas at a speed of seventy-five miles per second, the projectile didn't have the same range as a bullet, but from this close there was no way he could miss.

In front of the bosom of that white dress, a black form snatched the stake from the air. It went without saying who was connected to the arm that had reached over to make that catch.

"Why did you stop it, D?" the duchess inquired, and there seemed to be some amusement in her voice.

"We can't very well have a savior fighting the person she's trying to save," D said, tossing the stake back to Matthew. "Leave those guys to him."

"Oh, now you, too, would presume to interfere with me?"

"I won't interfere. But if you hurt him, Count Braujou won't stand idly by. And it won't do me any good if the count is destroyed in the fight that will ensue."

"You have a point there," the woman replied, a scornful expression skidding across her pale and beautiful visage. "Your good looks almost made me forget you're nothing but a hunting dog who lives by lapping up our life blood. You should just hold your tongue and watch. You make too much noise for a dog, but now I'll silence your barking."

The duchess's eyes met D's. Golden sparks formed in D's dark pupils. Suddenly, they wavered, grew slimmer, and shuddered like a death rattle a split second before they disappeared.

"Stop it," the giant called out to them; he'd sensed the unearthly aura emanating from every inch of D.

The duchess backed away two or three steps, as if her strength were spent.

"I realize this woman's been rude to you, but her power will be indispensable in the fight ahead. Without her, I may well fall to Valcua."

Perhaps on account of these words, D dispelled the eerie aura and turned his eyes toward the eastern sky. "It's nearly dawn," he said.

Knitting his brow, the count replied, "But it's still night. We'll set out right away."

Braujou turned around. Up to the point where he was swallowed by the darkness, his massive form moved without the sound of a footstep.

Watching him go in a daze, Matthew suddenly turned and noticed that there was no sign of the duchess, only a white fog billowing down the road.

He ran over to the four fallen thugs. When Adele joined him, she gasped. Could a Noble do this to someone without biting him, with just a touch? The quartet had possessed a vicious youthfulness, but now they were all withered old men with gray hair—they looked almost like mummies as they lay on the ground.

Behind them, the speechless pair heard footsteps heading toward the house. Matthew was just about to follow the Hunter when Adele stopped him.

"What is it, Mom?"

"He has Noble blood in him, too. I don't want him in the house."

"But—"

"It's the giant he's after. As long as the giant's guarding us, he'll stick around, too. That's bad enough."

Adele wasn't mistaken in her appraisal. Less than two minutes later the pair watched D straddle his black steed.

As the gorgeous rider turned in silence, Matthew could no longer restrain himself, and he impulsively shouted, "That was pretty impressive, you know! You sure are tough, mister."

Though the boy got the impression the Hunter shot a quick glance in his direction, D said nothing as he slowly rode away.

Certain that they hadn't seen the last of him, the boy still had feverish winds of emotion wreaking havoc in his heart. He called out, "What do you have to do to become a Hunter? To be a Vampire Hunter, I mean."

Before his mother could turn a look of shock and horror on him, D had gone off into the darkness.

Adele and Matthew were left standing there, shrouded in a desolation they couldn't even begin to describe. But it felt as if they had just learned they were the last two people left on Earth.

Matthew's mother pressed her face against his chest, and her lips began to tremble.

"What are we supposed to do now, Matthew? We're not cut out for anything but working in the fields. Now we've got no choice but to do like these Nobles tell us and leave our farm. I'm so scared," the mother said, her words giving way to sobs.

Matthew was gripped by a quiet surprise, but not because this was the first time he'd seen his mother this way. Rather, it was because he remained so incomprehensibly cool.

"It's okay, Mom," the boy said, gently clapping his mother on the shoulder. "We'll get by. Sure, we're leaving now, but we can always come back. And we can make a go of it anywhere."

A faint glow began to seep like water into the world. From the same direction the other three had gone—from the east.

Jessup the Beheader

CHAPTER 5

I

After giving first aid to the four barely breathing thugs, the Dyalhises brought them to the hospital. It was late the next morning before they were ready to head out. Their last piece of baggage was still in town.

Having treated all four of the boys by herself, Adele was exhausted and didn't talk much. When the hospital and the sheriff's office wanted to know about the quartet's eerie medical condition, Matthew maintained that they'd been found like that near his house. Apparently word of what had happened had gotten out, as every person the family passed gave them suspicious looks. There'd never been a case of any creature in the world sucking the life out of people without leaving a mark on them. From the state these four were in, the prime suspect was the Nobility. So why hadn't the Dyalhis boy testified to that effect?

The wagon that carried the mother and children took the main street through town, halting in front of the village's only inn. This is where the barmaid their father was so smitten with rented a room.

"Go get this stuff at Mr. Gamish's shop," Adele said, handing Sue a list before she climbed down from the wagon.

"Mom, you want me to go with you?" Matthew called out to her.

"If I had to bring my son along to drag out my drunken husband, I'd be a laughingstock. Whether you've got that shopping done or not, be back here in twenty minutes."

Her husband wasn't there. Seeing Adele walk past the counter and toward the staircase, the innkeeper told her Baird wasn't in. He said at this hour, her husband would be in the bar or at the coach stop, looking for handouts from travelers and acquaintances.

Closing her eyes and thanking him, Adele headed over to the bar. He wasn't there.

The coach stop was on the western edge of the village. Not everyone coming into town was necessarily an upstanding person. There was no guarantee a traveler wasn't an illusion beast that could read people's minds and take the shape of someone they knew, a camouflage creature called a magai, or a servant of the Nobility with orders to scout for fresh prey. Allowing coaches carrying all sorts of passengers to ride into the center of town might cost the villagers their lives—or their souls. Therefore, armed officials at the Somui coach stop checked every traveler.

When the stop, which looked like a large barracks, came into view further down the road, the coach that was halted in front of it tore down the path, leaving a cloud of fine dust behind. After Adele had walked on for another five minutes and was about thirty feet shy of the coach stop, men's shouts assailed her ears.

"There's no damned reflection!"

"Fire!"

Even though she couldn't see what was happening, she knew in an instant what it had to be. One of the travelers hadn't cast a reflection in the mirror held by an official.

The roar of an old-fashioned firearm overlapped their cries. Another thunderous shot rang out.

A man who looked like a farmer in his baggy coat and trousers had just come around the corner of the coach stop and into view.

He was running straight at Adele. Behind him, she could see two officials stained with crimson. One of them raised his gun and shouted, "Hit the dirt!"

As Adele leaped to the right, to her left the man screamed and leaned backward. The report from the gun reached her a split second later.

Still tilted backward, the man advanced another five or six paces, then dropped to his knees and toppled back as if forming a bridge.

Adele had already jumped up. Like a good Frontier woman, she held the bolt gun she carried for self-defense in her right hand. The man shuddered feebly, but he soon became motionless.

"You're not hurt, are you?" asked the official who came over, dragging one leg behind him, his gun trained on the man all the while.

"I'm all right. You got it worse than me."

Realizing that the man stained with gore from the waist down was alone, Adele turned toward the coach stop. The second man had slumped to the ground in the same spot where she'd seen him before. Doubled over like a snapped twig, his upper body seemed to be bleeding, and the blood dripped from his knees to stain the ground. The god of the soil would feed well.

By the time Adele turned her gaze back to the figure at her feet, it had finished dissolving with a foul stench. Its dissolution had come through a chemical reaction that took only seconds.

"This is a new one—some new kind of monster," the official beside her said, finally lowering his rifle. "I'll go get help. Don't suppose I could ask you to look after that fella, could I? See, that thing tore his chest to ribbons with its claws, and he's not gonna last long. There's no one else around."

"Sure."

Parting ways with the man, Adele hastened over to the coach stop. The man who sat there was dead. The wounds in his chest were more like punctures than slashes, reaching into his heart and lungs. It was a miracle he'd even made it that far.

"I bet he had some final words he wanted to say."

Kneeling, Adele clutched the rosary that hung around her neck and recited a prayer. There were a number of gods in the area. Instead of the one governing the colossal beech tree that stood next to the coach stop, Adele selected the one that represented the towering rock five or ten feet away. She felt that when it came to protecting someone called to heaven, the god of a rock would be much better suited to the task than that of a gentle tree.

Before the woman could end her prayer by calling out the god's name, she noticed somebody was coming up behind her.

No, it can't be. Please, God, anyone but him.

"Hey, Adele." There was no mistaking her husband's voice. "Fancy meeting you here. I sure am lucky it's you. Would you just shut your eyes for me for a sec?"

Averting her face from his boozy breath, Adele got up. Once more she wanted to close her eyes. Over the past twenty years, there'd been a number of times she wished she couldn't see anything, but never had she wanted it more badly than now.

She could see her husband clearly. The face puffy and pale from too much drink, the lifeless eyes of a dead cow, the scraggly growth of beard, and arms so scrawny the veins bulged from them. Her husband was already dead to her. She knew that well.

"What are you up to?" she asked as if she were interrogating a criminal.

Sheepishly avoiding her gaze, her husband replied, "Isn't it obvious? This guy's probably got some stuff on him he's not gonna need anymore."

Adele gazed at his profile. It was the face of a man who knew what he was doing was wrong and wanted to stop, but had done it so often that no matter how badly he wanted to change, he never would. He apologized, but went right ahead and stole anyway. He could swear it would only be this once, then turn around and kill someone. Her husband had become a monster.

Adele backed away a step.

Unconcerned, her husband wiped his sweaty hand on his tattered coat, straddled the dead man, and began going through the pockets of his leather vest. The left one was empty, but Baird found something in the right one. Opening the leather bag, he grinned. Pushing it into his own pocket, he said, "This'll keep me in drink for a while, I suppose. It'll be our little secret, Adele."

When he turned to look at his wife, Adele drove her knife into his belly. As Baird backed away, he clutched the hilt of the knife with both hands. He made an effort to pull it back out, but his face contorted with pain and he stopped.

"What the hell was that, Adele?" her husband said, his tone still sharp.

"Don't think that it was on account of what you just did, dear," Adele said, standing still as she spoke. "See, while your four little friends were being looked over, I heard what happened. Seems you had them all set to rob us as payback for what went on yesterday. And you told 'em if things got hairy, you didn't give a damn if they killed the lot of us and burned the place down when they were done. You must be out of your mind!"

"No," her husband said, his now-purple lips trembling as he denied the accusations. "That's a lie. I didn't say anything like that. Adele, you've gotta believe me. They're my kids . . . I'm their father!"

Her husband thudded down on the road, his face twisting with the shock.

"Only on the outside. Inside, you're a whole different person. The you the kids and I knew died ten years ago."

"Adele . . . Oh, Adele . . . ," her husband called out feebly, his upper body bending backward until he lay flat on his back. He was nearly at an end. The knife handle jutting from his solar plexus shuddered with each sharp breath.

"You can't go with our kids. But this is the least I can do. Better you be sent to your reward by me instead of being murdered by some Noble. Don't worry, though. Once I've seen that our kids are safe, I'll follow along behind you. After all, on the other side, you'll probably be back to your old self."

Adele turned her gaze toward the village. There was no sign of anyone.

"I'm so sorry. It's time to go," she told her husband, and then she put his body over her shoulder and jogged toward the path to her left.

It was a shortcut that would bring her to the general store without running into any villagers. She ran for all she was worth—she had to get out of town with Matthew and Sue as soon as possible. If she were to hide her husband's corpse somewhere off this path, no one would find it for a while.

Suddenly Adele had a strange sensation. Although she was progressing down the familiar path, it felt at the same time as if she were on another route. Stopping, she checked her surroundings, and it was the right path. The scenery to either side of it was familiar. And yet, something in the back of her mind whispered that it was different. Her husband's shudders were transmitted through her shoulder.

Going off the left side of the path, Adele slipped into thick woods. Suddenly, she came to a clearing. Nearly circular, the empty lot seemed to cover between one hundred fifty and two hundred square feet. Adele was sure she'd never seen this place before . . . nor had she ever laid eyes on the figure that stood at the center of the clearing. He wore a dark brown hood and a long robe, but whether the two were a single garment or not was unclear. About the same height as Adele, he didn't have a particularly muscular build, and the great ax he held with its blade resting on the ground seemed completely disproportionate.

What's he doing out here dressed like an old-fashioned headsman?

Not even a second after this question occurred to her, so did an answer.

Has he been waiting for me?

"I've been waiting for you," he said. Though he had the look of a man in his late forties or early fifties, his voice was terribly hoarse—much like the voice of an old man she'd met long ago who'd said he was a hundred and twenty. "My name's Jessup. I do all Lord Valcua's beheading."

"Valcua . . ."

Suddenly the name that had been part fantasy became a hard reality slamming down on Adele's mind.

"It's all true—isn't it?"

"You and the man you have over your shoulder belong to the family of an old enemy of my master, Lawrence Valcua, for which you must be executed. I don't care which of you we start with, but someone better come over here and put his neck on the block," said Jessup. His left hand wasn't touching the ax handle, but pointed down by his feet.

He stood near a U-shaped stand that looked like an iron plate bent from both ends with terrific force, supported by a sturdy pedestal about a foot high.

Realizing its purpose in an instant, Adele was terrified. Instinctively she tried to turn, but her feet wouldn't move.

"There's no point in trying to flee. You came here precisely so you might die by my hand. You walked the road to the beheader," Jessup said, his mocking gaze trained on Adele's feet. From his feet to hers, and over the ground Adele had just covered, lay a red cloth a foot and a half wide that ran down the path like a river of blood. She couldn't remember walking on it.

"Having set foot on it, you can't get away without my ax passing through that wrinkly neck of yours. Come here."

Perhaps there was some mystic power to his voice, or perhaps it was the bloody path she'd trod. Showing no signs of resistance, Adele began to walk toward the assassin in dark brown.

II

Of course, that's not to say she advanced of her own free will. But it wouldn't have been correct to say that she was fighting it the whole time, either. Perhaps the best description of the way she walked would be to say that it seemed natural—or even inevitable. Adele had fully accepted that she was walking toward her own death.

She stood before the chopping block. In this clearing that wasn't supposed to be there, sunlight draped through the gaps between branches like gorgeous lengths of fabric.

"Stick your neck out."

Adele set her husband down, knelt, and put her collar on the block with the semicircular scallop.

Seeing the woman's powerful, suntanned neck, Jessup's eyes narrowed with satisfaction.

"Here we go," he said in what was actually a somewhat pathetic tone, and he raised the great ax. He staggered a few times under it, a ridiculous counterpoint to his earlier boasts. Reeling under the weight, his body jerked from side to side as he swung the great ax toward the ground and regained his balance. A tree growing nearby got chopped halfway through its twenty-inch diameter trunk.

"Damn, that's embarrassing," Jessup said, cursing himself like someone in a comedy as he braced himself a little better this time and managed to pull his ax free. As he walked over to Adele, his gait was steadier, but still somewhat uncertain. Giving a huff, he cried out to focus himself as he raised the great ax high.

It was unclear what Adele was thinking, but she made no attempt to flee. Perhaps that was the true power of the bumbling beheader.

He raised the ax high, and then swung it down with all his might. A heartbeat later, a pale, thin stake flew out of nowhere and pierced his right shoulder.

"Waaaagh!" he shrieked, staggering and dropping the ax that was his very raison d'être.

As he pulled the stake out, he looked around and sputtered, "Wh-wh-who the hell did that?"

He needn't have bothered. On the red road to the beheader that ran through the trees stood a figure in black of inhuman beauty.

"That hurts, damn you. And I'm bleeding. What did I ever do to you, you bastard?"

But the cries he spewed suddenly died. He'd noticed how handsome his foe was. With golden light from between the branches shining on his face, the young man was not of this world.

"Who—who are you?" the beheader stammered.

"D," the man replied in a voice that could make the light freeze.

"Are you trying to—to stop me or something?"

"Not at all."

"What do you mean, not at all? Look what you've done. I'm bleeding!" Jessup said, sticking out his shoulder. "Does this look like not at all? Explain why you'd do something like this. If you don't, you'll be sorry."

D's form shimmered like a mirage. As he'd started walking toward Jessup, the glow from the sunlight spilling through the branches was there to watch over him.

"S-stay away from me!" Jessup shouted. He tried to raise his ax to menace D, but his legs wouldn't quite support him and he tottered drunkenly.

"Don't let your guard down, okay?" said a hoarse voice from the vicinity of D's left hip. "This guy's part of the advance guard for a Noble who came back from the stars. There's no way he could be such a mess. If he was, it'd make Valcua's blood boil having this clown guarding him while he slept."

"Does he even have blood?" D inquired in a monotone.

The voice fell silent.

To their side, there was a desperate scream as the great ax fell. If the blow launched from this weak stance had hit its mark, D's head would've been taken off at an angle. However, the Hunter's right hand caught Jessup's wrist with lightning speed and gave it an easy twist, sending the beheader flying neatly through the air to land head first on the grass a good ten feet away. Letting out a groan, he grew quiet.

"Oh, he's good," the hoarse voice remarked. "There's a method to his screwups. Be careful. Something's going on here for sure. This guy raised a blade against you. Take him out."

Saying nothing, D went over to Adele, who still had her head on the chopping block. He touched his left hand to the nape of her neck.

The woman jumped up and looked around restlessly.

"D? What are you doing here?"

"I was asleep, but something woke me up."

Adele dazedly murmured, "Here in these woods?"

"Outside the clearing. This place doesn't exist—it's a pocket dimension that man created."

"That makes sense. I was sure I'd never seen this spot before," she said, adding, "Don't tell me I was the one who woke you up."

"Yeah, at the coach stop."

Shortly after hearing these words, Adele's shock set in. Could it be that the gorgeous young man had seen her murder her husband?

Adele didn't get a chance to find out. D suddenly caught her shoulder and shoved her to the left. In that instant, a flash of silver skimmed past the tip of her nose.

After creeping up on the pair to launch a new attack, Jessup found himself once again evaded with ease when his second swing buried his blade in the ground. He was down for only a split second. Apparently he still had some fight in him.

Spewing expletives all the while, Jessup tried without success to free his ax, and then leaned on its handle as he fought to catch his breath.

D had been reaching for the hilt of his sword, but he brought his hand away. Even if this was all an act, D wasn't the kind of man who had to look for an opening before defeating someone.

Ignoring Jessup, D turned his gaze to Adele's fallen husband.

Adele closed her eyes. She heard a voice that sounded like a death rattle, and her fate changed once again.

Jessup had launched a third attack. It was wide of the mark, slashing through the air more than three feet from D. Who would've thought it could hack open D's back from the right shoulder down to the left hip and send bright blood gushing out?

Leaping back without a word, D reeled as he hit the earth. The fresh blood that poured from him slapped against the ground. Great as he was, the Hunter had no way to defend himself from someone

who could slash open his opponents without even aiming for them. Especially not after he'd successfully avoided two attacks by the same person and seen how pathetic his foe was.

"How's that? Now do you see what I'm really made of?" Jessup asked, but again he staggered and had to cling to his ax, the head of which was stuck in the ground once more. "When I aim, it never goes well, but when I don't, I do some cutting. This is what you get when you screw with me!"

Although he was putting on a bold front, his legs were wobbly, his face was slick with sweat, and his voice cracked uncomfortably high. Here was a rare case of a loser turning out to be a winner.

He stopped talking. His eyes went wide with disbelief, their retinas emblazoned with the sight of D standing like a vigilant deity.

Seeing that the wound had no effect on the Hunter, Jessup tried to flee. He dashed for the closest stand of trees with uncharacteristic speed, clumsily grabbing his ax and chopping block as he went.

As he ran, he swung his left hand out. A grayish lump flew into the bushes. But when a single streak of light zipped toward Jessup's back, the shape popped up again.

The rough wooden needle thrown by D was caught in the mouth of a lump about the size of a fist. With eye sockets like little caves and black hair that dangled like threads from the dried skin, it was a shrunken human head. Most likely Jessup had made it through some fiendish technique practiced on a head he'd personally lopped off. In midair it spat out the needle it'd clenched between its teeth, and then it whizzed straight at D, the wind swirling in its wake.

A second needle flew from D's right hand. The shrunken head bit down on it. But the needle kept on going, coming out through the back of the head. Its course rapidly thrown into disarray, the shrunken head fell at D's feet. Even after it fell, it continued to gnash its tiny teeth loudly and attempted to bite D's foot, but it soon became motionless.

"So, he can use the heads he's cut off? Must piss them off to be under his control. That little loser is something else!"

The weird little voice that spilled from the vicinity of D's left wrist brought Adele back to her senses. Even to a woman like her, accustomed to the strangeness of the Frontier, this deadly conflict had been like a nightmare. But the lifeblood that dripped from the back of the young man in black declared that it was all too real—as did the corpse of her husband, which lay at her feet. Adele still had to deal with that.

"D—I had to . . ."

A blisteringly hot pain pierced her back and chest. Falling just as she was about to turn, Adele was caught by D in time to see her husband sitting upright, his arm still posed from throwing the knife.

"A strong constitution was the only thing he had going for him—oh!"

Adele turned in D's direction. Hers were desperate movements—there were still things she had to do. She had to watch over Matthew and Sue. Once they'd made it through this unbelievable twist of fate, she had to see Matthew's bride with her own two eyes, and she couldn't die until she'd seen Sue properly married off.

"D . . ."

"Don't talk."

"Bring me over there—to my husband."

Adele asked to be set down by his side. Once that had been done, Adele pulled the bag of coins out of her husband's pocket. Grabbing D's arm, she pulled him closer. She shoved the bag against his chest. It was the money her husband had stolen from the corpse. Adele clung to it for dear life.

"Take this . . . to protect my kids . . . I can't . . . do it anymore. See to it . . . Matthew gets himself . . . a redhead for a bride . . . He's a real hard worker, that one . . . so his bride . . . can be lazy . . . just so long as she's kind . . . and cheerful . . . Now, in Sue's case . . ."

Saying nothing, D just listened. As he watched the dying mother, his gaze was the epitome of sternness.

"My daughter . . . She needs . . ."

Adele's hand slipped from D's arm.

Holding her body up, D asked, "What kind of man would be good for Sue?"

A single tear fell from Adele's eye.

"She needs . . ."

And then, all the strength left the mother's body.

III

As the siblings waited in front of the inn for their mother, all sorts of activity suddenly started up at the sheriff's office, and a crowd began to form. They saw a number of people run off in the direction of the coach stop. The sheriff's wagon headed that way as well. One of the people who remained walked over to Matthew, related what had happened at the coach stop, and told him that his mother was keeping a body company there and that he should go get her.

When they were halfway to the coach stop, the Vampire Hunter appeared on a black steed and informed them of their parents' deaths. Though they asked him how they'd died, he wouldn't say. Instead, he took them by a back road into the forest where the brother and sister saw the pair's corpses and finally accepted everything.

Once the lifeless husks had been loaded into the wagon, D told the children their mother had hired him, and that they had to leave town immediately.

"Before we do, let us go back to the farm," Matthew countered vehemently. "I wanna bury my mom and dad. 'Cause that's the house the two of them made into a home."

Oddly, a hoarse voice from nowhere in particular exclaimed, "What are you talking about, you idiot? As soon as the sun goes down—"

That's certainly what it sounded like, but almost immediately there was something like a short scream and it became quiet.

Turning in the direction of the farm, D tossed his chin.

Once they were closer to home, Sue—who was back with the bodies—started sobbing in a low voice. After they reached the farm, Sue couldn't stop crying. The two bodies were placed on the bed in their mother's room, and Matthew told his sister to stay with them before he went out back to dig a grave. The location had already been decided. At the top of a hill to the east that overlooked their land was a spot their mother had loved. When the weather was nice, she'd often set a table out there for them to eat dinner, and the three of them had never tired of watching the sun set behind the mountains to the west. As everything else was stained red, his mother's white apron waving in the breeze had lingered in Matthew's eye. Though she'd never once said she wanted to be buried there, the idea had occurred to Matthew as he recalled his mother's red profile gazing at the sunset.

A short time after he started digging the hole, Matthew sensed someone behind him and turned around.

D stood over the hole looking down at him, and he asked the boy if he could take his place for a while.

"I'll do it alone," Matthew said flatly. "This is our home. As long as even one of us is still alive, we don't need anyone's help deciding where to plant our own. Please don't take that the wrong way."

Saying nothing, D looked over his shoulder, and then remarked, "It would seem you're not alone."

Sticking his head out of the hole, Matthew looked in the same direction and saw Sue coming out of the barn carrying a shovel.

By the time they were done digging, the sun had disappeared, but enough light remained to aid them in their work. Since they didn't have any coffins on hand, they'd wrapped their parents in some curtains their mother had loved and gently set them at the bottom of the hole. After getting five years of use out of those curtains with white peach blossoms against a field of blue, their mother had said it was a waste to throw them out and had stuffed them into the back of a cabinet instead.

As she took up her shovel to cover them with dirt, Sue said, "Mom has to be happy to be together with Dad, don't you think?" She began to tremble and sob.

"Yeah, I suppose she is. After all, Dad has finally come back," Matthew lied.

There wasn't time to dig two holes. Even if there had been, if he'd dared to suggest burying them separately, Sue probably would have cried and made him stop.

Once they'd filled the hole with dirt, Sue laid some flowers she'd prepared on top of the grave, white ones. Matthew didn't know what they were called.

"Matt, say a prayer."

On hearing his sister's request, Matthew found himself in a bind. Though he'd been to a number of funerals, he'd never paid strict attention to the prayers said there.

As he stood with his lips buttoned, to his rear a voice like steel rang out. The words it spoke were a prayer from a distant land that he'd never heard before. The brother and sister traced the voice back to the young man in black.

The white flowers stirred in an almost imperceptible breeze.

Once they hit the road that led into town, Matthew halted the wagon. He'd seen the enormous car that was stopped up ahead before. The way it was dented all over made it easy to remember. No matter how solidly it might've been constructed, it was still unbelievable that it could remain intact after falling from such a height. If Matthew had known that this vehicle had dropped from an altitude of one hundred fifty thousand feet, he'd have been speechless.

The huge figure standing in front of the car raised one hand, calling out to them, "Perfect timing for our departure. But we seem to be short two people."

Matthew and Sue sat up in the front seat.

"I went into town, but Mr. Dyalhis wasn't there," the count continued.

The brother and sister looked at each other. The giant must have made a strong impression on the person he'd talked to. By now, the whole village would be in a panic.

"He's dead," D responded from beside the wagon. "So is their mother."

"Oh, my," the giant said, his eyes wide as he looked at the siblings and D. Though members of the Nobility were known for their disinterest in human affairs, he undoubtedly wanted to know what had happened. But he didn't ask, merely nodding instead.

"Okay, so there are two of you. I will protect you without fail. You may depend on that."

"Just so you know," D said, "their mother hired me."

For an instant, Count Braujou had a stunned expression, but then it became a smile some would call unsettling.

"This is a surprise! That means if we get crazed for blood and attack the children, the world's greatest Hunter of Nobility will be there to stop us." Turning that smile toward the brother and sister, he said, "You've got a very good guard. That must be reassuring."

No reply was forthcoming from the pair of stiff faces.

"Very well, then. Climb inside your wagon and get some sleep. I shall take the reins," the count said, and without waiting for the pair to reply, he went over to them and put one foot up on the wagon. Even standing on the ground, he was taller than the two seated in the driver's seat.

Matthew looked at D.

"Go on inside," D said, tossing his chin in the direction of the wagon's interior. "It's okay. He's not as heavy as he looks."

The siblings complied.

"Upsy—" the giant began in an all-too-human fashion. When his enormous form climbed up to the driver's seat, creaking sounds immediately emanated from various planks and metal fittings.

"—daisy!" he continued, but just as he settled into the seat, bolts tore loose and boards began to snap.

"You're gonna have to pay to have that fixed," D said. After all, the vehicle belonged to his employer.

"I know. Don't worry. But this thing is quite tiny, you know."

Finally getting his legs stretched out between the team of four cyborg horses, the count cracked the reins against the animals' rumps. Though he was easily three times the weight of the children, the horses began to move forward without any difficulty.

D rode along beside them. The count's car, driverless, followed behind.

"Whom did you tangle with?" the count inquired, his face still looking forward. "I can see the split down your back. Valcua had a bizarre ax wielder working for him. It was Jessup Tolleran—his official beheader."

D briefly recounted the situation.

After hearing the story, the count was expressionless as he said, "In the old days, Valcua had seven warriors. Speeny must've been one of them. I think it's safe to assume all seven have been brought back to life."

"Do you know the other five?"

"No, only Jessup. But I did hear tales about the eerie corpses they left in their wake—in my capacity as a Frontier sector controller, that is."

Twisting his upper body around, he turned toward the wagon's door. He was surprisingly flexible. Giving a light knock on the flap, he said, "Come out here—what I have to say will have some bearing on your lives from this point forward. You should hear this."

After waiting a while, the count made a sour face and remarked, "That's odd. I wonder why they won't come out."

"The flap won't open," D said with a toss of his chin.

The giant's enormous buttocks were blocking the entrance.

"Oh, that won't do. Can you hear me?" he roared in a raspy voice that echoed through the darkness. D's stare had unsettled him. "If you can hear me, answer. Won't you do that for me?"

Hearing a knock on the other side of the flap, the count was satisfied.

"Okay, the servants of the Nobility who are after the two of you have the following powers, going by the condition of the bodies they have left behind."

First, there were decapitated corpses—which would probably be the work of Jessup the Beheader. The incident with the shrunken head explained why the heads of those people had never been located.

Second, there was a lake that had filled with the bodies of drowned victims in the course of a single night. Nearly half of them had had their flesh shaved off as if they were roasted pigs. Undoubtedly that was the work of the water witch, Lucienne.

Third, there were bodies that had been mashed flat as if they'd been dropped from high in the heavens—that would be Speeny the spider man's handiwork.

Fourth—and from this point on, there was no intelligence regarding the guilty party—was the disappearance of the entire population of a town. One day, everyone in an eastern Frontier village of about twenty thousand suddenly disappeared. It was said that in the saloons, half-empty glasses were left on tables, and smoke still curled from cigarettes half-turned to ash. A resident who'd just returned from out of town discovered this disappearance. The situation was the same in every home, making it seem as if they'd all been going about their normal daily routines when something happened that made all of them decide to leave town for good—without stopping to see to anything else.

Fifth was an incident involving the army of a certain Noble. In a bizarre turn of events, roughly a thousand soldiers had committed suicide. That day, a certain singer from the Capital had paid them a visit, performing a dozen songs before leaving. According to the one soldier who miraculously survived—a man who'd lost his hearing in battle—nothing had been out of the ordinary during the singer's performance, but that night everyone else decided to die. On the word of this lone soldier, a search was made for the singer, but her whereabouts were never discovered. The army's commander was one of the Nobles who'd opposed Valcua.

"As for the other two—I don't know anything," Count Braujou said. "Of course, the aforementioned examples are things Valcua's seven are assumed to have done. At any rate, they're sure to be a troublesome bunch. My shoulder still hurts."

While he'd described Valcua's seven warriors as "troublesome," his remark would've made Speeny, the spider man, turn pale—for the giant remained fine after dropping out of the stratosphere. But the expression of the handsome young man in black riding beside him had not changed at all as he listened to the tale.

No matter what lay ahead, when they met the Ultimate Noble's assassins, clouds of blood were sure to fly. Whether this was something to be desired or mourned was no matter; the darkness ahead only grew denser, and an eerie breeze buffeted the two vehicles and the men that might be described as their dark guardians.

Dark-Magic Boundaries

CHAPTER 6

I

Over the next three days, Matthew and Sue learned a number of things about the Nobility. First, don't let them drive your wagon. By day, Count Braujou went into his vehicle to sleep, and it became Matthew's job to take the reins. The problem was the nights. Worried that they weren't moving quickly enough, the giant would settle his ten-foot-tall frame into the driver's seat and whip the horses' haunches. Realizing the strangeness of this nightly visitor, the horses galloped madly, chased by a fear they couldn't outrun. They certainly went fast. Over rough terrain or cobblestone streets they galloped at full speed. They even took corners at the same breakneck pace. The back end of the covered wagon would swing off the road from the centrifugal force and the sides would slam against rocks and trees. That alone was enough to put a man's heart in his mouth. One time, while they were driving along the side of a cliff, half the wagon was hanging over the edge. It was bad enough for Matthew, but Sue shrieked bloody murder, nearly fainting numerous times. She spent all of the next day sleeping.

"Take it easy, will you?" Matthew protested.

"You've seen the kind of people who're after us. Every second is as precious as gold," the other man replied, and the fact that the boy fell silent didn't have anything to do with the speaker being ten feet tall and weighing six hundred fifty pounds.

It was also for this reason that D remained quiet—even more than was his habit.

Second, they learned that the Nobility had no regard for any other form of life. If they found a shortcut, the count would have them gallop through a forest or up a rocky mountain without pause. Of course, such places were crawling with dangerous creatures. There were three-headed hydras that attacked from the treetops and the tribe of twisted mole men who lived in burrows underground, thrusting out giant spears to impale their foes. The bat people were just like humans with wings, except their emotional torment drove them to tear others to shreds. They had human voices that pleaded for mercy or cried out in pain, forcing the siblings to cover their ears.

D was just as ruthless in putting his sword to use, only colder, and while his aloofness as he hacked through everything didn't inspire anger in the human pair, the way the count seemed to enjoy the slaughter was more than they could stand. As the agonized cries of an impaled bat person showed no signs of ending, Sue pleaded with the count to put it out of its misery.

"It's serving as an example. The two of you might not know this, but they frighten twice as easily as any human. When they hear one of their own screaming like this, they won't come out of their lairs for three whole days. Our plan is to use that time to get somewhere safe."

That was a reason, and an extremely good one. As Matthew and Sue knew of the bat people's cruelty and how they would tear living humans to pieces, they thought it best to keep their silence. Nevertheless, on considering the hundreds of monsters that had been dispatched by D and the count over the course of three days, the pair was tormented by lurid visions of all the corpses that lay in the tire ruts behind their wagon.

Every time such thoughts troubled their spirits, the brother and sister seemed to seek salvation in the young man in black who raced alongside them—and his sternly handsome features. In a situation so ghastly it left them reeling, the Hunter's exquisite looks remained unwavering. Life and death were both far removed from this young man. All they found there was the kind of beautiful visage that rarely graced the world. Was that what it meant to be a Noble? The siblings would stare in rapture, but then they'd find a danger there that snapped them back to their senses.

The third thing they learned was the Nobility were immortal. This fact was the stuff of legend, and the siblings accepted it naturally enough. However, on seeing it with their own eyes, they couldn't help but be thoroughly chilled and horrified.

As they were racing along a road carved into the side of a cliff, they turned a corner and suddenly slammed into what was known as an "old man of the mountain." A mass of fur so thick it was impossible to tell whether it had arms and legs (let alone eyes, a nose, or a mouth), it was thirty feet in diameter. More than half its body hung over the edge of the cliff. Though the horses slammed into it head on, it sent them flying back. The car's control system proved useful in this situation, and the horses and wagon came through undamaged—but the count fell over the cliff.

The children jumped down from the vehicle and peered over the edge, only to find the Nobleman spread-eagled on the rocky surface fifty yards below. They didn't know whether they should be saddened or relieved. An armlike mechanism swung out from the bottom of the car and lowered a cable with a strap on the end. When it pulled the count up a few minutes later, there wasn't a mark on his body or his apparel. At some point, the old man of the mountain had disappeared.

And they'd learned one last thing—the feelings the Nobility had toward human beings might be described as paradoxical. While the count was there to help them, when he sat around the fire at night with the siblings, the look he gave them was icy cold. It wasn't scorn. In the same way that humans didn't despise beasts, he merely viewed human beings as a lower form of life.

But there was a moment when this disappeared. One night, while they huddled around the fire, Sue sang a song. Popular in the Capital quite a while ago, it had a soft melody and frivolous lyrics, but Sue's voice transformed it into a gem. On overhearing her singing in the kitchen, more than a few merchants and travelers staying the night at the farm had declared that if they took her to the Capital, she could be a first-rate singer; and, setting a bag of coins on the table, they'd asked to be allowed to manage her. Her singing was that good.

The count had been going to his vehicle, but then he walked back and requested, "Would you be good enough to sing another?"

It was little wonder that Matthew was astonished. All Sue could do was look up at the count with a face as blank as a doll's. They'd never heard of a Noble having any interest in a human song.

Matthew looked at D. D was gazing at Sue. And Sue couldn't take her eyes off the count. From his tone, she could tell his request was completely earnest.

However, she wasn't able to sing. The overcast sky suddenly called in a downpour.

As their legendary inability to cross rivers suggested, water was one of the vampires' weaknesses. The count hastily returned to his car. Since that night, he hadn't asked the siblings for anything. But Sue's mind kept returning to the expression on the count's face that time. It was like the one those travelers had worn when they put the bags of coins down on the table. When it came to the face of one pining for something beautiful, there was no difference between humans and Nobles.

In the wee hours of the morning of the fourth day, the two vehicles and the rider came to the road that led to what remained of the central Frontier.

D explained it had been a long time since men and horses had traveled the road. "There are other roads that lead there, but this is the most direct and least populated way."

The brother and sister had nodded at what D said, but when they realized what he'd meant by that, they got chills. He didn't want to run into anyone else—because he was expecting a fight.

"How long will it take to reach this 'fortress'?"

"Ordinarily, it'd be a month. At this pace, ten days."

Matthew couldn't help but grin wryly. By day, he took the reins, while at night he left them to the count, allowing the group to be constantly on the move. But the ride was so rough they couldn't get a good night's sleep in the wagon, and both he and Sue were positively exhausted. From what D had just said, deadly conflict lay ahead, and while the thought had filled them with terror, deep inside it had also come as something of a relief.

"Although it's been two thousand years since people stopped using this highway, there are three villages along it: Marthias, Janos, and Razin. Along the way, there'll be plenty of danger. It would be best to inspect our weapons."

"Right you are," the count said, his voice coming from his car. It was daytime. Undoubtedly he was speaking through a microphone installed in his vehicle. "Take a little break. We'll set off again in an hour. But you have to stay where we can see you."

As Matthew and Sue climbed out of the wagon, the count said in a quieter tone, "I wonder if Miranda's not coming." He seemed to whisper the words.

Saying nothing, D kept his eyes trained far back down the road they'd sped along.

"Appearances to the contrary, that woman's got a strong sense of duty. She's not the kind to forget a debt, even if it's one owed to a human being. I feel certain she'll catch up with us."

"If the enemy hasn't gotten to her first, that is," D remarked.

"The residents of those three villages aren't a threat, are they?"

"Not really," said D. "But Janos and Razin—well, the village of Janos produces poisonous herbs, while Razin subsists by crafting weapons."

"Do you mean to suggest the people there could be trouble? Good enough. If not for things like that, there'd be no point in having us along."

"That hardly sounds like the words of an antisocial old geezer who locked himself in his room for five thousand years."

"Did you say something?" the count inquired. Apparently his microphone had caught the mosquito-like buzz of the hoarse voice.

Not replying to this, D said, "The enemy is close."

"You're right," the count responded. As they'd been riding hard night and day, the brother and sister were surprised, but the one pushing them so hard apparently found it self-evident.

Just then, D raised his eyes.

The road stretched like a slender ribbon for ten miles, and then ran into a gorge. Dark clouds had quickly begun forming over it, and a shadow fell across the valley—a declaration of ownership, so to speak. The black clouds spread even further, and shadows fell on the faces of the human pair when they looked up. There was a flash. Light and darkness colored the world in rapid succession. Even when the black clouds formed a gigantic human face—easily a few miles long and wide—there was no change in D's handsome visage.

Sculpted from those black clouds was the face of a dignified young man. Thick eyebrows, nose and lips with lines so elegant a master painter could spend his entire life trying to get them right—all of them brimmed with dignity, while his eyes tapered to slits at the outer corners and were flooded with such coldness and pitilessness they filled those who saw them with a soul-devouring terror.

"I am Grand Duke Valcua," the cloud said. "Anyone who sets foot on this road will never reach his destination, nor will he be able to turn back. While the conspirators who drove me off among the stars have no choice but to continue on, you may leave, young man in black. I shall give you three seconds to do so. There's nothing more to be discussed. One."

At some point, Matthew and Sue had gone over to D, and now they were looking up at him.

The count's microphone kept its silence.

"Two."

The lightning gave D's face a pale blue glow. Like a gorgeous statue, he stood there, not making a single move.

"Three," the voice from the sky told him. Leaving no break at all, it continued, "Most unwise. So, you choose an agonizing death? With such an exquisite countenance, you're probably a fellow child of the darkness. Proceed, then. My soldiers are waiting at the end of the road."

There was a thundering sound that rocked the heavens: derisive laughter.

Suddenly the dark clouds sailed away, and the trio felt the morning sun.

"Are you feeling more rested?" D asked.

"Yeah. But this is no time to be worrying about rest," Matthew replied, and Sue nodded her agreement.

The count's voice said, "I'm surprised Valcua appeared out here. And even more surprised that he'd ask you to leave us. D, who in the world are you?"

As the gaze of the human pair and another set of unseen eyes fell on the Hunter, he merely replied in a cool tone, "Let's go."

II

That morning the chapel bell rang out in the sky over the village of Marthias. Among the villagers lived a huntsman with incredibly keen senses who was used to dealing with the supernatural creatures that lurked around their community, but the peals ringing across the empyrean vault gave him a feeling of dread, and probably made him want to spread an alarm. Most of the populace—which numbered under a hundred—were so surprised they ran outside, jogging toward the chapel before the huntsman (who'd been in bed with a fever the last three days) could make his appearance.

The population of Marthias had been about five hundred until, twenty years before, a traveling pestilence had invaded. The chapel had fallen into ruin when their priest succumbed to the illness.

Though they'd made repeated requests to the Capital and to the parish committee, no one was willing to relocate to the central Frontier (as was also often the case with physicians), so the people were forced to live out their cruel days without heaven's aid. They couldn't complain about someone going into the unsecured chapel—especially not when candles burned in the decaying sconces, an icon of a goddess they'd never seen before rocked against one wall, and a tall figure in ash-gray vestments stood behind the freshly dusted altar.

The people froze in the doorway. An unfamiliar priest turned to them with arms spread wide and said, "Welcome, everyone! Please, be seated."

His low voice was even clearer than the bell. While reserved, his tone carried a strength that would brook no insubordination.

Exchanging glances, the villagers seated themselves. The solid pews creaked but supported their weight.

"I am a traveling missionary. My name is Courbet," the priest said with a bow, and then he began flipping through the pages of a hide-bound tome on the altar. It was probably a book of sermons. Everyone on the Frontier knew that the traveling missionaries who moved from area to area, teaching people about the gods they worshiped, carried books of sermons that explained the basic tenets of their faith.

One of the villagers sheepishly raised his hand. It was the mayor. "Yes?"

Coughing to clear his throat, the mayor asked, "When did you clean the chapel? I've been awake since there were still stars in the sky, and I didn't notice your arrival. When on earth did you get here?"

Courbet smiled. For the first time the people noticed he had a long, horsey face and beady eyes. "Before you got up. The cleanup took quite some time."

"So, just what kind of gods do you believe in, sir?" asked a farmer's wife.

Living as they did, elbow to elbow with danger, the people of the Frontier were more inclined to embrace faiths as individuals than as groups. A missionary spreading the word of another god was something of a threat. In this very village people had killed each other on more than one occasion over religious differences.

"Stern but peaceful gods," Courbet replied. "But I can promise you this: My gods have nothing against whatever gods all of you may hold dear. You're under no pressure. Once you've heard what I have to say, if you all decide you don't like the sound of it, I'm willing to leave at any time."

A wave of relief spread over the people.

Flipping through more pages, Courbet halted at a certain section and began to address the group in a soft tone.

"My gods are called Braujou, Miranda—and D. However, you're not to mention this to anyone."

In the afternoon light, the sound of nails hammering home rang out like echoes.

D hadn't intended on halting the vehicles. They had sufficient food and water. Any place that might be used by their foes for an ambush was to be avoided or passed through as quickly as possible. Matthew and Sue had been told as much. Yet just as they were approaching the village, a young girl suddenly jumped in front of them. Letting loose a cry that was closer to a shriek, Matthew stepped on the brake, but she was too close. The girl fell under the animals' hooves.

"Whoa!" Matthew ordered the horses, and then he leaped down from the driver's seat. Some cyborg horses underwent operations on their brains that slightly increased their intelligence, and speaking was often the best way to communicate with them.

The girl who lay between the horses' hooves looked to be about the same age as Sue. Her simple dress was torn in places, and her exposed shoulder was bruised.

"It hurts!" she groaned. Her voice sounded pained.

"Are you okay?" Matthew asked frantically.

There was no reply.

As clouds of anxiety blanketed his heart, Matthew picked up the girl. But another surprise awaited him. A wall of people blocked his wagon.

"What's going on?" the boy said.

An old man in the front row of the crowd came forward with the aid of a cane and said, "I'm the mayor. We have a favor to ask."

"A favor?" Matthew said, furrowing his brow.

"Forget it," a voice like steel told the boy. "We're in a hurry. Set that girl down and get back in the wagon."

"But—" the mayor began, barely squeezing out the words, "that girl sacrificed herself to get you to stop. I beg of you—please, hear us out!"

"If she was a sacrifice, then it's on your heads," D said in a soft, cold tone. "Get back up there. We're moving out."

Matthew didn't know what to do. The girl at his feet had just groaned.

"We're begging you. Please!" the old man said, somehow getting down on his knees. The villagers behind him touched their heads to the ground in unison. "Someone has told us that gods are coming to rid our village of a misfortune. And we're certain he was talking about you."

The hands the old man clasped together trembled.

"So I beg you, just hear what I have to say. As you can see, we're down on our knees."

The old man and the other villagers all prostrated themselves.

"Out of our way," D said, his words raining down on them like a cold drizzle.

"D," Matthew said, turning to look at the Hunter.

"We don't have any time to waste. I have to honor the deal I made with your mother."

"We won't move!" one of the villagers shouted. "If you leave, we're all dead. So if you're going, you may as well kill us before you do."

The villager was serious. He wasn't going to budge, even in the face of death. However, principles and actually dying were two different matters. His heart caught in the talons of a terrific fear, he stiffened.

The young man on the black steed moved forward smoothly.

I'm about to get killed, the man thought. Riding before him was a grim reaper of unearthly beauty. Not about to take pity on him just because he was old, and not at all moved by the way this man was willing to risk his life, he was a gorgeous fiend who would think nothing of hacking his way through anyone who opposed him. The old man was in a kind of rapture as he imagined himself releasing a bloody mist beneath that sword. And that's probably exactly what would've happened if Matthew hadn't intervened.

"Stop it, D!" he shouted as if he were writhing in pain. "You said you had a bargain with my mom. Well, there's no way she would've abandoned these people at a time like this. And I don't want to, either."

The black horse halted.

"Then we'll hear them out," the Hunter said.

"Thanks," Matthew said in a terribly blunt fashion, and then he pointed to the girl at his feet. "Get this girl to a doctor."

Villagers ran over and carried her away.

The boy then went over to the prostrate mayor and said, "Let's hear what you have to say."

III

Matthew, Sue, and D went to the mayor's house. Though Matthew hadn't wanted Sue to accompany them, D had maintained that it'd be dangerous for them to split up. The ever-present sound of carpentry slipped in through the open windows. Leaving Matthew and Sue in the care of the mayor and several other villagers, D stood in the corner with his back against the wall. No one noticed that he was in the shade.

What the mayor had to say was as follows: "This morning a traveling missionary came to the village church. He was no ordinary human being. This man arrived in town before daybreak, cleaned the chapel, and was ready to greet all of us by dawn. I got up pretty early myself, and there were others who were up all night in the saloon, too. And none of them heard him walk into town or any kind of commotion from the church. From the moment he called us together with the sound of the church bell, I knew what he really was. And on top of all that, he was so happy to tell us all about these strange 'gods.'"

"Strange gods?" Matthew said, getting the feeling that this was going to be trouble. But it was his own impetuousness that had gotten them involved with these gods. What did any of this have to do with them, anyway?

"According to him, these gods are named Braujou, Miranda, and D. Though he did say we weren't supposed to tell anyone that. Your name wasn't mentioned, but if D works for you, you'd have to be even more important than a god."

Having spoken, the old man finally showed them a smile. The others laughed.

D's connection to the siblings had already been explained. The purpose of their journey had not.

Perplexed, Matthew turned to D. The young man in black had melted into the shadows in the corner like some dark, supernatural blossom given human form.

"What are they putting together?" the Hunter asked. He was referring to the carpentry.

"That's the rub," the mayor said, slapping his knee. "It's a shrine to honor these gods. Of course, it's no more than a plank-covered shack, but the missionary said that would be fine."

"What's his name?"

"Courbet."

"So what the hell is he trying to do? He comes here this morning, says D's a god, and tells you to build a shrine—what's he got in mind?"

Matthew's question made the mayor and villagers look at each other. Suffering and uncertainty flowed around their wrinkled features like a gas.

"Where is he?" D inquired.

The mayor, Matthew, and everyone else trembled. Sue even put her hand on her brother's arm. She'd felt the unearthly air D's soft tone had carried.

Matthew asked, "You think it's them, D?"

"Yes."

The mayor was reflected in dark eyes that could only be described as awe inspiring. The old man backed away as if trying to escape something, stopping just as he was about to fall over.

"I don't know," he said, his face like that of a dead man. "Before he left, he said he'd be back tonight. Told us to have the shrine ready for the gods by then. A number of us went after the missionary, but there was no trace of him."

"And those were his only demands?"

"Yeah, that was it," the mayor replied, lowering his gaze.

On noticing this, Matthew said, "He threatened you, didn't he? What did he say?"

The mayor gnawed his lip. "If we don't do as he's asked, the curse of the Nobility will be on our village."

"What kind of curse?"

"If you were to go to the church now, you'd find a bloodstain on the floor. A villager who laughed out loud was crushed when a piece of stone from the ceiling fell on top of him. And all that bastard had to do was wave the book of sermons in his hand. He laid it out for us. If we didn't follow his instructions, the same would happen to everyone in the village. Then he added something else—said the only thing that could save us was these gods. And right then, we decided we had to come clean. To be honest, we don't know what he's after. We figure you folks would know more about that than us."

"Where's that girl from earlier?" D asked, oddly enough.

After a pause, the mayor replied, "In the town hall. We don't have a doctor, but we've got medicine there."

By the time he'd said this, D had already left the shadows and was headed for the door. He looked like a beautiful shadow.

Matthew and Sue hurriedly stood up.

At the town hall some five hundred yards from the mayor's house, they witnessed a miracle. The girl who'd fallen under the hooves was there with her mother. When D put his left hand against her forehead, her labored breathing was gone in a heartbeat and her fever passed. The girl recovered in seconds.

As mother and child hugged each other, beside them D said, "I've fixed any damage my employer has done. Now we'll be leaving."

Dumbfounded, the mayor shouted, "Please, wait! We've been completely honest with you and asked you to save our village. If you leave now, we'll be annihilated. He'll get us. Do something about him. After all, you're the reason he came here, aren't you?"

D looked at Matthew.

Thinking for a few seconds with the expression of a much older man, Matthew nodded and said, "If you were to put him down, it'd make things easier for us, too. D, let's give it a shot."

The young man in black remained silent as the group went outside.

"I'm going to the chapel," D told them, and then he started walking over to where they'd parked the vehicles.

Halting in front of Braujou's car, he turned toward the door and said, "This concerns Matthew and Sue. Keep them safe." His tone was the same as always.

When a hole opened in the seamless body of the vehicle, Matthew and Sue stared at it dazedly.

"Stay inside until I get back. No matter what happens, don't let them out, Braujou."

"Leave it to me," Braujou responded in a sleepy voice.

The pair were shaking all over, but D somehow managed to get them into the vehicle, and once the hole in its side had vanished, he began to head back to the village.

Completely ignoring the group of people that had formed in front of the mayor's abode, the Hunter went into the chapel. The villagers froze at the doorway.

The stone interior was quiet and cold. Crude stone statues stared at D with the faint outlines of eyes. Though the villagers believed in different gods, they apparently worshiped here together. Between the second pew and the wall, a bloodstain remained on the floor. A bloodied chunk of stone had been set beside the door. Putting the palm of his left hand against the stone, D raised it toward the ceiling.

"No doubt about it—it definitely fell from the spot right above him. The whole ceiling's in terrible shape," his left hand said. "But the piece that fell wasn't rigged in any way. It seems like it was a complete coincidence that the only part to collapse was right on top of a nonbeliever. As you can probably tell, there's no trace of any spell or telekinesis, either. That's one weird trick he's got."

"You remember anything like this?"

"Not—" was all the hoarse voice managed before D's hand was tightly squeezed into a fist and the Hunter went outside.

The sounds of carpentry echoed in the air without a moment's respite. A number of colorful kites danced across the sky. It must've been some of the community's few children amusing themselves.

"Hey! Where are you going? You're not gonna saunter right into this trap, are you?" the hoarse voice asked frantically.

"The trap's not very well laid."

"Yeah, that's true—but that's no reason to jump into the lion's den for the fun of it."

Not replying to this, D took the road up a slope. As he came within view of the wooden structure that was nearly fully framed at the top of the hill, hurried footsteps and a taxed voice chased after him.

"Wait! Please, wait just a moment . . ."

D turned, and the mayor finally halted in front of him, taking several deep breaths to calm himself.

"You don't seriously . . . plan on . . . going into that thing . . . do you? I thought I . . . made it clear . . . that it's dangerous!"

The old man's winded delivery only served to demonstrate his sincerity.

"It's not finished yet. If it's meant as an obstacle for us, perhaps I should destroy it."

"If you were to do that now, the villagers would all be in danger," the old man said, looking to D for agreement, but then he held his tongue. His expression quickly grew clouded with fear. "Oh, that's right . . . You don't give a rat's ass about the people in this village, do you? All that matters is that the lot of you finish your journey safely."

"That's my job."

"We told you everything, regardless of the danger we were putting ourselves in. Don't you think leaving us to fend for ourselves would just be heartless?"

"The person who hired me asked me to protect her children with her dying breath. Nothing else concerns me."

Leaving the mayor standing there awestruck, D walked away.

Though only the frame was standing, this was clearly going to be a house. It was square, with each wall thirty feet long, and just a little bit taller. Five villagers hung from the wall and ceiling beams. As soon as they noticed D, two of them let out screams and fell to the ground, while the rest clung to the closest post or beam for dear life. The reason their compatriots had fallen was obvious: D's good looks had robbed them of their souls. The other three soon ran over to pick those two up, and luckily they'd landed on their asses and were okay.

"At this rate, they'll only have the outer walls done by tonight," the hoarse voice said. "So, what do they hope to accomplish by sealing you inside?"

D looked back at the mayor.

The mayor was backing away, as if he'd seen something horrifying. His body sank unexpectedly—the earth had subsided. He sank down to his waist, and then stopped. The old man braced his arms and tried to pull himself free. But when the villagers started to race toward him, his screams made them stop. His hair stood on end, his upper body went into fierce spasms, and then his eyes rolled up into his head. At the same time, bright blood shot from his mouth and nose like a ruptured hose, sending up terrific splashes when it hit the ground.

Telling the paralyzed villagers to step aside, D moved forward. Ignoring the mayor, whose head had slumped limply to one side, the Hunter slowly started down the hill.

A quiet murmur from the villagers came after him. The bloodied mayor had jerked his face back up and then fallen forward. There was nothing left of him from the waist down. His body had been brutally sliced in two below his hips. The villagers' terrified murmuring was reignited like a flame when the old man's upper body dug both hands into the dirt and pulled itself toward D like an insect.

"Behind you!" someone shouted, but the upper body had braced itself in a pushup position, and then it sprang up over D's head like a bug. It was unclear whether D noticed the single line that stretched between the torso and the ground.

The Hunter made a silvery sweep behind himself, while the mayor's torso reversed direction in midair and landed with a thud on the ground. Ignoring the vain twitching of the fingers curled before its chest like claws, D took to the air like a supernatural bird, exquisite and black, coming down to assail its earthbound prey. Backed by the force of a leap that carried D from a spot fifteen feet away, plus the acceleration from his descent, the blade he gripped struck with precision. His longsword sank halfway into the earth, and as he pulled it free, a black fluid shot out of the ground with terrific force. No one there noticed it was blood.

D made a horizontal swipe to his right with his sword hand. The gleam collided with a black, sickle-shaped object that appeared from the earth, making the strangest sound in the world. Fifteen feet long, the sickle made a tearing sound as it was cut free. When it was finally embedded in a boulder that lay by the side of the road, it proved to be indeed a giant, steel scythe.

"It's a subterranean doll master!"

"No, it's a corpse rider!"

It was difficult to say whether the terror in the voices of the villagers who'd witnessed this was inspired by the creature with giant scythes that had just expired underground, or by the young man in black who'd sheathed his blade and turned back toward the mayor's remains.

Without a doubt, a fearsome subterranean creature had just breathed its last—a creature that burrowed underground, killing anyone who fell through the last bit of earth it left over its pit, then sending one of its "control lines" into the nervous system of its victim so it could be in command of the deceased and hunt for food up in the surface world it was fated to never enter.

"Hmm. To be honest, I've had a suspicion all the villagers were under something's control, but it looks like such concerns were groundless," D's left hand said in a voice that he alone heard.

When the Hunter walked toward the partially constructed hut once more, no one stood in his way. As if they were watching a demon that appeared in broad daylight, the villagers opened a path for D, and he stood in front of the hut. A wind was stealing up on him.

Raising his left hand, D caught something borne on the wind. A sheet of paper. The vermilion characters scrawled on it seemed to be written in blood.

If you lay a hand on that hut, the villagers will all die in horrible accidents.

There was no signature.

Before he'd finished reading it, D turned around. In the direction the wind had come.

Deadly Banquet, Scarlet Banquet

CHAPTER 7

I

Roughly thirty feet from the road up the slope were remnants of a stone wall that stretched for fifteen to twenty feet. It was more than six and a half feet high.

There was a silvery flash.

From the other side of the partition came an agonized cry.

D hung in the air. The stone wall he'd sliced through at an angle toppled over with a dull thud—and the Hunter landed beyond that piece without a sound, facing it. Between D and the wall was a figure in vestments clutching his right shoulder. Bright blood spilled between his fingers, leaving vivid red stains on the ash-gray fabric.

"Are you one of Valcua's henchmen?" D inquired in a low tone. He didn't ask the man his name. This was someone he had to slay. All that mattered was whom he served.

"N-no, I'm not . . . ," the figure in vestments replied with a desperate shake of his head, but his pale complexion said more than that.

D took a smooth stride forward. An instant later, two things happened. D's stance shook ever so slightly, and from the sky high above him a colorful object swooped down. A flash of light danced out, and the form became a bisected kite that fell to the ground.

Ordinarily, the Hunter's blade would've reversed direction and gone for the robed figure—splitting Courbet's head open. However, his target flew away from the path limned by the tip of his sword. The man raised his right hand high, and his body floated up into the air, flying off into space at a speed D couldn't hope to match. D hurled a rough wooden needle after him with his right hand, and the robed figure clutched his throat. His groans streamed through the air, but his form swiftly dwindled, becoming a speck that was swallowed by the blue sky.

As the Hunter sheathed his blade, free as usual of a single drop of gore, there was the sound of several small footfalls on the road up the hill.

"There it is!"

"Oh, it's been cut!"

"That stinks!" a chorus of children's voices cried.

Picking up the kite, D headed toward them. The faces of the paralyzed children were tinged with fear and admiration. Just a glance told them there was nothing ordinary about this young man. For these children who'd never be able to leave the Frontier, outsiders were the object of adulation.

"Whose kite is this?" D asked.

The children backed away, as if threatened by the Hunter's gaze.

"It—it's his!" they said, shoving one boy forward.

He was a little redhead about eight or nine years old. Apparently shy, he lowered his eyes, and his body tensed from nervousness.

There were five children all told.

"Sorry about that. Let me pay you restitution," D said, pulling a coin out of an inner coat pocket. Just as he was about to put it in the boy's hand, the boy hurriedly pulled his hand away and shook his head.

"That's too much—I couldn't take it."

"Then in return, you can also answer a question for me. Did your kite cut somebody's string?"

Kite flyers normally crashed their kites into others, trying to slash each other's strings.

Eyes still lowered, the boy shook his head and said, "Nope. It got cut."

"I cut it," said a pudgy girl behind the boy, inflating her chest proudly.

"I see. Thank you," D said, giving the boy the coin and walking away.

Reaching the road up the slope, he turned to look back. Right behind him, the children halted. He started walking again—and turning, found the children stopped again and staring at him.

"Seems you're Mr. Popular," the hoarse voice remarked with amusement.

"Can I do something for you?" D asked.

Glancing at each other, the children fidgeted. Still, they couldn't hide the youthful curiosity and adoration that burned in their eyes.

Looking determined, the same pudgy girl from earlier asked, "Mister—are you a Hunter?"

"Yes."

"A Vampire Hunter?"

"That's right."

Before he'd even finished answering, the children broke into cheers.

"Wow! A real, live Vampire Hunter!"

"That's so cool."

"You know, as soon as I saw you, I knew that's what you had to be for sure!"

"Awesome!"

The chubby girl asked, "So, how many Nobles have you cut down?"

"Well—a lot."

"Excellent!"

"Does it make you happy that a lot of Nobility have been destroyed?" D asked.

"Of course it does!"

All the children nodded their agreement.

"I hope all those monsters get turned into dust."

"Yeah, me too!"

The tall boy who seemed to be their leader asked, blushing, "Um—do you think I could be a Hunter, too?"

"Do you want to be one?"

"Sure."

"Then give it your best."

"You bet!" he replied, his previously drooping head shooting up high.

On his way back to the vehicle, the Hunter passed a number of villagers running up the hill. Apparently the men doing the carpentry had let the others know of the mayor's demise.

"Go on home," D said.

The children showed no signs of leaving.

"Go home now."

When his tone became sterner, it came as little surprise the children quickly scattered, but they continued to watch the Hunter from behind statues and stone walls.

"Looks like you're a hero here," the hoarse voice chided.

"When that kite fell, I stepped on a stone and was thrown off balance," D said.

The hoarse voice responded, "And as a result—that bugger got away. To all appearances, it's just a coincidence. The ceiling collapsing on the villager in the chapel and the mayor falling through the ground were coincidences, too. Plus, there just happened to be a corpse rider underground. Hmm . . . It all seems a little too convenient. Still, you stepping on that stone was undoubtedly a coincidence, and so was the kite. Makes me wonder."

"You think he can control coincidences?"

After a short pause, the hoarse voice replied, "Could be."

"If he can, will it prevent me from cutting him down?"

"That's a distinct possibility."

Someone with the ability to control coincidences might cause wind-borne leaves to block an attacker's field of view without even needing to think about it, or a split second before receiving a blow, that same opponent might happen to notice he hadn't strapped his armor on correctly.

"We'll have to find some way around that, I guess," the hoarse voice murmured grimly. They heard the faint sound of a motor, and then the door to Count Braujou's car opened. Matthew and Sue stepped out and stretched. Obviously they'd been released because D had returned.

D inquired coolly, "Did the count tell you to get out?"

Dismissing that with a wave of his hand, Matthew replied, "No, it wasn't like that. We asked him to let us out. It's one big room in there, real lavish like a castle or something, but with the artificial lamps and all, it feels kinda stuffy."

Beside him, Sue nodded but said nothing.

"What happened?" the count's voice finally asked.

Once D had explained the situation, the Nobleman remarked, "That's a strange ability he has. Is he one of the foes we know about? Or is he one of the two about whom we know nothing? Eh?"

The count's gloomy monologue was interrupted by the village children, who had gathered once more around the Hunter.

D remained silent, but the leader of the group finally said to him, "Um, mister—you're gonna leave town, aren't you?"

"I suppose."

"Then I guess we'll never get another chance to meet a Vampire Hunter again. So, um . . ."

"Oh, don't even think about it," the hoarse voice said. It was a special remark that D alone heard. "There's no money to be made showing these brats your tricks."

"You want to see something?" D asked.

"You bet!" the children exclaimed.

Matthew and Sue looked at each other, and then trained curious eyes on D.

"Oh, you big dope!" said the voice the Hunter alone heard.

"Show us anything. Anything at all," the children cried out.

D pointed down at their feet. "Pick up some rocks and throw them at me. Throw them whenever you like, from wherever you like."

The children complied with his request, but they were reluctant once they had the stones in hand.

"Don't hold anything back. I'm a Vampire Hunter."

D's words stoked the flames of battle in the children.

"Everyone—we'll all let him have it at the same time. Spread out."

At their leader's command, the little combatants ran out all around D. D stood right where he was. A thread of tension connected the children. This wasn't a game. This was war.

"Let 'im have it!"

With the leader's shout, rocks flew at D from all directions.

What exactly was it that the children saw? Thin streaks of light spun around D as he stood perfectly still. Even when they heard the ring of hilt against scabbard, that light remained burned into the children's retinas along with the gorgeous figure in black. They didn't notice that the rocks they'd thrown with all their might had rolled right back at their feet. It was several seconds before they took note and finally exhibited normal human surprise again.

They were left speechless by the shock, but D bent over to pick a stick up off the ground—a tree branch about a foot and a half long.

He told the children, "Take a swing at me."

"What?" they said, their youthful faces more excited than surprised. Who would've thought they'd get to practice with a Vampire Hunter? It was understandable that they hesitated to take the stick.

D waved his right arm, and the stick jabbed into the ground at the feet of one of the boys. It was the same boy who'd had the string cut on his kite. The boy wasn't looking at D. His downturned eyes beheld only the ground.

Several seconds passed. And then the boy's face rose little by little, looking toward the branch. He grasped the stick with both hands.

"Wow! He's usually got less nerve than anyone!" the leader exclaimed, his eyes going wide. "No matter what we do, he always holds back, always goes last. He's the slowest kid around! But he's going first. Hey, Slowpoke, you sure you know what you're doing?"

"Good for you! Give 'im hell, Slowpoke!" the chubby girl said, clapping her hands, and the other children followed suit.

The boy's face flushed, and then he made a manly expression of what was clearly determination. The boy they'd always called "Slowpoke" had kept something hidden in his heart, and now it'd become a fire. Without anyone telling him what to do or ordering him, he let out a youthful and ferocious cry to focus himself for battle. Making a thrust, he passed by the Hunter on the left. To the children, it looked as if he'd passed right through D's body. Desperately trying to slam on the brakes, the boy dug his feet into the ground as he turned around.

D's right hand was going for the hilt over his shoulder. Seeing where he'd be coming from, the boy adjusted his stance with the branch.

A faint shadow skimmed across D's lips. A smile.

The Hunter tapped the toe of his boot lightly against the ground. The stick, except for the part the boy gripped, fell to the ground.

A rumble that wasn't quite words spilled from the mouths of the children—and from those of Matthew and Sue.

When had he drawn his sword and made the cut? More than that, how had he managed to not move at all while avoiding the boy thrusting straight toward him? All these things remained a mystery. However, the children accepted them. This was a Vampire Hunter—a man who slew the Nobility.

D stood before the boy, who was so stunned he still hadn't left his combat stance.

"You know what happened, don't you? I took a hit to the waist."

When the Hunter's hand touched the stick, the boy released fingers that were wrapped so tightly around the wood it seemed like part of him, and the branch was transferred into D's hands. He picked up the half on the ground as well. Though the branch was a piece of wood, the cuts on either end had a sheen like metal. Sticking them together, D held them for the span of two breaths or so, and then brought one of his hands away.

The branch didn't fall apart.

Placing it back in the boy's hand, he said, "Give it a swing."

The boy made a hesitant swing with it.

"Give it all you've got."

The boy swung it high, and then swung it low. It whistled through the wind. But the stick remained in one piece.

Surprise and another emotion glowed in the face of the boy—and in the faces of all the children. They were quite impressed.

"That's all," D said. "You scored a hit on a Vampire Hunter. Never forget that."

There was no reply.

The boy knew that D had purposely let him get that hit in. The other children were fully aware of it as well. However, the boy wasn't embarrassed, and the other children had no complaints. What they'd been focused on wasn't what D had done, but rather the boy's actions as he took up the branch and charged at the Hunter. Whether D had let the boy hit him or not, that was good enough for the children.

Clapping the boy on the shoulder, the leader said, "That was pretty good."

"I won't be calling you Slowpoke anymore," the chubby girl said, grinning.

By the time a smile spread across the boy's whole face, D was already walking off toward Matthew and Sue.

II

When the last hint of red decorating the rim of the western mountains had been lost, Count Braujou appeared.

"This Courbet fellow seems to be connected to the spider man who attacked me," the man who'd fallen from the stratosphere pointed out. "In which case, we should prepare ourselves for air-to-air combat. But before we do—we have to brace ourselves for being worshiped as gods, I suppose."

"Are you really going?" Matthew inquired with dissatisfaction.

"That's what you wanted, isn't it? The whole reason we stopped in this village is because you wanted to look good."

"That may be true, but it's still got me kinda worried. You guys aren't gonna get beaten, are you?"

The count smiled widely. "Now there's something that God only knows. It may be shabby, but I don't think this shrine has been constructed on a whim. They must be fairly sure they can kill us."

"Are you gonna be okay?" Matthew asked, both his voice and his expression growing even more uncertain. "The folks from the village seem to be on pins and needles. Apparently they blame you guys for the death of the mayor."

Glancing at D, the count said, "How is that my fault?" His tone was sly. In this regard, the Nobility didn't differ at all from human beings.

D didn't answer.

"There are three gods—D, Miranda, and myself. But Miranda isn't here. If only two of us enter this shrine, I wonder if will incur the wrath of their true god."

Looking at the brother and sister, D said, "Wait in the count's car until we return."

"Is it gonna be okay? Will you really come back?"

"What a nuisance you are, boy. If you tell us not to do this, we could save a lot of wasted time. Which will it be?"

"Well—we already said you'd do it."

"In that case, relax," the count said, clapping the boy on the shoulder.

Still, Matthew had his doubts. "But you don't both have to go, do you? I mean, in case something happens."

"Matt," Sue said reproachfully. "You made the call. Pull yourself together."

"I've got myself together," Matthew countered heatedly. "But this isn't like the farm or our village. There's no one here to protect us except these two. If we lose them, what do you think will become of us? These people are out to kill you, too. You wanna end up like Mom?"

"Don't say that to me at a time like this," Sue said, her cheeks stained bright red. Not with anger, but with embarrassment.

"I suppose it'd be asking too much for you to have a little faith in the Nobility," the count said, smiling and clapping Matthew on the shoulder again. Though the boy stood six feet tall, he was like a mere child beside the ten-foot-tall giant, and the slap tossed him violently.

"You'll be safe if you remain inside my car. Though you're still young, I suppose you drink wine, at least. The Nobility's drinks are exceptional. So, shall we go?" Braujou said to D, swinging the long spear he held in his hand and walking toward both the Hunter and the village.

A half-moon rose, and there was some wind.

Villagers were already keeping watch on the situation from their homes or out on the streets, but they hurriedly shut their doors and windows, or else ducked behind buildings.

"Hmm. So the Nobility are still the object of fear, are they?" Count Braujou remarked, his tone conveying a certain amount of pride.

"I don't know if that's it," said D.

"Oh, you mean they think we got their mayor killed? Wouldn't it be best to dispel their misconceptions?"

The count continued on in this manner, but D didn't reply, and the two of them came to the road up the hill. Only four villagers were waiting there.

An old man a bit larger and a bit older than the late mayor bowed his head and said, "Right this way."

They followed him up the hill. The other three were also gray-haired and gray-bearded old men—making it seem like a procession of the dead.

Just before sundown the sound of hammering had ceased at the shrine, which stood quietly in the light of the half-moon. The two men who stood by its door bowed. Despite its rushed construction, the windowless shrine was remarkably well built.

"So, all the other houses are mud brick, but not this one. Wood burns, you know."

The count seemed to read the intentions of the one who'd ordered its construction, laughing and looking up at the sky. The village leaders followed his example, having heard the manner in which the missionary had fled when cornered by D. The man who'd vanished into the heavens would probably be watching the ground from on high. But would he descend from the heavens again?

"Is there anyone inside?"

At D's query, the men all shook their heads. The middle-aged man who stood at the fore turned to the two men who'd been guarding the shrine.

"No, not a soul. Not even a mouse could've got by us, right?"

The other man nodded repeatedly at this.

Everyone there was utterly terrified. None of them had actually seen a Noble before. What's more, this one was ten feet tall. And they knew about the other man who stood beside him—the young man darker than the darkness and more exquisite than the moonlight. They could tell he was a dhampir.

"Very well, then—"

The count extended his right hand, and a spear seemed to grow from his fist and jabbed against the door to the building. Creaking on its hinges, the door swung inside. A bit over twelve feet high, the doorway would allow the count to enter without any difficulty.

Side by side, they were walking toward the flickering lamplight that filled the doorway when the count narrowed his gaze and exclaimed, "Dear me! It would seem mice have taken to wearing perfume these days. And Noble perfume, at that."

Both men stepped into the building at the same time.

The ceiling, floor, and walls were all made of wood, with the flames of a single lamp dancing against each of the four walls. Aside from that, there was nothing else . . . except for the lithe, alluring figure in white that lay sleeping at the base of the wall ahead of them.

From the vicinity of D's left hip, a hoarse voice exclaimed, "Oh, is that Miranda I see?"

The woman who lay there with her sensuous form draped in a white dress was indeed Miranda.

"Who brought her here, and when, and how?"

The two men most likely shared the same questions as the hoarse voice. This female fiend's husband had long ago challenged the Ultimate Noble, along with Count Braujou and General Gaskell. It would've been easier to believe the whole world was crumbling than to think the same tried-and-true Noblewoman who'd effortlessly fended off the water witch back at the Dyalhis farm could be put to sleep so easily or left there so defenseless.

The two of them halted simultaneously. Nodding, the count said to leave this to him and raised his long spear.

Did he seriously intend to impale Miranda?

D showed no signs of trying to stop him.

Whistling through the air, the iron spear lanced right through Miranda's abdomen. The count hadn't hurled the spear. Rather, he'd kept it in his hand and made a thrust, like a spear fisherman. Was this cruelty the true nature of a Noble—the true nature of a vampire? He certainly felt the agony of Miranda's silent contortions transmitted from the spearhead down the weapon and through his hand, and what should arise on his refined countenance but the bloodthirsty grin of a demon.

Wasn't D going to stop this?

The Hunter stood stock still as the hoarse voice said, "Hmm. Interesting approach."

It was at that moment the beautiful woman stopped moving. Concentrating a glowing red gaze on the spear and the bright blood spilling from her abdomen, she then slowly turned to one side and looked up at the count, eyes agleam with malice and mocking laughter.

"What a pleasant way to awaken someone," said Miranda. Gouts of blood spilled from her mouth to paint vermilion patterns on the floor.

While it had indeed awakened her, the devil himself couldn't have come up with a more disturbing manner of rousing someone.

Her gore-stained mouth shouted, "Hurry up and take that thing out of me, you rude man!"

Shrugging, the count smirked as he pulled his long spear back out of her.

The wound closed immediately—not only that, but the fabric seemed to drink up the lifeblood that had seeped from the duchess; in the blink of an eye it all vanished. The men could only gaze at her in surprise as she rose in a pure-white dress without a single spot on it. A displeased look flitted across the graceful features of the Noblewoman the moment she saw Count Braujou lick up the blood she'd left on the tip of his spear.

"How did you get here?" D asked. It was a natural question.

"How indeed," Miranda said, smiling seductively and looking up at D. "I myself don't know. I spent all day resting in my coffin, and the next thing I knew, I was here."

"Can you recall ever traveling subconsciously?"

The count was referring to the ability of Nobles to unknowingly travel through space. Since their history had begun, on a few extremely rare and freakish occasions Nobles had traveled from the idle darkness of their enclosure out into the blinding light of day without realizing it, and when it was concluded that this phenomenon was linked to a central mechanism of the Nobility's own psyche, it caused an absolute panic among the Nobles. Even after an investigation conducted by the Sacred Ancestor's personal team of physicians determined the cause to be a subconscious longing for the light, many Nobles tried their best not to believe the findings. But that was what the count had been asking about.

"No, I do not," Miranda replied disdainfully, but the smile never left her face. "Which isn't to say it couldn't happen. That's probably what occurred here. If not, how could I have come to be in such a wretched place without knowing it?"

"Then you came by coincidence?"

D's murmurs caused the two Nobles to turn.

"It couldn't be," the count said. "Not even Miranda could appear before us just at the right time. She doesn't even know where we are."

"Have you ever seen this place?"

At D's question, the Noblewoman gave an alluring shake of her head. "No, I've never been here before."

Lovingly stroking the shaft of his long spear, the count said, "Then, could this be the work of someone with powers we don't know about working for Valcua?"

"It might be Valcua himself," D said, his words freezing the very air.

III

Whoever brought the sleeping Miranda there could've ended her life if they'd chosen to do so. The fact that she was still alive spoke volumes about the supreme confidence their unseen opponent had in how perfectly he'd laid this trap.

It was Miranda who fractured the frozen air.

"The three of us can't just stand around this doghouse discussing matters. That conversation will keep until later. I'll be going now."

The hem of her dress whirled as she headed toward the entrance. Her shoulders were trembling slightly, perhaps due to the humiliation of not only being abducted by their foe with such ease, but not even noticing it at the time, and then having her two compatriots witness that fact. However, the proud Noblewoman halted before she'd taken three steps.

"How did you two enter this place?"

Her query caused the two men to turn, and Count Braujou gasped.

The place where the door should've been was a plank-covered wall. There wasn't a single crack to indicate an entrance.

"Dear me. This is a fine amusement they've prepared for us. Do you want out, Miranda? Just wait. Now—"

The count raised the spear over his head. It made the wind swirl so fiercely the hastily erected shack seemed likely to blow away. Amid that roar, they heard an impact.

Pulling the spear back, the count stared at the wall to his right. There wasn't a scratch on it.

"I struck it. What do you think, D? Do my eyes deceive me?"

The young man in black turned his handsome features in the same direction and replied, "No, it really is shrinking."

It wasn't strange that the nearly twenty-foot-long spear would strike the wall. The count had taken that into account when he swung the weapon.

The ceiling was approaching the trio's heads, just as D said, and the walls were definitely drawing closer.

"What a quaint setup," Miranda said with a bewitching smile. Even the most resolute human would've been bewildered at this situation, but the way she seemed to actually enjoy their predicament was true to the Nobility's dauntless nature. "Count Braujou, can't you do anything with your cherished spear?"

"Hmph," the gigantic Nobleman snorted, but there was something about his expression and bearing that suggested he, too, was enjoying this. Without a wasted movement, the count swung the long spear toward the wall to his right. Its path was clearly shorter than last time, and it bounced off the wall with a strident sound.

"Oh my, I may have given you too much credit," Miranda sneered as she looked at the unmarred wallboards.

The count's lips twisted as he took a new stance with his spear.

The Noblewoman told him, "Just so you know, even if you stop the walls to our left and right, there's still the other two to contend with. What's all this?"

That last cry of surprise came when she saw D step forward. His right hand flowed toward his shoulder—and a silvery flash split the dancing lamplight.

A line had been carved in the wall.

Miranda and the count gasped.

The line immediately faded.

Sheathing his blade, D stepped closer to the wall and pressed his left hand against it.

"Hmm. It seems to absorb gravity," the hoarse voice said. "Think of the house itself as a kind of black hole. Beyond the boards—no, actually the boards themselves have had their neutrons and electrons fused to form an incredibly dense material. If we don't do something, we'll eventually be absorbed by the house and become part of that black hole."

"Goodness," Miranda said, ceremoniously raising her hand to her mouth. True to her high station, she clutched a handkerchief in it as always.

"My, but this is becoming rather trying, wouldn't you say?" the count said. His voice resounded over D's head.

Staring up at the giant, who'd been forced down on one knee, D pulled a fistful of dirt from one of his coat's inner pockets.

"Did you bring that just in case? It's not like you to be so well prepared. Oof!"

Pushing the palm of his hand—and the human face that'd surfaced on it—into the tightly packed ball of earth, D took a step to the left. The count's spear had managed to stop the walls in front of and behind them, but it would be difficult to do anything about those to the left and the right, and the ceiling had already dropped to about six and a half feet. The count lay face down on the floor.

"Pardon me," a sweet voice said at the same time a softly perfumed sleeve came into contact with D. Standing to his left, Miranda had been pushed closer to him.

"From what we just saw, it looks like we can depend on you. Is there anything you can do?" she asked, her fragrant breath falling against D's face. It was like a bare tree in winter.

"Give me a hand," D told the count.

"But I—I can't get up very well," the count groused.

"Your hand," D said, bending over and taking the count's left hand. As the Nobleman furrowed his brow, the Hunter unbuttoned

Braujou's cuff, exposing his wrist. D forcefully flicked his little finger against it and caught the lifeblood that poured out in the palm of his left hand. Not a single drop was wasted.

"Oh, that's a bizarre little thing you have there."

"How unusual," Miranda said. Her face and that of the count, both nearly pressed against D's, displayed astonishment. It wasn't clear whether or not they realized how distressed they appeared.

"Okay," the left hand said, while D ran the same finger across the count's gash. The blood and the wound both disappeared.

"Hold your breath. I'm gonna suck up some air."

Air whistled into the mouth in his left hand.

All three of them asphyxiated simultaneously. The mouth of the weird-countenanced carbuncle had drawn in every bit of air in the room with a single breath. A pale blue flame flickered in the depths of its tiny maw.

Earth, water, fire, and air—all four elements had been assembled.

Miranda trembled. Her face was pale. Did she sense something from D?

The ceiling was just above D's head as he crept on his belly. The space was fewer than six feet from left to right.

"Pardon me," Miranda said, sprawling across the back of the prone count as D began to creep forward.

The walls were closing on them from the front and back. The long spear was bent to its limits. The ever-shrinking confines of the hastily constructed shack-cum-black-hole must have put hundreds of millions of tons of pressure on either end of the weapon. Both this trap and the spear were mind boggling.

The ceiling dropped even further.

"You know, this is beginning to hurt," Miranda's voice called out behind the Hunter.

The top of his traveler's hat hit the ceiling. Now lying completely flat, D drew his sword. It was pitted against ultradense walls that wouldn't allow even electromagnetic waves or light to escape. There was the sound of bones creaking behind him.

D thrusted his sword. Miranda and Count Braujou saw it slide into the wall like a mirage. Glowing cracks spread out around them. No one knew how the black hole collapsed.

Above the three people lying in a tiny lot, the half-moon glowed starkly. D was the first to rise.

A murmur went through the villagers, who'd been watching from afar.

"The gods are safe!"

"They might be, but why are they sprawled over there?"

"At any rate, they must be worshiped!"

Kneeling on the ground, they raised their arms and bowed deeply.

Sheathing his blade, D looked back at the other two.

The gigantic figure stared intently at his terribly bowed spear, and then said in a distressed tone, "Hmph. There'll be no fixing this."

The weapon had endured billions of tons of pressure. It was a miracle that it hadn't snapped.

Apparently giving up on it, he shifted his gaze to D, and his eyes had a hint of fear in them as he asked, "Just who exactly are you, sir?"

"I should like to know that as well. You're just fantastic," Miranda said as she stood beside the count, both hands folded together and her body trembling. "It's almost as if—as if I were looking at the great one in his youth. The first time I had the honor of meeting him, he already seemed as timeless as the universe, so I can only imagine what he must've been like. But verily, in his younger days he must've resembled this regal knight—"

"He's a Hunter," the count reminded her, both his tone and his expression morose.

"Oh, dear!"

"But that's not to say there isn't some resemblance," the Nobleman continued.

Two pairs of eyes crawled over every inch of D with obvious interest and curiosity.

Footsteps pounded up the hill. It was one of the villagers. Ignoring the old men asking what had happened, the villager ran straight to

D and said, "Your car's been stolen. I was keeping an eye on it with a bunch of the others. Then that missionary came along and whispered something to it, and it sped off all by itself down the highway that runs west!"

"Didn't anyone go after it?" one of the old men cried out, his jowls quaking with the words.

"It all happened so suddenly. And that car's terribly fast."

"What became of the missionary?"

"I don't know. We were all focused on the car, and the next thing we knew, he wasn't there anymore."

"Excuse me," Miranda said with a cough before turning to the count. "Are you certain this isn't due to some negligence on your part?"

"It can't be," the count spat angrily. "That car is under the complete control of a proton computer. Its recognition sensors can check five million points in a half a millionth of a second to see if a person is me or not. It would never operate on anyone else's instructions."

"And yet, it left."

"Oh, shut up!" the count said. Those who could see in the dark saw his face darkening with rage.

As the villagers stood paralyzed, thinking the allies were about to fight among themselves, one of them noticed something. D was looking up at the sky.

Following his lead, the villagers gasped aloud. By the time the count and Miranda looked up in the air, grumbling spilled from the foremost rank of villagers like a bank of clouds.

"What's that?"

"The half-moon just became a full moon."

"The top half wasn't there. Hey, are those letters I see?"

Indeed, there were letters darkly stained into the top half of the brightly shining moon.

"Wha—what's written up there?"

A hoarse voice that the villagers straining their eyes would never hear said in a murky tone, "Come to Galleon Valley tomorrow at one o'clock Afternoon. If all three of you aren't there, the hostages' lives are forfeit."

"What's this Galleon Valley place?"

When the count's query rained down on him from above, the villager who'd raced to notify them replied in a quavering voice, "It's a valley just two miles west of here. They say the Nobility used it as a testing ground long ago, but no one's been out there as long as this village has been around."

"Hmm. I don't care where we have to go, but traveling by daylight is going to make things a little difficult. D, do you have any ideas?"

There was no reply. D would obviously be going with them. However, could even the Hunter put up a good fight against foes with the power to turn a board-covered shack into a black hole, or inscribe words on the half of the moon that should've been in darkness, especially when his two allies were forced to take refuge from the sunlight?

"Well, do you, D?" the count inquired again. The wind made the hem of his clothes and Miranda's dress dance before reaching D's hair.

The unearthly beauty of the young man in black's face glowed in the moonlight as he asserted in a low voice, "I do."

Tyrant's Stars

PART TWO

The Diva in Janos

I

"Someone's on the move," a voice called out by the flickering light of a single candle. At the same time a number of people squirmed to life. They looked up in unison.

A glance at the rough but simple beds lining the walls made it clear this was an inn. Up by the ceiling floated a man; he was upside down about ten feet off the floor. His body excreted a thread that those on the ground could never make out, no matter how they strained their eyes, and the man entrusted his full weight to it, curled up and dangling like a spider. His arms, his legs, and the fingers he presently used to scratch at his chin were disproportionately long compared to his body. This was the man who could even do battle in the stratosphere—Speeny.

"One of the threads I strung around the village just broke—the one on the route north. Which would mean they're headed for Janos, I suppose."

"Who is it?" asked the monklike figure—Courbet. His right arm hung in a sling looped around his neck.

"Judging by the way the thread was cut—it'd have to be D."

"For what purpose?" came a woman's voice.

In a corner of the dilapidated room was a ceramic pitcher filled to the brim with water. Although there was no sign of anyone, that was where the voice originated. It had to be Lucienne.

"I don't know," Speeny replied.

Almost simultaneously, another voice said, "I thought this might happen."

Ringing with both the composure of age and the power of youth, it made all the others turn in its direction.

"Oh!"

"Is that Curio the Preacher?"

"Has he joined us at long last?"

Courbet, Lucienne, and Speeny spoke in near unison, so afraid they couldn't help but say something.

The figure in the doorway—which had stood permanently open since the automatic doors lost their power source—wore a hooded robe like the "missionary," Courbet, but the color of his was a far more sinister vermilion, and he was shrouded in a weird air that left the group of freaks stunned and reluctant to approach him. Apparently he was one of the most powerful of the seven assassins.

As another figure on the floor was about to rise, he insisted in a tone overflowing with dignity, "Don't."

Coming down to the floor from the ceiling, Speeny said, "Well, then—why would D go to the village of Janos alone?"

"If you consider for a moment how they earn their daily bread in that village, the answer will soon come to you. Such is to be expected of the greatest man on the Frontier, with his nearest competition light years behind. Oh, but he's a shrewd one."

"How—how so?"

"I heard your plan through Speeny's thread. From that, I can only assume he's gone off to get Time-Bewitching Incense."

A murmur spread from the mouths of the other three.

Time-Bewitching Incense—a scent that could turn day into night for the vampiric Nobility, it was a two-edged sword that at times saved their eternal lives from destruction, while at other times left them critically exposed during what should've been the inviolate night.

"Ah, so they'll turn day into night?" Lucienne said, her tone carrying anger. "If they do that, then even by day they can have triple their expected numbers. I suppose even Count Braujou and Duchess Miranda have never seen a night so filled with daylight."

"Well, then, we must do something to stop him," groaned the other man in a vestment—Courbet.

"What can you do, wounded like that?" Curio remarked coldly. He looked down at the figure who lay on the floor. The person who'd lain moaning and groaning but otherwise unable to move since Curio's identity had become clear was Jessup the Beheader.

"From what I can see, Speeny's also been wounded, and Lucienne is hardly unharmed. As for those three—two of them are dyed-in-the-wool Nobility, and the other seems to possess power every bit as great as a Noble's. The lot of you would have no easy time slaying them now."

"But we can't just stand back and do nothing. We were instructed to wait until you arrived, and now we have to strike a blow against them. To be honest, I was beginning to wonder what we'd do. Of course, if we had to, we could slay all three of them easily, but now that D's alone, I thought this would be the perfect opportunity to engage him."

"Precisely. That rascal's gone off to Janos alone in the hopes we wouldn't notice. But now that we're wise to him—"

These two objections were voiced by Courbet and Speeny, respectively.

In response, the figure in the vermilion robe said, "Callas is on the way there."

There was an explosion of astonished voices.

"Oh—the Diva?"

"Has she been brought back, too?" Speeny said, and his joy was so great that as he descended from the ceiling head first, a victorious smile was already on his face.

"Her songs might do the trick," Lucienne said, her voice not sounding pleased at all, but rather ringing with fear.

"And I'll send along one more for good measure."

"Who?"

The figure in vermilion moved, and a yelp arose from the floor. He'd delivered a kick to the plump shadow.

"You're not wounded all that badly, you layabout. I've already notified Callas. Hurry off to Janos. If you don't, I'll treat you to a sermon."

Shrieking, the fleshy figure of Jessup the Beheader leaped up without any further hesitation.

It was late at night when D entered the village of Janos. The moon glowed like a fire in the night sky. Still, it was nothing compared to D's handsome features as he sat astride his steed. Though the moon merely glowed by reflected light, D's beauty was the source of its own luminance.

Perhaps the villagers did their utmost to hide their presence from passing travelers, as the air was free of strange scents, yet D could detect the faintest traces of bromine that couldn't be concealed. Rows of houses made of stone and Quonset-hut-styled buildings covered with vinyl awnings slumbered in the moonlight. The latter were domes for growing extremely poisonous herbs, the mere smell of which could spell death, while all the fields around the town also displayed lovely expanses of poisonous flowers and plants.

Taking the main street through the center of town, D halted his steed in front of a certain house. It was just an ordinary building, with nothing to distinguish it from any of the other houses.

Getting down from his horse and rapping on the wooden door, the Hunter had to wait a short time before a masculine voice cursed him through the wall, "Just what hour of the day do you think it is, you daft bastard? I've got a good mind to douse you with poison goo!"

"Sorry, but this is urgent."

"Shut your hole, you—"

The wrathful voice faded away suddenly. It was like the tide quickly ebbing. When the man spoke again, it was in a tone of fear and surprise—and nostalgia.

"No, it couldn't be—is that you, D?"

"I've come to ask a favor of you."

"H-h-h-hold on. I-I-I-I'll open right up."

On the other side of the wooden door, there was a rattle and a great clamor that gave way to a cry of pain. Apparently the man had banged into something. The bar was lifted, and the wooden door opened inward with a creak.

The silhouette against the light quickly resolved itself into an unusually scrawny man with gray hair. His wasn't the face of an old man. However, his dry and lusterless skin and exposed bones made him look terribly old.

"What in blazes is it? It's been three whole years. Never thought I'd be seeing you like this."

"I need a favor."

"You need a favor from me? Fair enough, since it's thanks to you I'm still alive. Not that I've done a hell of a lot with my life, but I never forget a debt. Go ahead and name it."

"I want you to make Time-Bewitching Incense," D said.

The man's jaw dropped. It fell with a vigor almost unthinkable for a man in his condition.

Taking a step back, the man allowed D to enter his house. After bolting the door again, he led the Hunter to a cramped room. They sat in crude chairs on opposite sides of a round table.

"You ask the damnedest things, don't you? But you being the man called D and all, I guess there's no helping it. I'll get started on whipping it up right away," the man said, having finally recovered his calm.

But D told him coolly, "I'd like you to do something special to it."

"Really? What?"

After D had finished explaining what he wanted, the man inquired in a strangely soft tone, "When do you want it?"

"I have to bring it back to Marthias by noon tomorrow."

"Which means I've only got tonight, until daybreak." The man shrugged his shoulders, saying plainly, "It can't be done."

"That's why I came to you, the Frontier sector's preeminent toxicologist—Karim Mubbe."

"I'll give it a shot," he said, donning a grin so intrepid it seemed he must've intended to help all along. "Well, I'm gonna hole up in my workshop. But my wife and kids are sleeping. Try not to make any noise."

The man didn't wait for a reply, but disappeared behind the only bronze door in the place. Once the door had been locked, he opened an iron panel set in the wall to the left of it and peeked inside. On a rustic bed, his wife was stroking the hair of their six-year-old son and four-year-old daughter. As Mubbe turned and was about to shut the iron panel, his wife shot him a glance.

"Dear . . ."

"It's okay."

And saying this, Mubbe closed the panel.

His workshop was lined with shelves filled with innumerable glass jars of poisonous herbs, and the greenhouse connected to the west wall was used for raising other virulent plants and insects. The jars and greenhouse were all made to double or triple thickness, because even the slightest crack could turn his entire house into a hell on Earth.

"Now then," he said, taking a gas mask off the wall and putting it on so it covered his head and chest. Donning gloves, he opened the door that led to the greenhouse. There was an airlock just large enough to accommodate a single person. Entering it, he shut the outer door, and then opened the inner one. There was a second airlock. After he'd passed through a third airtight chamber, he finally reached the greenhouse. In there, the air itself was a toxin.

The profusion of fearsome flowers was a thing of beauty. This toxic hell was adorned with crimson and indigo, purple and pale blue, and luxurious shades of green that seemed like nothing that could possibly be of this world. But Mubbe didn't even glance at these blooms, of which he never tired, going instead into the center of the greenhouse.

Roped off on all sides, there bloomed a stark-white blossom. Its soil was a strange hue, due to special care and nutrients. Though it resembled a lily, it had two petals more and a much softer overall impression. Even here in Janos, famed for its poisons, no one but this man knew the transparent sap that dripped from the stalk was a component of Time-Bewitching Incense.

"You only put out a stalk once in a hundred years—come on, baby," Mubbe said, gently beginning to push the soil away from the plant with his gloved hands. The slightest scrape to the stalk or leaves would cause the components of the plant to change in an instant.

Gently, patiently, and with almost mechanical precision, he continued what he was doing, stopping only once to say the strangest thing: "I'm really sorry about this, D."

II

A lovely sound drifted out of the depths of the night. Twined in the wind, pushed along by the moonlight, the sound took a long time arriving. Before the door to its destination, the sound let out a faint sigh but slipped in through a crack without the slightest pause.

In the room, a figure leaned against one wall. There was nobody else there.

Three o'clock in the morning. Everything was draped in a false death.

The figure against the wall suddenly opened his eyes. His pupils were so black, a dark gleam seemed to spill from them. Turning his gaze to the doorway, D quickly pulled away from the wall.

Once outside, he heard it clearly.

From the vicinity of his left hip, a hoarse voice said, "That's a hell of a fine voice. I've heard of sirens singing to enchant captains and get them to smash their ships on the rocks, but this singer's got them beat. Watch yourself, D."

D was already advancing on foot. Had the hoarse voice's warning been in vain? Had the nocturnal song already robbed him of his senses?

Advancing with silent footsteps, the vision of beauty in black was beckoned to the central square of the village. A well stood in the center of the cobblestoned expanse. And beside it stood a woman. Her seemingly naked form stood out in the moonlight. D's eyes were able to see that her diaphanous dress was a pale purple.

Stillness descended, for the woman had shut her lips. She didn't seem particularly proud of the song that had flowed thinly but deliberately all the way to Mubbe's house, and D displayed no emotion at all.

"I am Callas the Diva," the woman said, the black hair above her brow adorned by a golden circlet that glittered in the moonlight. Near its center, the circlet rose in a relief of a bizarre creature's face, the eyes of which were set with blue jewels.

"But then, I can't expect that you'll answer me," she continued. "You've heard my song, after all. Haven't you, D?"

There was no reply.

Perhaps taking this as proof of her spell, the woman formed her thin lips into a grin. It was a transparent smile.

"We've long since figured out what you're up to. I'm an assassin sent to slay you. Normally, I'd have waited until the Time-Bewitching Incense was completed, but I happened to see you when you came into the village."

A mysterious emotion resided in the woman's eyes. Perhaps it was grief—or passion.

She continued, "You were simply too gorgeous. My heart threatened to burn down to nothing when I saw your handsome features. But that will prove to be your misfortune. Any man capable of inspiring love in me would surely attract other women as well. And if you're truly a man, you're bound to capitalize on that. Alas, that I couldn't bear. Still, I can't help but picture it. Laugh at me if you like, D. But I would rather do away with you than have you love any other woman. Here and now, without waiting for you to get the Time-Bewitching Incense."

A dagger appeared in the woman's right hand, both sides honed razor sharp. Raising it with an elegant motion, Callas hurled the blade. It sped toward D's chest, but halted a split second before hitting him.

"What?"

As the diva's eyes went wide with shock, the figure in black told her, "I've heard of Callas the Diva. Now, tell me the name of the other assassin."

"But you—didn't you listen to my song?" the woman groaned in astonishment.

"I heard it."

The Hunter's answer came from midair. The bounding D swung down the sword he held overhead, and he seemed to slice the woman in half from the top of her head down to the breastbone— but she remained motionless in her dress while D's blade narrowly missed her left shoulder, slicing only air. A second slash mowed through the night air and her torso, but the blade relayed no resistance to D's hand, and Callas only laughed haughtily.

"It would seem that you did indeed hear my song. And having done so, there's no way for you to strike me."

Like the sailors bewitched by the sirens of legend, were those who'd heard Callas's song drained of their souls without even realizing it . . . or perhaps left cowards?

"Take your own life," the lovely lady whispered.

After the horizontal swipe of his blade, D had taken a stance with his sword held out straight at eye level, but he kept his eyes gently closed.

Disbelief squirmed into Callas's expression. She'd gotten the impression the gorgeous young man who'd swung his sword with such deadly precision had suddenly become a completely different being.

"You're . . ."

Before she could say another word, D opened his eyes. They gave off a blood light.

As the singer shrieked, the Hunter's blade danced out over her head once again. It was exactly as before, but this time it would be the end of Callas.

However, a heartbeat later, D reeled wildly in midair. Fresh blood gushed from his back, falling on him like a heavy spring rain when he landed and dropped to one knee.

"Heh! How do you like that?" another voice laughed from the same direction D had entered the square. Grabbing the handle of the ax he'd driven into the ground, and still somewhat off balance was Jessup the Beheader.

"I just got here and was looking for a place to conceal myself, and what should I happen across but this scene! Callas, I hope you know you owe me for this. Sing me one of them songs that got you piles and piles of gold. Oof!" he grunted, finally managing to lift his ax but still unsteady on his feet—but D knew better than anyone how fearsome he was with an ax that never hit anything. The Hunter's backbone was shattered.

Though this man appeared at first glance to be incompetent, he was truly worthy of being counted among the Ultimate Noble's seven assassins if he could hack open D's back, even if the Hunter had been entirely focused on his deadly battle with Callas at the time.

"But, you know," the beheader continued, "you're quite a piece of work too. I thought I'd completely blindsided you, but it seems you saw it coming after all. Normally, your torso would've been chopped in two."

Jessup warped his lips into a smirk.

"Well, did you have a nice taste of the great Jessup the Beheader's 'dark-cloud chop'? I can cut you without even aiming for you," the man declared.

Planting his unsteady feet, he raised his ax. Though his eyes were trained on D, his ax was pointed in a different direction.

"From this distance, not even you can reach me with your blade, D. But my ax can cut you. Hey, watch this, Callas. I'm about to take the best-looking Hunter on the Frontier and chop 'im to pieces! I'll start with his right hand."

In the moonlight, the Hunter's coat spread like the wings of a black bird. D had pulled in one arm and leaped into the air. His fist was aimed at Jessup's face.

"I'll fix you!" Jessup shouted.

The ax limned a silvery arc. With a thunk, D's fist was chopped off at the wrist. Black blood spouted out.

D kicked off the ground, just like a mystic bird soaring across the surface of the moon—or an enormous and exquisite bat.

Staggering, Jessup was still able to launch his next attack—this time at the Hunter's left leg.

But down by that foot, a faint, hoarse voice murmured, "Figured him out?"

The reply to that was a flash from Jessup's ax.

D's thigh split open, and fresh blood gushed out. Blood from his right leg.

A flash of white light pierced Jessup between his surprised eyes, and something black sprayed out as the beheader tumbled backward. The man's eyes were still wide with disbelief as they watched D turn to go after the diva.

"She got away?" the hoarse voice said from the ground as D approached it. Callas had vanished.

Sheathing his sword and retrieving his left hand with his right, D pressed the severed limb against the wound and let go. The wound vanished in seconds, and the surface of his palm rippled like water. What formed there was a little face with eyes, a nose, and a mouth. It looked like nothing in this world.

The little face looked down at Jessup on the ground and scolded him with relish, saying, "What, you didn't think we could figure out the pattern after you screwed up three times, you dolt?"

Although Jessup's "dark-cloud chop" seemed to cut his opponents when he swung his blade in the wrong direction, his swings were not entirely haphazard. If that were the case, no one could ever beat him.

Having been cut twice, D had let his left hand be severed by the third blow in order to discover the relationship between where

Jessup struck with his ax and where the cuts appeared. The second wound had been dealt to him when he was entirely off guard, but he used the ones before and after it to learn to read the pattern, twisting in midair so that his leg was dealt no more than a shallow cut. And the reason he'd drawn the beheader's attention to his left hand was because he needed his right to wield his sword.

The slice in the peculiar material of his coat had long since closed, and it seemed that D himself had also made a full physical recovery.

"That's one down—what, six to go? We've got a long haul ahead of us," said the face in his left hand. Its tone was far from light. Based on the one who'd just been slain and the other who'd escaped, it could tell with great certainty just how fearsome the remaining five would be.

"I wonder where that woman disappeared to. She's probably hiding behind something, waiting for a crack at us."

Bending down, D picked up a stone off the ground and threw it into the air. The parabola it traced was intersected by another line that cut through it at an angle. The stone dropped to the ground.

"You're still under the effects of Callas's song, eh? You got off lightly. Anyone else probably would've killed himself a hundred times over. You'd better slay Callas before it comes to that."

"Fix me up."

Picking up Jessup's body, D hurled it toward the wooden fence at the southwest side of the square. The enormous corpse looked to weigh in excess of two hundred pounds, but it whizzed through the air like a fastball to fall in a thicket far beyond the fence. The Hunter didn't have the least bit of regard for the remains. His cold-blooded demeanor was that of someone who didn't consider it even an empty husk.

"I'm already on it. The problem's your spinal column. This is gonna take a little while."

Not replying to this, D started to walk back the way he'd come. The movements of this man who'd been chopped through the backbone were so elegant, they could've made the moon itself swoon.

III

When he returned to Mubbe's house, the owner just happened to be poking his head out of the back room.

"I've done it," he said.

Perhaps due to the materials he worked with day in and day out, his fingernails were melted and the joints on his right hand were swollen, but in it he gripped a single blue candle.

"Genuine Time-Bewitching Incense! It was a rush job, so it might not be a hundred percent effective, but it should work for your purposes. Not that I have any idea what those purposes would be."

The toxin specialist wore the smile of satisfaction of an artist who's put his whole body and soul into his work. D stared at him and said, "Try lighting it."

"Excuse me?" Mubbe's mouth fell open. Shaking his head, he said, "Hey, it's night right now. If I were to light this thing . . ."

Night would become day. As a dhampir, D wouldn't experience the same hellish agony that a Noble might, but it would still be a rather painful ordeal.

"Light it," D said, a steely ring of intimidation to his voice.

Gazing stupidly at the Hunter's handsome face, Mubbe finally shrugged and replied, "Okay. Just don't come crying to me about how bright it gets."

Taking one of his homemade matches off the table and striking it, Mubbe brought the pale blue flame to the candle's wick. The instant a small light sparked, a great shudder passed through D. Though he had human blood in his veins, the sudden change from night to day wasn't one the Hunter could withstand effortlessly. His blood reversed its flow, and his metabolism was thrown into disarray. Noble blood couldn't escape its fate. More than a few dhampirs had been driven mad by as much.

Several streaks of sweat rolled down D's paraffin-pale cheeks. As his body trembled weakly, the organs within it screamed and squirmed with white-hot agony.

"Damn—I'll put it out!"

Unable to stand it any longer, Mubbe reached over. No sooner had he felt a gust of wind like a cold breath skim by the end of his nose than the fire was extinguished. His body's senses told him it was night again.

Turning to look at D, Mubbe saw the left hand the Hunter had raised to the candle open to take it in its grip. Though he got the impression he'd glimpsed something like a human face in the palm of D's hand, he soon forgot about it.

"Are you okay?" he asked D.

"I'll manage," the Hunter replied coolly, not a mote of discomfort in his tone. "Karim Mubbe, you've certainly done your job."

Taking a coin from his coat pocket, D laid it on the table.

Mubbe was puzzled. For something like Time-Bewitching Incense, the going rate would be fifty golden Mircalla coins. But the sight of the slightly larger and thicker coin triggered something in his brain. His eyes opened wide.

Murmuring, "It can't be," Mubbe slowly picked it up. His hand was shaking. As he held the coin in his palm and stared at it intently, the shaking spread to the rest of his body.

"This . . . this is a Sacred Ancestor coin . . . ," he said in a tone choked with wonder and fear. Faint as his words were, they hung in the air for a long time.

"They were minted in the Capital to commemorate the ten thousandth anniversary of the Sacred Ancestor's birth. As I recall, only fifty were made—a real treasure among treasures. Anyone who got one—even a human—had something so valuable it was as good as being dubbed a Noble. D—where the hell did you get this? Hell, even if you wanted to get one, you couldn't. Unless you had it from the very start, that is. D, just who are you?"

"I've given you your reward," D said, taking hold of the candle and getting up.

A short time after the unearthly beauty of that darkness in human form had gone and the door had closed, Mubbe's wife appeared in the doorway to the back room.

"Did I wake you up?"

Shaking her head, his wife said in a tone that was practically a song, "No. I was out anyway."

"What about the little ones?"

"They're asleep," she replied, and then she smiled. "No, that's not true. Don't you remember? We don't have any kids."

Amazed and numb, Mubbe shook his head.

That's impossible. But she's right. We never had any kids in the first place . . . Has the little woman always been this sexy? She's supposed to be squat and tough, with the smell of dirt and sweat about her . . . Wait a minute. Come to think of it, she took ill during that epidemic six years back, and then—

"Everyone's dead," Mubbe mumbled, convincing himself.

"That's right. No one's left here to keep you company. Can you stand being all alone? No? Then take your own life," said the woman who until a moment ago had been Mubbe's wife, bringing her lips to his right ear.

A low, gentle melody flowed between her lips and his ear. A song.

"This song calls for your own death . . . even if it didn't work on D."

Before long, the woman pulled away from him and gave him a seductive smile. There could be no mistaking Callas the Diva.

Mubbe got up and stepped through the door to his workshop on rubbery legs. Going over to the row of gas cylinders by the wall, he reached for a valve. It contained the most powerful poisonous gas imaginable, a colorless and odorless mixture of toxins extracted from three thousand varieties of plants.

Shortly thereafter, there was the hiss of escaping gas and the sound of a body falling. Once she'd heard that, the lovely and wicked diva slipped through the doorway and into the darkness as if seeking fresh applause.

A morose air drifted through the dilapidated boarding house.

"Jessup was slain, was he?" the missionary Courbet practically groaned.

The elegant woman who responded with a quiet nod was the fiendish diva Callas. She'd just finished recounting the events that had transpired in the village of Janos.

"And D definitely got his hands on the Time-Bewitching Incense—is that right, Callas?"

Four faces turned to the source of that question—Curio. His tone was cool, composed, and genial, as if trying to aggravate the woman in her bleak yet explosive mood.

"Indeed," the diva said with a nod. The beautiful woman responded as if he'd struck a nerve. Even in ordinary conversation, it almost sounded like she was singing. "However, I disposed of the one who made it."

"It sounds like you really enjoyed yourself," another voice remarked, and all the rest looked at each other. They'd expected her to put in an appearance. The source of the voice then drew the gaze of them all, just as Curio had done.

It came from just above the ground, from the ceramic water pitcher. A woman's face rose above the lip of the container like a disembodied head. It was the water witch, Lucienne.

Drilling Callas with her eyes, she said, "It sounds like Jessup died protecting you. Shouldn't you be more distraught over his loss than any of us?"

"Regardless of what you may think, my heart is filled to bursting with sadness," Callas said. It looked like a grin was rising to her lips; it sounded like she was singing a song.

"Surely you all heard her. And the look on her face every time she mentions D—it's as if she were speaking about the love of her life! Are you sure you haven't been won over by his looks?"

"Everything you say is correct, Lucienne. He's a gorgeous man. So cold, but with such sorrowful eyes, a nose more perfectly sculpted than that of Adonis, and lips like icy roses that make one pine for even a drop of blood. I'm not the sort of woman who's so inured to beauty I could ignore such things. But this I swear to you: I can't allow so exquisite a man to live. I, Callas the Diva, will slay D—with my song."

Her declaration was so soft yet forceful that Lucienne's disembodied head couldn't speak for a moment.

The next remark came from the ceiling.

"Hey! A swift horse approaches from the village of Janos. It just broke through my thread and entered the boundaries of Marthias."

This time, it was Speeny who drew the eyes of all.

"Is it a man or a woman?" Curio inquired.

"Well, my thread tells me it was a man."

"The part about coming from Janos worries me." After a moment's contemplation Curio continued, "I think I'll go have a look," and headed for the door.

A rumble went through the rest of them. Even his allies were frightened by the prospect of this man heading out.

"Curio, sir—do you have a horse?" asked Courbet.

"Don't worry about that."

"But he's so fast—you'll never catch up to him," Speeny added from the ceiling.

"There's no need for you to worry, either."

The figure in the vermilion robe pushed the door open.

Once outside, he slowly started walking down the highway. Any Frontier person might've frantically called out to him to ask if he'd lost his mind, but no one would've ever left his house to check. The darkness of night on the Frontier was composed of nothing save pure danger.

After going about sixty feet from the lodging house for workers in the abandoned farming community, Curio heard the ferocious beating of wings overhead.

"My mount is here."

He looked up, but instead of stars, his eyes beheld an enormous shape spreading out to attack him. A split second later, he was flying through the air. Sharp claws dug into his shoulders, and the nocturnal giant hawk with a thirty-foot wingspan flapped its wings, ready to carry its unprepared prey off to its nest in the north. But it almost immediately pointed south—swinging around in the direction of the village of Marthias.

Was this what Curio considered a mount?

Like an obedient steed the giant hawk did indeed carry Curio to his destination. As Curio was borne up to the heavens, his prayerlike words were only heard by the enormous bird.

Would there really be that much difference between racing across the ground and soaring across the sky? In less than a minute, Curio spotted the horse and rider advancing down the highway that stretched like a thread in the moonlight. Pointing at his target, he said in a monotone, "Crush his head."

Stranger than that remark was the fact that it seemed to be an instruction for the giant hawk. The bird instantly went into a dive. It beat its wings once to change direction and then merely glided. When it next flapped its wings to pull up again, the rider would be missing his head.

Due to their great speed, Curio's face warped from the air pressure. With thirty feet to go, they were closing on the rider, who was bent low over his steed and riding as fast as he could.

At that second a long spear zipped through the air. Severely bowed, its curve had been taken into consideration and it landed right on target, piercing the great hawk's abdomen. The rider turned at the sound of the creature's death screeches, and the giant hawk went into a tailspin as it fell, slamming into the ground and rolling two or three times like an enormous ball of rags, plowing into a vacant lot by the side of the highway and sending grass and dirt flying before it finally halted. Though it'd breathed its last, the giant hawk was still twitching when Curio crawled out from under its body about a minute later.

As Curio staggered to his feet and shook his head, a low but dignified voice weighed heavily on the night air, saying, "So, it shielded you with its wing?"

Not seeming particularly agitated, Curio looked up at the giant who towered some fifteen to twenty feet away.

"You're . . ."

"Now, why would a hawk do such an admirable thing on an empty stomach? You're one of Valcua's seven, aren't you?"

"Whatever could you be talking about?"

"I was covering D on his way back from Janos, expecting to stop someone from attacking him, and it looks like here we have our first rat in the trap. The nerve of asking us to come out in the daylight! Don't you have the courage to fight a Noble now, at night? I am Count Braujou."

Galleon Valley

CHAPTER 2

I

He was up against a great, ten-foot-tall man—a veritable giant. Even the bravest warrior would suffer a heart attack from the shock. But the preacher in the vermilion robe didn't seem the least bit afraid as he said, "Please allow me to introduce myself. I am one of Valcua's seven—Curio is my name."

"What kind of tricks do you have?"

"That's a trade secret."

The giant guffawed at this. His was completely unrestrained laughter.

"You're an amusing fellow. However, since you mentioned Valcua, I can't let you leave here alive."

"I might very well say the same thing to you."

"The blazes you might!" Count Braujou bellowed, his right knee rising before he slammed his foot against the ground.

A line ran straight toward Curio. Halfway to him it split to either side, opening into an enormous crack.

Wringing a cry of terror from the bottom of his heart, Curio leaped to one side to escape. At his feet another crack opened, swallowing him up.

The count brought his foot down again.

Having seen his success, the giant's eyes narrowed with satisfaction when he saw Curio trapped chest deep in the crack. The split had opened no further.

Letting out a deep sigh, the count made a light bound, landing next to the giant hawk. Artlessly extricating his long spear, he licked at the bird blood that clung to its tip. His eyes began to glow with blood light.

"It's been a long time since I had a fresh meal," he said, running his tongue around lips that already had a pair of fangs peeking from them. "I aimed for the hawk. You see, there are a number of things I want to ask you. I know the abilities of four of the seven of you. And I have a good idea about another one. As for the other two— of which you are one—what powers do you have? What's the other one look like? And what's his or her name? I stopped that crack you're in. But I can make it swallow you with another tap of my foot. So you'd better start telling me what I want to know, unless you want to be smashed flat as a pancake in the depths of the earth."

"I have nothing to say regarding the other member," Curio replied. His tone was soft.

That only angered the count more.

"However," the preacher continued, "as far as my own abilities go, I shall be more than happy to give you a demonstration. You see, it wasn't you who stopped the crack, Count."

"What?"

In the darkness, the Noble's prim and proper countenance blackened with rage. He pounded a foot the size of a throw rug against the ground. But his ears caught Curio saying, "Stop that."

Quaking, the crack widened a bit, and then stopped.

Firmly planting both hands on the ground, Curio slipped out of the deadly maw.

Oddly enough, the count didn't launch his next attack. Shutting his eyes, he grimaced as if he had a headache, and he leaped back at essentially the same time Curio escaped from the fissure. It was difficult to tell what the Nobleman was thinking as he jabbed his long spear into the ground and put his hands over his ears.

"So you've discovered how my sermonizing power works? I should've expected as much from a Noble. Now that you're powerless to do anything, you can just stand there while I destroy you."

The preacher in vermilion drew a machete from inside his robe. For travelers or wandering holy men whose travels took them to trackless wastes, it was an essential implement for hacking through the forests that stood in their way or slaying beasts.

Raising it high, he shouted, "Forgive me," and hurled it toward the giant. It pierced the Noble through the heart with amazing accuracy.

Count Braujou's face grew paler in the moonlight. As the light faded from his eyes, his skin lost its luster and countless cracks spread across it, as if it were a dried-out riverbed. When the flesh fell off, the giant's body was reduced to dust that spilled from his clothing to form a great pile on the windless ground. His clothes collapsed, and the dust, glittering in the moonlight, scattered.

"A confirmed kill," Curio murmured, turning his eyes toward the village. He was perfectly calm, as if he'd fully expected this outcome. His demeanor might even be described as bored.

Was this any way for someone who'd slain a Greater Noble such as Count Braujou to act? How had he even managed to kill the count?

"I suppose there's no point in giving chase now. Guess I'll just have to be satisfied that I've destroyed one of our foes. That leaves D and the duchess—two opponents to make my blood run cold."

While he wasn't disparaging them, his tone was nevertheless one of supreme and unwavering confidence.

He sauntered over to the giant hawk. The chest still rose and fell in the body that Count Braujou's spear had pierced.

"Well, I still have transport," Curio remarked, bending down in front of the hawk's face. A low mumbling flowed out into the night air.

About two minutes later, powerful wings began to beat. It was the giant hawk. The nearly dead bird began to climb up into the sky once more. Curio clung to its back. The wind stirred up by its wings swirled and dispersed the ash on the ground in all directions, and when that finally stopped, the moon alone was left dazzling in the darkness of night, with no sign of the hawk anywhere.

†

A bell announcing noontime could be heard in the distance. The man in the vermilion robe suddenly looked up, turning his eyes toward the massive crack in the wall sixty feet from the floor. A skinny figure with spidery limbs stood at the edge of the fissure, looking outside.

"Are they here, Speeny?" Curio the Preacher called out to him.

Speeny crossed his arms over his head to signal no, but suddenly stopped.

"Yes," he replied, his answer flying down from on high. "They're as good as we thought. I had threads strung all through the valley so they couldn't get the drop on us, but this is D we're dealing with here, and the woman is a Noble, sure enough. They came straight down the middle."

"Yes, they would, wouldn't they," Curio said with a nod, a look of philosophical contemplation on his face. "That's just what they'd do. If they didn't, this fight wouldn't be much fun."

"Well, then—I'll be on my way," Speeny said.

"Yes, you run along. Thank you for acting as lookout—now get as far away from the valley as you possibly can."

As soon as Curio finished saying this, Speeny leaped outside. But he didn't fall. His body rose, zipping up past the crack and swiftly disappearing. Anyone who knew what Speeny was capable of would've found his haste quite strange and even cowardly.

Still facing the crack, Curio grinned, but it wasn't a scornful smile. Rather, it was sympathy and understanding that drifted to his lips.

"Has he run off to the stratosphere? That's probably not enough to allay his fears. Why, I see that even my own knees are shaking," he said, his smile becoming a wry grin.

After turning his gaze to the right, where Matthew and Sue lay on the glowing floor, he looked back and finished what he was working on.

The crack had grown beyond sixty feet. It now stretched all the way to the top of the five-hundred-yard dome. The corridors that surrounded it were wide enough to accommodate a pair of small buildings side by side, but there wasn't a single window in them. Normally, the temperature of this massive dome would've been kept at absolute zero, but the machinery responsible for doing so remained inoperable.

Curio now raised one hand and mumbled something to an immaculate machine that resembled a gigantic icicle. Three hundred feet tall, it was a colossal computer, and the base on which Curio stood was a good thousand feet in diameter. Once it was called Sigma, and it had reigned over this valley as a "god" the Nobility had created. Now it had lost its defensive systems and was covered with gray dust from the millennia that had passed since it had been discarded, but it retained its anthropomorphic dignity. It made a strong impression—even the Nobility had gotten goose bumps when they looked up at it—and that impression was not one of a mechanism, but rather that of a ruler.

What was Curio doing before this machine, a machine that might even be considered sacred? He was whispering. If one listened closely enough, she could make it out.

"Awaken. That is your mission. Rise now from the five millennia of sleep that have lain over this valley. That is your mission."

Perhaps it was drained of energy, because the machine continued to lie still, but Curio's words kept creeping toward it like a serpent. Like an admonishment, forceful but patient. Oh, so that was why he was considered a preacher . . .

Since dawn, he'd spent over seven hours in part of these magnificent ruins invoking the massive computer to come back to life. Tirelessly, he repeated the words again and again, speaking of how necessary and justified this awakening would be. As if there were no question that a dead, inorganic construct was capable of listening and understanding. Though his face was sweaty and the shadow of fatigue hung heavily on it, there was no despair or resignation there.

"A foe is coming. Coming to destroy both you and us. A fearful foe the likes of which even I have never encountered. To save yourself, and to save us, please awaken."

Just as he finished chanting this prayer for the thousandth time, a grave echo shook the dome. Spinning around in amazement, Curio looked up to Sigma's summit.

"Ah, at last—now the valley is awake again."

His face was bleached white by light, and a long shadow was thrown across the floor. Every inch of Sigma had begun to glow. There were indications that something, somewhere, had gone into motion. The antiproton furnace. The defense systems. The cosmic-ray-analysis circuits. And more. Much more.

A few minutes later, Curio turned around. He'd given the machine all the information he had on the foe it needed to slay. The brother and sister being held hostage had also been dealt with. All that remained was to leave things to Sigma and the valley it controlled.

Speeny had escaped, and now the preacher fled as fast as he could too.

Curio found himself running down a road made of metal. Above him stretched a sky devoid of a single cloud. The rows of buildings to either side remained exactly as they'd been when they were created. That in itself was proof they had nothing to do with the daily lives of the Nobility.

In constructing factories and other installations, the Nobility brought all their science to bear, building things that would last forever. Factories had framework made of the greatest metals known to science, were built of parts and materials that would never rust or decay, and were permanently coated, while the most critical parts were each equipped with their own repair facility to guarantee them against failure. In contrast, the homes and gardens the Nobility inhabited by night, as well as their cottages and carriages, were often made of natural materials—wood, stone, and metal. This vividly illustrated the strange disposition and obsessive whims of these Nobles blessed with eternal life. Perhaps those who couldn't be destroyed longed for destruction?

As Curio ran, he was painted white by the torrents of light surging at him from all directions. Robbing even the sunlight of its color, the light was proof that the valley had come back to life. A groan like an earthquake reached him through the soles of his shoes, and the ions in the air jabbed at his skin like lightning. He had to wonder if perhaps he'd made a terrible mistake. A feeling that resembled fear flitted through his heart.

Galleon Valley—not even his lord Valcua would explain what had transpired there.

We can't begin to fathom what our lord might be thinking. Someone that grand could destroy this entire planet on a whim. All he said was this: *Use Galleon Valley to slay D. Order Sigma to do away with him.*

Suddenly, Curio halted. A pair of figures had appeared on the glowing road ahead. Had they been standing there all along? No, they'd definitely come through a nearby entrance to the valley, but in Curio's eyes, their gorgeous forms gave him the impression they'd been standing there for a very, very long time.

Stopping again, he bowed respectfully and said, "A pleasure to meet you. I am one of the seven, known as Curio the Preacher."

"I'm D."

The Hunter's voice and his handsome visage made the same man who'd brought a dead machine back to life again after five thousand years tremble with rapture.

II

"If you're a man, I'll thank you not to get weak in the knees upon seeing another man," the woman in the white dress beside D said in a mocking tone. "I am Duchess Miranda. If you're human, at least show us proper courtesy."

"Please pardon my manners," Curio said with a bow. "It is my utmost pleasure to make your acquaintance."

"Much better," the duchess said, grinning with satisfaction and looking at the blue candle D gripped in his left hand. Though its tiny flame melted into the sunlight, drops of wax were dripping from it clearly enough. Its nature was easily deduced from the fact that Duchess Miranda was out in the sunlight—it was Time-Bewitching Incense.

"Where are the two kids?" D asked.

Curio knew the young man would have nothing else to say. Any other words were unnecessary, and D was far too exquisite to say anything superfluous.

"I might ask you where your other member is, but I'd be a fool to do that. You see, I had the honor of slaying Count Braujou last night."

"Oh, how cruel. He really was a gentle person," Duchess Miranda said, but she seemed somehow pleased. "You're a nasty one. But we shall soon return the favor by decreasing your group's numbers by one."

"Ah, that would be most appreciated. I could finally bid farewell to this disagreeable material world."

As Curio said this, he felt his back growing cold and hard.

Why am I having this conversation? Is it because I don't want to stop talking to the young man before me? Do I wish to hear his voice again?

That was ridiculous—it was a foolish thing to do. Look at the Hunter. The eerie aura that turned the preacher's spine to ice declared that the young man had no use for anyone who wouldn't answer him.

D stepped forward.

Imagining the pain of having his backbone severed, Curio shouted, "They're in the central building up ahead. And they're both still fine!"

D turned to run.

Curio tried to move away, but the glint in the Hunter's eye made him freeze.

"Stop it," he said reproachfully.

It's no use, he thought, badly shaken. He'll cut me down!

He felt the pain of steel biting into the top of his head before he saw D move.

"Aaaaah!" he cried, but, strangely enough, the cry was accompanied by a feeling of relief. The deadly blow hadn't fallen on him.

Opening his eyes, he looked up and muttered, "Was that a dream?"

The Hunter in black and the Noblewoman in white had vanished. Still reeling with relief, Curio conjured a vision of D's handsome features as he charged forward in the unearthly air with blade in hand. Ah, such beauty. For an instant, a strange emotion skimmed through Curio's heart. He didn't realize it was a desire to be cut down. Perhaps he'd seen a vision of the future.

D sped onward through the darkness. Curio no longer occupied his thoughts, and Miranda had vanished. In the instant he'd started to bring his sword down on Curio's head, he and the Noblewoman had both been drawn into another space. He guessed the hole in space that had appeared without warning was the work of whatever controlled this valley. The Time-Bewitching Incense was in his pocket.

"You probably already know this, but our velocity has reached the speed of light," the hoarse voice said. It didn't sound at all shocked, but spoke as if this was the sort of conversation they had all the time.

D and the source of the voice were in a space that had been distorted four-dimensionally; they could have kept going forever.

"Looks like we're gonna break the speed of light. If we do, it'll be trouble," the voice continued. "I'll connect us to another extradimensional space. We've gotta escape. I ate some dirt earlier. Fire we can manage. Water I'll leave to you."

D transferred his blade to his left hand and extended his right arm.

"But the problem will be wind," the hoarse voice said in a tone that conjured up a vivid image of a worried countenance.

Though they were moving at terrific speed, there was zero air resistance—it was like they were falling through the void of outer space. Yet they weren't suffocating.

Bright blood gushed out. D had used the blade in his left hand to cut his right wrist. Returning the sword to his right hand, D used the palm of his left to catch the spilling blood. That was their water. Not a drop of it was wasted.

"Okay!" the hoarse voice exclaimed, and at the same time the Hunter's left hand stroked the wound. Seconds later, all that remained was a faint red line that immediately faded.

"We're passing the speed of light!" the hoarse voice called from the left hand D had extended. "And we've got no wind. Brace for impact!"

A tiny mouth formed on the palm of his hand. In it appeared a howling blue flame. Space twisted as the tiny mouth inhaled. The left hand vanished. At the same time, D felt a violent impact.

"Congratulations on breaking free of my sealed dimension," an austere male voice said. "But it must've been quite hard on you. You're under a spell, aren't you?"

D was standing inside a huge dome. The voice issued from the tower that loomed before him.

"My name is Sigma. I'm an antiproton computer."

"There are supposed to be two children here," D replied. Talk of "Sigma" or "antiproton computers" meant nothing to him.

"There certainly are. Right here."

A golden line appeared in the floor not three feet from where D stood, and it rose without a sound to create a space ten feet high and six feet wide. It had no depth and was invisible when viewed from the side. Matthew and Sue were inside it. Apparently they noticed D, because they reached out their arms and started to run. No matter how they pounded across the ground, they never came any closer. Though less than three feet lay between that space and D, the distance between the children and his dimension was infinite.

"D!" Sigma called out. "Earlier, I saved from your blade the man who awakened me. The command that man gave me was to dispose of you. However, as strange as it seems, another force has given me different orders. And five millennia later, I may now act on these instructions."

"What kind of instructions?" D inquired. It was little surprise this had piqued his interest.

"To give you a test."

At that point most people would've asked what kind of test, but D said, "Who gave you these instructions?"

"Grand Duke Valcua."

If Count Braujou, Duchess Miranda, or even any of Valcua's seven had heard the computer's reply, they would've undoubtedly been astonished. The orders to bring Sue and Matthew to the Galleon Valley and awaken Sigma had been personally given by Valcua. Had he foreseen five thousand years ago that D would come here? If so, was that the reason why Matthew and Sue had been taken? No one would've ever thought it necessary to go to such lengths. As the assassins had said, Valcua's aim was to have his revenge on the Dyalhis children.

"Valcua took an interest in you, did he? And five thousand years ago, no less. Things are starting to get interesting," the hoarse voice murmured in a tone eddying with curiosity.

"Is there someone with you?" Sigma inquired, its ears apparently catching the murmurs. "Ultimately, I must follow the directions of my creator before acting on the command to eliminate you. D, you shall take the Sigma test. I'll hold onto the two children until you've finished. Afterwards, you may take them with you—if you pass the test, that is."

The dimension that imprisoned Sue and Matthew vanished, starting with the opposite end from which it'd first appeared.

"Let the test begin," Sigma declared in a richly patinaed tone.

A heartbeat later, D stood in a wasteland of reddish-brown sand that went on forever.

"It seems to be a phantom reality zone," said the voice from the vicinity of his left hand. "Transferring you into it was quite the sleight of hand. If it were a Noble, only one of the very oldest of their kind could manage something like that."

Before the hoarse voice had finished speaking, they heard the echo of iron-shod hooves. A knight on a black steed approached with a black lance in one hand. The armor that covered him from head to toe was also black. The horse was covered with armor, as well. No matter what D did, it didn't seem he'd be in for an easy fight.

About sixty feet away, the knight reached for his visor with one hand and opened it.

"I'll be damned," the hoarse voice exclaimed, and there was nothing feigned about its surprise.

It was Matthew.

"It's the work of these hallucinatory systems. Don't be fooled by 'em."

Perhaps taking what the hoarse voice said as a signal, the knight with Matthew's face kicked his black steed's haunches.

As his foe charged in a cloud of dust, D gazed at him, with his sword lowered. He showed no signs of moving. Ordinarily, D would easily dispatch a foe like this. However, when his opponent wore the face of a boy he was supposed to rescue, how would the Hunter respond?

The vacant look on Matthew's face suddenly contorted. His mournful expression seemed louder than the thundering hoofbeats as he shouted, "Save me, D!"

The lance gleamed in his right hand.

"My hands, and my whole body, are moving on their own. Please, you've gotta stop me!"

His voice was joined by a cry that was even more morose.

"D, don't kill my brother!"

The voice belonged to Sue.

"That's an illusion too," the hoarse voice told him.

What did D make of these three voices? As he stood there, still and vacant, he didn't demonstrate the tiniest inclination to fight back.

Matthew shifted the lance. Despite his words, murderous intent filled every inch of him.

"Please, stop it!"

Matthew bent backward.

"Stop it, D!" Sue cried out.

"They're just illusions, I tell you," the hoarse voice muttered, and a second later D was swallowed by the rumbling of the ground and the cloud of dust.

The lance flashed out.

A cry from Sue that would make anyone want to cover his ears streamed through the air.

D was in the air, too. Just before those iron-shod hooves could trample him, he'd dodged the lance and bounded over Matthew's head.

Over what head? It was gone. As the horse galloped on, there was still a knight on its back. But his head had been cleanly removed, and fresh blood spouted from his neck. Some of that blood became a vermilion fog carried by the wind.

As D landed without a sound, there was a dull thud to his left. It was likely the head hitting the ground.

Not bothering to watch the horse run, D looked up, hearing the flapping of wings overhead. He saw the tiny form of a bird rapidly approaching. In less time than it took to draw two breaths, it became a great eagle with a wingspan of more than thirty feet. Beating its wings fiercely to remain at a height of sixty feet, the bird opened a beak that seemed almost metallic. Inside it was Sue's face. A face drenched with tears and fear.

III

"You killed my brother, didn't you?" Sue shouted, tears flying through the air to accompany her cries.

One of them fell on D's shoulder. As he turned his striking features to look at the winged form above, there was nothing on them that might be termed an emotion.

"You killed him even after I asked you over and over not to. Kill me, too—do it!" she cried.

The giant eagle went into a dive.

"Stop! Don't kill me!" Sue screeched as they fell.

D didn't move.

The great eagle's talons snapped open. A white flash mowed through the air. Bones snapped, and then the enormous talons went flying, severed from the bird. It was the giant eagle's left leg. The right one caught hold of D's shoulder, and the bird began to fly with terrific force.

As it beat its wings mightily, the giant eagle craned its head to look at D. From its mouth, Sue was heard to whimper, "D—please help me. I—I'll be eaten up. I beg of you. Hurry! Quickly—you have to save me!"

Her usually determined face was a mess of tears as the Hunter's sword shot toward it. Instantly killing Sue with a thrust that penetrated her throat and went all the way to the brain stem, D pulled his sword back out and directed another slash toward the giant eagle's right wing. The great bird let out a death rattle.

They'd already climbed to an altitude of over three hundred feet. Although the creature made a desperate effort to keep flying, it went into a tailspin.

"Jump!" the hoarse voice bellowed. It was shouting at D. "Are you gonna jump or ain't you? We'll crash!"

Seeing that it got no response, it continued, "As landlords go, you sure are a pain in the ass!"

Just as it muttered that remark with disbelief, the earth swallowed up the gigantic bird.

Saying nothing, D found himself gazing at Sigma. It was clear that everything he'd just experienced had been an illusion created by the machine. And the young man had consented to what had happened and what he'd done.

"So, is the test over or what?" the hoarse voice whispered.

"Only the first part. However—"

The computer's voice broke off.

"Is this the emotion they call surprise? My creator gave me the ability to feel it, but this is the first time I've actually experienced it. For the two situations I just presented, I hypothesized five thousand and twenty-five possible reactions you might have to each. And you've done a remarkable job of exceeding all of them. Truly you are a man to be feared . . . Who are you?"

"Return the children," D said.

"The test is not over," Sigma replied. "And if you should still live when the test results are in, then I shall dispose of you in keeping with my second directive."

The world turned white.

The snow gusting at D already came up to his knees, and the north wind was so cold it threatened to freeze everything it touched as its howls shook a heavy, gray sky. Every breath froze his lungs, and they'd nearly ceased to function. Yet the steps he took through the snow were strong and precise, as befitted a dhampir.

"We're almost to the summit," his left hand said to him. "He should be waiting up there. Hope you've still got some strength left."

In lieu of a reply, D halted. At the summit of the graceful white slope, the wind and eddying snow hindered his vision, but a figure had come into view. In D's eyes, he looked like a towering black wall.

"So, you've come?" said the voice that fell from the sky—the voice of a great being. "You've done well to make it this far. However, you won't be leaving, D. Not unless you slay me."

A white light connected heaven and earth. The falling thunderbolts enveloped D, striking every inch of him with blistering waves of electromagnetism. In the depths of the white light, his left hand rose. The light wavered like a heat shimmer, churned, and sucked like a glowing mist into the mouth that opened in the palm of the Hunter's hand.

D kicked off the ground. When he landed in the snow, he left no footprints. Perhaps he knew where the figure's weak point was. The sword he swung from high over his right shoulder caused the sound of cutting flesh and ribs as it bit into the form.

Soundlessly, the figure and all signs of his presence disappeared.

D landed on the opposite side of where the shadowy form had been.

"It felt like you made contact," the hoarse voice said. "To give him some lumps—or a slash, in this case—you really must've got—"

The voice broke off when it noticed what D was looking at.

About fifteen feet from him, a figure in a white dress stood in the snow. Snowflakes clung like white jewels to the black hair that billowed in the wind, but they quickly faded away. Dark eyes as clear as a holy night quietly reflected his image.

D! she said, her voice every bit as lovely as her eyes. *Lay down your sword. And come into my waiting arms. I never got to hold you even once.*

The woman opened her arms, and then looked up in the air in wonder.

The young man came down like a supernatural bird, showing no hesitation as he sliced through the woman from the top of her head down to her crotch.

"You cut down your mother, too?" Sigma said to the young man in black, the machine's voice carrying all-too-human emotion. It had never imagined he'd do such a thing. "Where do you come from, and where are you going? Who—or what—are you?"

"Give me the children," D said. "Your test is finished. If you won't give them back, I'll take them."

The young man took a smooth step forward. He was imbued with force and an unearthly air. Sigma's components began conjuring up the emotion known as fear.

A thin beam of light from the ceiling speared D. The Hunter's expression warped with pain, and his body melted away.

"That enzyme dissolves bodies—your mind is deeper and stronger than I'll ever know, but your flesh isn't . . ."

A warning signal resounded somewhere in Sigma's electronic thought centers. An intense "pain" shot through it, and its "eyes" were drawn to the blade of a sword stuck halfway into its casing. Blue electromagnetic waves stretched from it in all directions.

"That's my . . . vital spot . . . You really are . . . something else."

A puddle of ooze lay on the floor where D had been. It stood up. For an instant, it was only visible as something wearing clothes, but Sigma knew the strapping figure with dark eyes could only be D.

"DDDwhowhoareareareyouyouyouuuuu?—you?—you?—you?"

Sigma's field of view rapidly dwindled to a spark of light in the Hunter's dark eyes, and before long even that had faded into complete darkness.

"You cut your father, killed your mother, even did this to me," Sigma said, its voice sounding a million miles away. Undoubtedly that was what a machine that had come to know great sadness sounded like. "Is this the thing human beings term 'fate'? The test has ended. You may go, D. Your demise I shall leave to the assassin I'm about to produce."

Once again the golden space appeared between D and Sigma. Sue and Matthew stumbled out of it. The boy managed to catch himself, but his sister collided with D's chest before she finally stopped. As she slowly slid down him, he scooped her up to keep her from falling. The threads of strength that had been pulled taut had all been snapped by her relief.

D gazed at Matthew for a few seconds as the boy's shoulders heaved in his battle to catch his breath, then said, "Let's go," and tossed his jaw.

Though the direction he indicated wasn't the same way he'd entered, it was the right door nonetheless.

†

There were three cyborg steeds tethered at the entrance to the valley—horses purchased in Marthias. D had intended to bring the two children back all along. Sue had somehow managed to regain consciousness, but the Hunter put her on the back of his horse and pulled the extra mount along behind them.

From a distant rock pile, a trio of figures watched.

"This is a hell of a thing. All three of them are fine," Curio the Preacher groaned in amazement, making no attempt to disguise his shock.

Beside him, one of the others said, "It would appear the effects of my song have faded. But that's no reason to be ashamed. He's incredibly powerful. It really is unavoidable."

It was the fiendish diva Callas. As she watched the rider who'd dwindled down to the size of a pea, her eyes and her voice—which had caused Curio and Speeny to look at her so suddenly—seemed to melt away into rapture. But the two fierce gazes of condemnation returned to normal when the woman declared in the same delirious tone, "I won't fail a second time, though. This fearsome man has made a mockery of my song and myself—and I, Callas, shall see to it that my song brings about his end."

"But I don't understand this. Did my sermon not work? There's no way that could be."

"Everyone makes mistakes," Callas said, a faint grin rising on her lips. She wasn't trying to console him.

"Why did Grand Duke Valcua tell us to take those children hostage? Wasn't his goal to kill the two of them?"

This was something the assassins had already discussed at great length. And they hadn't reached a conclusion.

"At any rate, let's go back. We must form our next plan. Speeny!" he called out to the third member.

There was no response.

Turning, he found no one there.

"Where has he gone?"

A thought bubbled up in the preacher's brain.

"Well, now. I think I'll be going," Callas said, and though she looked around, it was apparent at a glance the action was purely perfunctory. Of all the assassins, this beautiful woman was the most lacking in the spirit of cooperation.

As dignified as any philosopher's, Curio's expression was tinged with something that resembled sorrow as he said, "Don't tell me that idiot's doing what I think he's doing."

The Weapon Master of Razin

CHAPTER 3

I

"Hey, Sue!" Matthew called out, and the girl, who had her hands around D's waist and her forehead pressed against his back, lifted her head. She sensed irritation in her brother's tone.

"You're fine now, right? Get on that free horse."

"I guess you're right. Okay." Before she could change her mind, Sue told D, "Stop, please."

The gaze she trained on the Hunter's back held a sort of dependence. But as she put both hands against the horse's rump and started to lift herself up, D told her, "Wait."

"Why?" Matthew asked, his lips promptly tightening in a scowl.

"You get over here, too," D said.

"What?" Matthew exclaimed, sticking his chin out defiantly. "On your horse? Can it even carry three?"

"It'll carry us. Come on."

"You're crazy. I thought you were only after Sue."

Sue grew pale at her brother's horrid remark.

"Matthew—what a thing to say!"

"Well, it's the truth. Something's been bugging me for a while now. You've gone sweet on him, haven't you, Sue?"

"Matthew!"

"Now hear this: There's no way in hell I'll—"

Matthew's tirade cut off. A black form had sailed through space, pushed him back, and taken a seat in the saddle. The horse broke into a gallop.

"Holy!" the boy managed to exclaim, frantically grabbing D around the waist. The Hunter held Sue under his left arm.

Behind them, a terrific flash of light exploded.

"Get down!" D shouted, ducking.

Not sure what was going on, Matthew followed suit.

A massive rock hit the ground in front of them. The instant they went around it, a wave of blistering heat struck Matthew's back. Melted rock whizzed noisily through space.

"Where the hell are you going?" Matthew bellowed, because they were clearly galloping toward a cliff. However, had he looked over his shoulder, he wouldn't have had any cause to complain. Behind the trio, flames and shock waves were closing on them. Again the blistering heat struck Matthew's back, and a second later it burned the back of his neck and head.

"Holyyyyyyyyyyyyyyyyy!" he cried again, in fear of the reality that greeted his eyes.

They were falling. Flying off the cliff, the cyborg horse plummeted like a stone toward the water flowing fifty yards below. Matthew shut his eyes, and then he lost consciousness.

Wrapping his right arm around Matthew, D dismounted the cyborg horse in midair. He'd decided the load would be too much for the steed to bear.

Holding the siblings upright, the Hunter was just about to enter the water feet first when a terrific shock jerked up all three of them.

D let go of Matthew, and the boy fell the last three feet to the water without incident, instantly regaining consciousness. On madly rising to the surface, he saw that flames licked at the sky from the chunks of rock falling toward him. He dove underwater and swam down for all he was worth. A smoking piece of rock struck him square in the back. Matthew was the lucky one.

A thread had descended from the sky and wound around D and Sue. After releasing Matthew, D had grabbed his sword and struck the thread without being able to cut it, and now he and Sue were rising higher and higher at a speed of one hundred and twenty-five miles per hour. They'd already reached an altitude of six thousand feet, and showed no signs of stopping. Sue had fainted.

"Time for me to do something?" the hoarse voice from D's left hand asked, trembling with expectation. "It's been decades since I got to do a kissing scene. Hey, don't cramp my style now!"

D gazed into space without saying anything.

They hit ten thousand feet.

Fifteen thousand.

Twenty thousand.

Thirty thousand.

Fifty thousand.

The sky had a deep purple color.

At an altitude so high it was impossible for human beings to breathe, D met a lone, spiderlike man hanging in midair.

"I'm Speeny," the man said by way of introduction. His voice didn't reach them. But D's ears could catch the slight movements caused by the sounds. "Welcome to my battlefield. I hate to do away with such a handsome fellow, but let's just call it my worldly obligation."

Taking a quick glance at Sue, the spider man narrowed his eyes.

Although it would be impossible to prevent a human being from suffocating in the stratosphere without using some kind of mechanical device, D's left hand was covering the girl's nose and mouth.

"What a strange thing you're doing there. I thought it would rattle you if I made the girl suffer, but it seems I missed the mark. You should be in a lot of pain, however."

Even D couldn't put up much of a fight in the stratosphere, where the temperature was sixty below zero and there was essentially no oxygen.

"If I did nothing right now, even a dhampir like you would die. If you were returned to the surface, you'd probably come back to life, but don't worry—I'd stab you through the heart before that could happen. Do you think you can cut this thread? Well, you can't. A very important person gave this grand thread to me. The only things that can cut it are the fingernails the great one bestowed on me!" Speeny said, holding his right hand in front of his face for the Hunter to see.

As ridiculously tapered as his arms, the nails had been filed to razor sharpness at the tips and along the edges.

"The line you're hanging from comes from me. But you can't tell where the line I'm on comes from. It actually stretches from the moon. I was born in a lab in the Nobility's Lunar Palace. Of course, I only learned that when a messenger from the great one came to offer me a position as a bodyguard in the Lunar Palace. Up until that point, my mother and I had lived in the slums. I thought I was dreaming. I was sure I'd end my days in that lousy pigsty, but in a solid-gold room in the palace, the great one informed me of my pedigree and ordered me to serve as one of Valcua's bodyguards. You understand what I mean by pedigree? I, the great Speeny, am the cream of an elite crop, manipulated from the time I was an embryo to be a superman. When I was just a kid in the slums of the moon, where they say only one in a hundred survives to adulthood, I got into murderous brawls of a hundred on one and never lost once, but I never suspected it was due to the power I'd received from the great one. D, you should consider it your misfortune to have made an enemy of him. But I can't give any credence to what Curio said. What did the antiproton computer in the valley do? Granted, you did escape my meteorite attack. I can't help but respect you for that. Oh your eyelids are getting heavier, are they? Okay, have yourself a peaceful sleep. When you wake up, both you and the little girl will be in a better place." Speeny laughed mockingly.

His confidence sprang from the thread he used, one end of which was connected to a spot on the moon about two hundred thousand miles away.

"Ah, yes," Speeny said, breaking into a truly evil grin. "I just thought of an amusing game. I'm going to throw some knives at you and the girl. Try to dodge them if you can with your head and body in that state. I suppose the game can go on and on until you're both dead."

Before he'd finished speaking, Speeny started hurling long, thin knives with a snap of his wrist. D knocked away three aimed at Sue and took care of three more intended for him, but the fourth one sank into his chest.

Speeny was ecstatic. He'd slain a foe Sigma couldn't destroy and even Curio had feared. He danced for joy on the unseen thread, and then dropped smoothly down toward D. He was halfway to the Hunter when his own heart shrank with an audible sound. Even in the purple sky, he could see the black raiment spreading out.

He couldn't possibly do anything in this cold, could he?

The question that flashed through Speeny's mind was the last thought he ever had.

Grabbing the thread and making a leap, D drove his blade through the man's brain and all the way down to his legs. Speeny shuddered violently in midair, then immediately grew still. The blood that gushed from him gave off steam, but it quickly froze.

Dodging those icy fragments as they fell, D swung his sword once more. The thread connected to the surface of the moon that Speeny said the great one alone could cut was easily severed, and the three of them fell back to earth at a ferocious velocity. The Hunter's frozen coat and hat, instantly heated by friction with the air, started to smoke.

"Here we go!" the hoarse voice said with excitement, the words muffled by the fingers of the left hand D held clamped over Sue's mouth and nose.

"That Speeny was a bold fool to challenge D on his own," the missionary Courbet said, spitting the words like a curse.

"But the explosion that rocked us was undoubtedly caused by one of Speeny's meteorites," a woman's voice remarked.

As if in response, everyone looked around. The walls were crumbling, there was a great hole in the ceiling, and dislodged beams stabbed into the floor. This seemed like no place for a human being to be, let alone live, but of course the group that was assembled consisted of people who were something other than human.

"Could even D take that kind of impact? If Speeny took the battle into the stratosphere, I think his odds of victory would increase to 80 percent."

That claim was countered by a luxuriant and scornful laugh in a voice like a golden bell. It was Callas the Diva.

"You think an unsightly creature like Speeny could triumph over that young warrior? Surely you jest. A man like that only comes along once in a thousand years, perhaps even once in ten thousand years. A miraculous jewel born between heaven and earth, he's not the sort to lose his life in Speeny's world, of all places."

As she spoke, Callas stared at a certain spot in the room. There was no one there—only a bronze decanter. It was a rusty water pitcher that had sat there from the time they'd taken this as their temporary strategy center.

A female voice came from it, saying, "With friends like you, who needs enemies? The moon that glows by night watches over Speeny. By now, D has been reduced to a fireball burning up as it drops back to earth from the stratosphere."

Callas's eyes glittered. Silence shrouded the air.

They heard a hard knock coming from the crack in the ceiling. There was the sound of something knifing through the wind.

"Out!" Curio cried.

The shadowy figures dashed for the windows and holes in the walls. Immediately after, an object that fell from the heavens punched through the roof of the dilapidated boarding house, scattering parts of the building in all directions like an explosion. The fiends were forced to take to the air or hit the ground to escape the wave of rubble flying at them.

After the dust settled, they went back to the smoking, flaming remains of the dilapidated building. There they saw a depression pounded into the earth and the charred portion of a corpse lying in it.

Once, Count Braujou had fallen from the stratosphere because of Speeny's machinations, but the immortal nature of the Nobility saved him. This was not the case with the object that now rolled to the feet of the group.

"The dropper ended up being the one who was dropped—it's like a bad joke," Courbet groaned. He sounded crushed. "Perhaps they took each other out?"

"The stratosphere was Speeny's kingdom. And since its king was defeated—well, it's not entirely inconceivable, but I think it highly unlikely," said Curio.

It was so still, even the flames seemed to have lost their sounds. Before long, Courbet murmured, "But Speeny got his thread from the great one—how could D cut it?"

"If anyone could do it, it's him," Callas said, her voice melting into rapture.

No one grew angry or contradicted her. The assassins, who'd just lost a second compatriot, lingered silently in the sunlight.

II

That evening, there was no one to see D and his companions off as they left the village of Marthias. When it was time for them to go, the villagers seemed to remember that these people had been the cause of all their trouble, and that they had also caused their mayor's death. While they weren't exactly being stoned, as D and Matthew gripped their respective reins, they got cold rejection in lieu of farewells. In place of parting handshakes, they received emotionless stares through doorways or from behind curtained windows.

"What's their problem?" Matthew grumbled from the driver's seat as he worked the reins. "They're the ones who asked us to stay and help them in the first place. And now that they don't need us anymore, they just toss us like trash?"

"That's right," D said from astride his cyborg horse, which was alongside the wagon. "You're traveling with a dhampir and a Noble. It's only going to get tougher from now on."

Matthew spat and turned away in disgust. He'd never had much patience, a fact that had caused his mother to worry endlessly. It was something of a mystery that he'd never gotten sick of farm life and run away.

"Stop it, Matt. Mr. D's right," Sue said, coming out of the covered wagon and laying a hand on her brother's shoulder as if to steady him. She'd heard the entire exchange from inside.

Pressing her cheek against her silent brother's shoulder, she took a glance behind them and said, "Still—it is kind of sad."

Was she referring to the fact that they had no well-wishers to see them off, or talking about the car beside them? She'd heard from D that its owner, Count Braujou, had been slain. Duchess Miranda was missing, and she might not be in perfect shape either.

"Sad, eh?" the left hand D wrapped around the reins said in an intrigued manner. "If ol' Braujou could hear that, he'd probably weep bloody tears of joy. There ain't a human in ten million who'd be broken up over the loss of a Noble."

With the sound of creaking wheels, the wagon and car set off. In their wake they left only tire tracks.

When they were only about sixty feet from the edge of the village, a number of shouts and footsteps closed on them from behind. D turned, and a toss of his chin told Matthew and Sue to have a look. The two of them leaned out of the seat and looked back.

Nearly a dozen children stood in front of the defensive palisade waving their hands.

"Goodbye!"

"Mr. Hunter!"

"Take care!"

"I'm gonna be a Hunter, too!"

"Goodbye!"

The children shouted as loudly as they could, something sparkling in their eyes. This wasn't a brief parting with someone who was coming back. They knew they'd never see him again.

Sue turned to D and said, "That's for you, D."

The exquisite young man just stared straight ahead. Sue knew he'd never look back.

As the wagon and car disappeared into the darkness down the road, the children left one or two at a time until only the last and smallest figure remained. It was the boy D had encouraged. Even when the blue darkness was painted over by a still deeper shade, the boy kept his eyes glued to the end of the highway. Perhaps he had a hunch that handsome young man would be coming back.

After a while, the boy's mother appeared and tried to bring him home, but the boy cried and resisted her. Grabbing him by one thin wrist, she tried to drag him away. A hard, sharp pain shot through her hand, and she let go of him. The boy stood in a combat stance with the slim branch he'd picked up from the ground at his feet. It was the same stance the young man in black had taught him.

Clucking her tongue, his mother told him he'd be getting no dinner that evening. The boy stuck his tongue out. His mother cursed his unruly behavior as she left, and then the boy looked back down the highway, still holding that same stance.

There was no one there.

Shouting as loudly as he could, the boy made a thrust with the stick. After repeating that action three times and catching his breath, the boy focused his gaze again on the highway now sealed away in darkness.

Riding without respite, the group reached the boundaries of the village of Razin around daybreak.

Matthew had been twitching his nose for a while, and just as the defensive palisade came into view he could take it no longer, coughing loudly and saying, "What the hell is that smell?"

On his instructions, Sue had taken cover inside the wagon.

"Razin oil," D said.

"What the blue blazes is that?" Matthew asked, glaring at D while the Hunter swayed in the saddle.

"A high-grade oil used in all the weapons manufactured in their village. You'll get used to it soon enough."

"Give me a break! My stomach's turning somersaults!"

"Stay here," D said.

"Huh?"

"If anything happens, give a shout. I'll hear you."

"Wh—where do you think you're going?" the boy stammered.

"I smell blood mixed in with the oil."

"What?"

Giving a kick to his mount's flanks, D galloped off as Matthew watched in a daze.

Their map showed it was still five or six hundred yards to the village. And it was a windy day. Despite it all, D could detect the smell of blood.

"Sue, this is starting to scare me. Dhampirs really are monsters, just like the Nobility."

At the clearing before the gates, D halted his steed. In the light of dawn, it looked like the village was sleeping. However, there was no sign of anyone in the lookout tower: a bad omen.

"That sure is one powerful scent of blood. We're not talking one or two dozen people here," the hoarse voice remarked, but it sounded amused.

D advanced on his horse.

Just then, the gates slowly opened inward. A horrendous stench of blood tainted the very molecules of the air.

A human figure appeared, about six and a half feet tall and covered in armor. His helmet's steel mask shielded his face, his arms and legs hid beneath plates of riveted steel, and with every step the sound of metal grating on metal resounded from his joints. The right arm was equipped with a machine gun, while there was a sixty-millimeter grenade launcher attached to the left. The armor showed faint marks from welding. Anyone would recognize it at a glance as a combat suit. The best weapon makers in Razin had developed weight-absorption technology that made it possible for a human being to control a nearly one-ton mass of iron from the inside.

After halting at the gate, he spotted D. He paused for about two seconds, and then there was the clank of metal as he entered the clearing. The cold sunlight starkly illuminated the vermilion springs that shot from the chest portion of his armor. He was a little over twenty feet from D.

The man in the combat suit raised his right arm, training the barrel of the machine gun on D's face. A black gale flew to one side, while the head of the cyborg horse was reduced to a bloody mist. The bullets ripped through the air and vanished into space.

The top half of the combat suit turned to the right, and the black gale raced directly at D. It was followed closely by a burst of flames. D twisted his body out of the way, as if he knew the path the fiery blast would take. His movements were far quicker and more agile than those of the combat suit's motorized upper body. As the combat suit turned to face D, a diagonal slash of his sword cut through the shoulder and chest of its fifth of an inch of iron plate as if it were tissue paper.

The suit halted its movements for a second, and then its right hand made a jerky movement as it reached for its mask. Lifting it revealed the face of the person within. It was a young man with a drawn-out countenance. Neither his vacant eyes nor his slobber-covered lips showed a hint of pain. Yet D's blade was apparently stuck in his body.

"He's crazy, isn't he?" D's left hand said.

Just then the combat suit moved its left arm. The barrel of the grenade launcher turned to D, right in front of him. The madman grinned slightly.

A crimson beam of light pierced the suit through the chest from behind.

D jumped.

The burning-hot laser beam had gone through the ammo stored in the suit. A fireball much larger than the suit of armor ballooned out, along with a cloud of choking, oily smoke. Behind him, the Hunter heard the sound of more explosions and falling pieces.

When stillness returned and D picked himself off the ground, white smoke rose from the back of his coat in several spots. It had been kissed by flames and pieces of burning iron. D twisted his upper body, his coat whirled through the air, and the smoke vanished.

D's eyes reflected a figure standing at the top of the palisade. He had short hair, a tanned face, and a black eye patch covering one eye. The brown fatigues he wore were the kind used by anti-Nobility guerrillas, and they were now a rare sight.

"You okay?" the man called down to him. "I don't mean to tell you your business. But you should take off instead of getting any closer to this place. Razin's a dead village now."

D turned toward the gate without answering the man. As soon as he was through it, he saw a person lying in the road, and then another, and still more beyond that. Redness seeped from the bodies of the fallen.

"So, you came in anyway? Suit yourself," the one-eyed man said from the lookout tower behind the palisade as he peered down at D.

"What happened?"

At the same time D posed this question, the man leaped down, landing right beside the Hunter. He touched down without a sound, as if he had wings. This was no ordinary farmer.

"I don't really know. I've been in the Capital for a while, and just got back three hours ago. The fog was still heavy, so I couldn't tell what was happening in town."

He'd found it very strange that there was no one in the lookout tower, and ignoring the immovable gates, he'd climbed over the palisade. He'd gotten the impression the fog was tinged with red. There'd been that much blood.

"I knew straight away there'd been a whole lot of killing. The stink was so fresh, it had to have been within the last hour." And with that, the man turned to D and introduced himself, saying, "I'm Greed—I work for the village as a warrior."

III

D went back to Matthew and Sue and told them they'd be leaving right away.

"Hold on! We've been riding all night, and we're beat," Matthew protested. "Maybe I'd be all right, but Sue can't take this. Let us get some rest."

"It's dangerous here. The village has been annihilated."

Matthew's eyes went wide. "That's preposterous!" he said. "I've heard about this place. If it's not the best-armed village on the Frontier, then it's a close second. Bandits won't even attack the place. No way could it get—"

"I saw it for myself."

Matthew fell silent.

"Let's go," D said, wheeling his steed around.

"We can't. Sue needs to rest!" Matthew yelled out shrilly after the Hunter.

Standing defiantly in the driver's seat, the boy almost seemed possessed as he twitched from head to toe. Words flew wildly from his bloodless lips.

"She's always been weak, since the day she was born. It's a miracle she's made it this far. I've got a responsibility to look out for Sue. I say we take a break here."

Quietly watching the ranting boy, D said, "If we leave now, we can reach an outpost by night."

"Outposts" were lodging facilities constructed by Frontier administrators to protect travelers from monsters and bandit attacks when the distance between villages was great enough to necessitate camping out overnight. They were stocked with food, water, and weapons, and in many cases they also had a caretaker.

"Sue can't make it!" Matthew said, stamping his feet angrily in the driver's seat.

"There's something funny about this clown," D's left hand groused in a low tone.

"Stop it, Matt," said the frail figure who appeared from the covered wagon's interior. Though her dainty face certainly had a haggard look to it, it wasn't the kind of patient-at-death's-door look that would've warranted Matthew's behavior.

"Mr. D is right. I'll be fine. Let's keep going."

"But, Sue!" Matthew began to protest again. Sue leaned against her brother's back.

"Please, Matt."

"Okay," Matthew said, patting the back of his sister's hand and nodding.

Just then, there was a great rumbling sound in the distance. A short time after that, a shock reached them through the ground. It continued for a long time.

"That came from the highway," the hoarse voice said.

But D had already told the pair, "Stay right here," and dashed off.

Just a thousand feet from the village, the road between the community and the highway was buried under chunks of rock. Someone had blown up the cliffs by the side of the road.

Looking up at the top of the pile of boulders, each up to ten feet high, the man in the guerrilla fatigues scratched his chin.

Halting his new horse beside the man, the first thing D asked was, "Was that you?"

"Huh?"

Greed pointed to the top of the rock pile, then at himself, frowning and shaking his head.

"It was the same monster that slaughtered the villagers. I didn't see any sign of it, but I had my suspicions, and this makes it pretty plain. This is the work of the Weapon Master."

"The Weapon Master?" a hoarse voice inquired. It didn't reach Greed's ears.

"The lifeblood of the village is the weapons they craft here. Buyers come from all over the Frontier. To keep anything from happening to the goods, they're all stored in a single location. And the Weapon Master is the one in charge of 'em."

While Greed's expression could be described as intrepid, he began to look a little pale.

"Not only had the villagers been forced into the center of town, but the warehouses and factories were torn apart, too. No one but the Weapon Master could do something like that. Gotta be hiding around here somewhere."

"What'll you do?"

"I'm gonna settle up accounts," Greed said, smacking his laser gun. "Nothing to do with that murderer but have a hanging. Before I do, I've gotta hear why the hell it'd do such a thing. I'm a warrior, after all."

"You don't have an employer anymore."

"I took the job, just the same."

"How's this Weapon Master armed?"

"That's top secret in any village like this. No one but it and the mayor would know. From the rumors I've heard, it's packing a sixty-millimeter particle cannon and two hundred guided pencil missiles, a pair of flamethrowers, and a needle gun, but apparently it's also got a couple of secret weapons to be used against Nobility."

"That's a formidable opponent."

"Damn straight," Greed said, scratching his head. "So you shouldn't just be strolling around out here. Since the road's been blocked, the bastard must mean to kill you, too. The only reason it ain't showed itself is because it got hit when we exchanged fire. If I get killed, you folks have gotta find some way to get outta here."

"Come with me." D indicated the back of his saddle.

After returning, with Greed, to the Dyalhis children, D explained the situation and told them to go into the village. Sue was to stay inside the covered wagon until he gave the word.

Not even asking why, Sue simply nodded.

Still suspicious, Matthew pointed to Greed and asked, "You sure we can trust him?"

"Hell, no," Greed replied. "Do whatever the hell you like. I've got a job to see to. D, that's one swell employer you've got there."

And with that, he walked off. From the look in his eyes, it was clear he didn't think much of Matthew.

Passing through the gates, Matthew gazed, dumbfounded, at the bodies lying around.

"This is just sick. Who'd do something like this?"

"Apparently it was someone known as the Weapon Master."

"The Weapon Master of Razin?" Matthew said, apparently having some knowledge on the subject. "Tell me it ain't so. If that's the case, we're in deep shit. D, we've gotta get outta here right away!"

"The road's blocked. You have any explosives?"

"Well, I've got charges for blasting irrigation ditches. I'll go get 'em."

Climbing into the back of the wagon, he emerged with yellow cylinders in his hands. He had a dozen.

"They're not all that powerful. They couldn't blow a rock like that out of the way."

"Find an inn."

Saying this, D started forward on his horse.

"Wait. What do we do if it finds us? Shouldn't we hide or something?"

"It already has found us. Apparently the Weapon Master's equipped with high-powered radar."

"Then what are we supposed to do?"

"Find the best place you can to roost."

Matthew couldn't say a word.

"Right now, the Weapon Master is repairing the damage Greed inflicted, but sooner or later it'll be back. Until then, get some rest."

Wiping the sweat from his brow, Matthew said, "Where are we supposed to look for a good place to roost when the whole town's soaked in blood?"

Just then, Sue stuck her head out of the wagon. Seeing the scene around them, she grew deathly pale and shut her eyes.

"Get back inside!" Matthew shouted.

"No, I'll be fine. I have to get used to things like this. Say, Mr. D, there's a good inn."

Looking at D, the girl had a gleam in her eye that made Matthew's face turn to stone.

In front of the community center, the three travelers stopped the vehicles and horses. It hadn't been destroyed, and there weren't any corpses around. As the building doubled as a hotel, they knew it would have soft beds and fresh food.

Once the wagon and car had been deposited in the parking lot, D quickly appeared, racing off in the same direction from which they'd come.

Watching him go from the window of a spacious room, Sue said anxiously, "I wonder if everything will be okay."

"It's too late to worry about that. This is where you suggested we stay. There's no one left, but it looks comfortable enough," Matthew replied as he surveyed the surroundings.

"That's not what I meant!"

On hearing this rare angry outburst from his normally reserved sister, the boy quickly turned in her direction.

"Don't tell me—" Matthew began, his expression growing more intense. "You really are sweet on him, aren't you? Sweet on that dhampir—that monster!"

"Stop it! He's keeping us safe. Why don't you grow up?"

"You're the one who needs to grow up!"

Grabbing his sister's wrist, Matthew spun her around so she faced him.

"What are you doing, Matt?"

Jabbing a finger at his terrified sister's nose, he said, "I'm only saying this because I'm your brother. Don't you ever make nice with that freakin' dhampir again. You've gotta keep some distance from the hired help."

"I don't want to!"

Matthew became furious. His sister had never disobeyed him before. And he'd never acted like an overbearing older brother, either. Everyone who knew the two of them always sighed and said they couldn't believe how well the siblings got along. But a young man of unearthly beauty had caused a split between them. Matthew struck out with his hand, as if he could bat the rift away.

A hard smack resounded from Sue's cheek, and she fell.

Matthew had swung his fist at her.

"I'm sorry, Sue! Are you okay?" he asked, laying a hand on her shoulder, but it was viciously knocked away. "Sue?"

"Don't touch me! I hate you!"

Suddenly, Matthew felt completely isolated, like he was all alone in the world. Everyone had turned their backs on him, leaving him far behind. His father, his mother, and now even Sue.

"Sue . . ."

When the girl at his feet looked up at him, his face was no longer that of his normal self. Extending both hands, he slowly bent down toward his sister.

Something was reflected in the corner of his eye.

The window faced the parking lot and the center of town, where little paths crisscrossed fallow barley fields. A bizarre object stood on one of those paths.

The simplest way to describe it was to say it was a lovely young lady riding on a black sphere about six and a half feet in diameter. Her long, blond hair was tied back, and she had the kind of refined good looks and pale skin rarely seen in farming communities—she was the kind of girl who'd undoubtedly make the hearts of the village lads beat faster. The high-necked yellow shirt that covered

her pale nape still displayed her curvaceous figure. And the weapons mounted on the pylons that ran through the center of the sphere—a high-caliber beam cannon, flamethrowers, miniature missile-launcher boxes, a needle gun and its ammunition—were the sort of dangerous business that hardly seemed to suit such a person.

Matthew realized something instantly.

She's it. She's the Weapon Master!

The eyes of the lovely young lady on the sphere were devoid of anything that could be called life. She had to be a mere sixteen or seventeen years of age, but just one look at her beautiful face would've told anyone she was insane.

With the sound of meshing gears, a particle-beam cannon took aim at the community center.

"Don't!"

Just as Matthew frantically clamored on top of Sue, a raging crimson stream streaked out under the blue sky to score a direct hit on the wall of the center, spreading a boiling-hot field as it ate its way through the reinforced plastic and concrete.

The cyborg horses that were tethered nearby went berserk, snapping the reins and galloping away with the wagon still behind them.

The beam cannon took aim at the pair on the ground.

A streak of white suddenly stretched from the girl's temple: a needle of unfinished wood. Over a foot in length, it punched cleanly through her right temple to poke out below her left ear.

The girl turned her face to the side.

About thirty feet away, on the path to her right, darkness in human form sat astride a black steed. Was darkness born beneath a blue sky always this gorgeous?

"AnD yOu . . . WoUlD bE . . ." the impaled girl murmured in a robotic tone of rapture.

The lovely Weapon Master who'd destroyed an entire village was linked to D by a ghastly will to kill.

Friends and Foes

CHAPTER 4

I

"You can't answer that?" D asked. It was in the same low voice as always, but his foe, a good thirty feet away, still heard it with perfect clarity.

For a heartbeat, a stunned expression spread across the lovely young girl's maddened countenance. But it didn't last long. The sphere didn't appear to move as it rotated so that the girl and D faced one another. Did she realize D had chosen the community center to lure her out?

Completely expressionless, the girl fired her beam cannon.

The instant the stream of blistering heat produced a heat shimmer near the weapon's muzzle, D started his horse galloping with all its might. But when D abruptly disappeared from the melting, steaming path, the Weapon Master didn't think it strange. It wasn't her crazed brain that sensed this; it was her intuition.

There's no way such a gorgeous man could exist in our world.

As D left his horse and sailed down, the girl's survival instincts repelled the Hunter's sword. D bounded in the same direction as the blade and at the same speed, not losing his balance in the least as he touched back down to the ground.

"That's an electronic barrier," the hoarse voice indicated. "With that last needle, you caught her off guard, but now she's got her eye on you. Her survival instincts have been triggered."

The sphere backed away without a sound. The scenery that was visible behind it was distorted, undoubtedly due to the force field.

D suddenly felt a terrific weight across every inch of his body.

"Oh, no! She's pinning us down with this force field—we've gotta make a break for it!"

Before the hoarse voice had finished speaking, white smoke gushed from the back of the sphere. Trailing long plumes of that same smoke, thin objects reflected the sunlight as they climbed steeply. Dazzling flames spouted from their tails as the pencil missiles followed their sensors into the force field—into the powerful hand that was outstretched . . . and the mouth that had opened in it. All thirty missiles were inhaled, and the instant the last had been swallowed, thirty feet of flames and black smoke stretched from that tiny mouth.

A meaty little face formed on the hand's surface and groaned with great pain, "That was a hell of a meal."

D closed the distance between himself and the Weapon Master in a single bound. His blade came down in a deadly diagonal slash—and vivid sparks flew from the surface of the sphere. It'd literally escaped by a hair's breadth. Not halting there, it retreated toward the center of town.

And D was still ready to give chase. He started to take a step, but then halted. The scenery before him was distorted—a force field had been activated. It was like a black hole, with the power to reduce even a steel battleship to its constituent atoms the instant it made contact. Not even a void existed within it. It was a parting gift from his opponent.

"So, she took that needle from you, no problem? Must be a cyborg or some kind of amplified human being," D's left hand murmured as the Hunter returned his sword to its sheath. "But those kids—that was just too bad."

D turned toward the community center. Flames had begun to spring up in various parts of the collapsed building. Sue and Matthew were nowhere to be seen. D had left the two in an extremely dangerous situation, and then failed them.

Giving a small whistle, D summoned his cyborg steed. Just as he settled into the saddle, a crimson beam of light skimmed past his right cheek. D turned around.

This young man could even sense the murderous intent of a machine. That was why it was practically impossible to get the drop on him. But he hadn't dodged the shot.

A jeep was approaching from the end of the path that ran to the west. Coming down the trail, it stopped beside D. The wagon and car remained in the community center parking lot.

Behind the jeep's wheel, Greed turned his gaze from the blazing community center and the still, vapor-shrouded barley field and back to D, saying, "Fought the Weapon Master, didn't you?"

As he looked D over from the top of his head down to the tips of his boots, the man's good eye swiftly filled with admiration.

"And yet, you don't have a blessed mark on you. What are you, some kind of monster?"

Greed's one good eye bulged as he trained his gaze on the vicinity of D's hip. He thought he'd heard low, hoarse laughter. However, he immediately looked up and grinned as he said, "I think you'd best go into hiding after all. Having two monsters running around here would just leave me on edge."

Apparently the warrior was still determined to fight alone.

When he looked at the collapsed community center, a sad expression came to his face, and he asked, "You don't mean to tell me they were in there?"

D nodded.

"Damn," Greed said with a shrug, and then he clapped D on one shoulder. "Those were some good kids, weren't they?"

After that remark, Greed asked, "Where'd the girl get to?"

"The center of town."

"Thank you kindly. Don't take it so hard. And stay the hell out of this!"

Getting back in the jeep, he started the engine and raised one hand in parting. He wore an affable smile.

The jeep raced off down the path. After watching it go for a while, D got back on his cyborg horse and headed over to the car and wagon.

There were too many things Greed couldn't understand. He didn't know how or why the village's entire populace had been slaughtered. When he'd returned to the village, everyone had been stained with red. Most of the villagers had died in their houses, but those who'd noticed something was wrong and tried to run had been murdered in the streets. The Weapon Master could do it—he realized that in an instant. But why?

He'd learned of the madness while he was searching the village, when the other warriors attacked him. The reason he'd somehow managed to fight them off was because they were mainly armed with gunpowder-based firearms, while Greed's weapon was a far more powerful and accurate laser rifle, and as they'd approached him, they'd made no attempt to remain silent.

But where had this madness come from? On rare occasions, humans became infected with a virus that caused insanity. However, as only the warriors and the Weapon Master were affected, it was impossible to deny the possibility that it'd been induced artificially. He'd told D as much.

And when I find out who did this, I'm gonna tear them to pieces.

The faces of the village mayor and his daughter Vigne rose in Greed's mind. When he'd come to the village as a drifter seeking work, the other villagers had mocked and berated him, but the mayor had given him a menial job on his farm. For a whole year he did manual labor in exchange for three meals a day, and then the mayor selected him to be a warrior. Greed still remembered the words he'd said: "I'll never forget what you've done for me."

If he would have said he'd never wanted to run off during those days of hard physical labor, it would have been a lie. But whenever his exhausted body transmitted that thought to his brain, Vigne had always miraculously appeared. And each time her pale, slender hands had held a boxed lunch. "From my papa," was all the girl said as she handed him the box, and though she turned around immediately, for a second their eyes met, and she didn't try to look away. Greed remembered well her plump, pink cheeks and the large eyes that had reflected him. *The world ain't all bad*, he'd thought. *Why not try toughing it out a little longer?*

In this village festooned with blood and corpses, the very first place he'd gone was the mayor's house. The mayor lay in the foyer, while Vigne had fallen in the hallway in front of her bedroom. The mayor had been shot through the heart; half of Vigne's face was missing. The damaged portion was charred to a crisp—she'd taken a savage blast of heat from a beam cannon. The remaining half of her face wore an oddly peaceful expression, and that was the only thing that kept Greed from losing his mind. At the very least, it left him ready to fight with a cool head.

He'd slain each and every one of his foes, and kept from getting killed in the process. He knew a lot about the Weapon Master. In truth, he didn't want to fight her. But it was the sight of the mayor and Vigne dead that madly fanned the flames of vengeance in his heart.

I'll kill 'er if it's the last thing I do.

Trembling with rage as he steered the jeep, he had a lethal gleam in his one good eye. Though he drove around the center of town, there was no sign of the Weapon Master. Undoubtedly she was repairing the damage D had dealt her.

Could it be she'd left the village?

Greed turned his vehicle toward the gates. In less than two minutes he was there.

A figure in vivid vermilion garb stood at the entrance to the village.

"What the hell . . . ," he muttered, unconsciously leveling his rifle.

Halting the jeep about fifteen feet from the figure, Greed called out to him, "Who the hell are you?"

The robed figure started to take a step forward.

"Freeze. You can do your talking from right there."

"My thanks," said the man in the robe. He had a low voice that carried well. "I've been following the waterways to my destination, but I'm terribly tired. They call me Curio."

"This might be a stupid question, but are you the one who did this to the village?"

"You are correct, sir. Kindly stop that."

The instant the man had finished the first remark, Greed had started to pull the trigger. But his finger wouldn't move.

"We both need to be prudent in our actions. Let's discuss this at length."

The Weapon Master had concealed herself in a secret location known only to the mayor and herself. There was a weapon warehouse on the northern outskirts of the village, and the rock beneath it had a natural cavern large enough to fit an entire factory. Having already climbed down from her transport, the Weapon Master lay on a simple steel bed. The space around her was filled with lockers and racks full of weapons and ammunition. Scattered about were various tooling machines. The warehouse aboveground was just camouflage, and here underground was the real storage facility, as well as a factory for weapon production and repair.

Her head hurt terribly. Pierced by D's needle, her brain had long since ceased to function; a spare electronic brain had taken control of her body. The thoughts of the electronic brain were almost entirely limited to combat, but to allay the risk of danger, it'd been adjusted to allow a few normal thought processes. An engineer who'd come from the Capital did the work. After finishing the job, he stared intently at the Weapon Master and said rather emotionally, "I used to be in the service of the Nobility. As a result, until a year ago I was a rolling stone. Looks like you're in the same boat. Outcasts have always gotten a raw deal, and they always will." And then he'd left.

Nothing was known of the Weapon Master's roots. As an infant, she'd been abandoned in front of the village gates while they were changing guard shifts. At the time, the village was in the midst of a famine, and there wasn't enough to feed an outsider. Normally, she'd have been left out—without mercy—to be eaten by monsters or supernatural creatures. A single, authoritative declaration from the mayor that she might one day prove useful had saved her. The baby was dubbed Eris, and she was raised by a widow in the village. The mayor footed the bills for her care.

From the time she was very young, anyone could see that Eris demonstrated outstanding abilities. She had excellent reflexes, coordination, and mental faculties. "If she had the physical strength of a man, she'd be positively superhuman," a member of the Frontier Medical Corps had declared during a periodic call on the village. And when Eris turned fifteen, she was appointed Weapon Master.

Villagers or merchants promptly sold most of the innumerable weapons manufactured in the village, but the village warehouse held some extremely advanced weapons and items so dangerous their sale was prohibited. It would have been impossible to list all of the villages that had been slyly infiltrated or even openly attacked by thieves or bandits who learned of such bounty. On such occasions, the village's Weapon Master would arm himself or herself with the most potent munitions in storage and bring the fight to them. The Weapon Master only emerged once all the warriors had been slain.

Regardless of how lethal the armaments might be, if the Weapon Master was a human being, his or her performance in battle would be limited. In this village, they decided to make their Weapon Master a cyborg to overcome those human limitations. It was left to the mayor to persuade her. Eris silently agreed. The widow who'd raised her had informed her of her destiny, and as she'd grown up she hadn't really planned on going anywhere or doing anything. She was an orphan the village had taken in. So she would work for the good of the village.

The price Eris paid for her refreshingly earnest decision was an electronic backup brain and highly sensitive sensors implanted in her body. In place of her womb was a singular weapon, the only one of its kind; it'd been decided during its testing stage not to use it. Thus, the most dangerous item the girl defended was implanted in her own body.

Cut off from her crazed brain, her electronic brain retained memories of what had happened during her insanity, but allowed her to function normally again solely in her capacity as the Weapon Master. She'd returned to her senses. Eris now decided that she would rest her weary flesh, then repair her conveyance and make adjustments to her weapons.

Feeling terribly thirsty, Eris got out of bed and went over to a spigot close by. The facility inside the cavern consisted of materials that had been brought there in secret and improvements made over the years by a series of mayors, their families, and the Weapon Masters. The water drew from a subterranean source.

She twisted the valve, and then filled her cup from a vigorous flow of water. After emptying the cup and returning it to its place on the shelf, Eris walked toward the tooling machinery in the back. She went ten or fifteen feet before she halted. Her electronic brain and other sensors had detected a presence behind her.

As she turned around, she simultaneously drew an oversized firearm with an ammo clip in the front.

The first thing to catch her eye was a dress evocative of watery-blue depths. Needless to say, the woman's good looks were startling, as was the fact that she was dripping wet from the top of her head to the hem of her dress. Come to mention it, even her skin was like water. If left to her own devices, she might have turned back into water or perhaps evaporated.

"WhO . . . aRe YoU?" the Weapon Master inquired mechanically.

"I'm known as Lucienne."

II

Respectfully bowing her head, the water witch said, "There's no place water goes that I can't enter. And I arrived here in the village faster than another individual—a certain murderer—by following this aquifer underground."

She'd no doubt imagined what the most likely question from Eris would be.

"ThE wArRiOrS aNd I wEnT mAd AfTeR hEaRiNg A sErMoN bY a MaN iN a RoBe. WhErE iS hE? If He'S oNe Of YoUr CoMpAtRiOtS, hE cAn GiVe YoU tHe LaSt RiTeS nOw."

Suddenly, the firearm howled. The weapon's report echoed off the rocks, and a tiny hole opened in Lucienne's forehead. Fluid gushed from her brain—but it was all water.

"It's no use."

Quickly running to the wall to her left, Eris got a flamethrower. Grabbing it by the pistol grip attached to its nozzle, she pointed it at Lucienne.

"WhIcH wIlL WiN, tHe PoWeR oF fIrE oR wAtEr? LeT's SeE."

This time, there was nothing else to discuss—and the water witch caught a six-thousand-degree blast of flames in the face. Steam roiled up. Lucienne leaped to one side. She didn't have a head—the flames had seen to that. A heartbeat later, a semitransparent lump bubbled up on the stump of her neck. The flames besieged the water witch once again. The right half of Lucienne's body was reduced to steam and vanished.

Still in that horrible form, the water witch retreated toward the spigot. The flames pursued her ruthlessly. Water splashed against the floor. The instant Lucienne touched it, her body melted away, becoming a large volume of water that slapped against the ground. The flying droplets were carefully dried up by six thousand degrees of fire.

"What have we here?" someone said, giving a few little sniffs.

Lowering the temperature of the flames, Eris gave a blast to the spigot, evaporating every last drop of water before tightening the valve and going back to bed. This monster could appear at will anywhere there was water. The one who called herself Lucienne and another one had come to the village ahead of someone else, and as a result, she and the warriors had gone insane and slaughtered the villagers. Apparently it was Lucienne's compatriot that had caused them to do so. Eris would definitely kill both this person and Lucienne.

However, she got the feeling something wasn't right. She'd gone over her memories repeatedly, but there was a section that was completely blank. Even her electronic spare brain couldn't fix it.

She wondered what that woman had come here to do. Perhaps she'd believed that Eris was still under her compatriot's spell and had arrived to give her new instructions.

After she'd had some rest, she would arm herself and eliminate them for sure. Her memories of the slaughter of the villagers left a twinge in her heart as her spare brain deleted them.

Eris fell asleep.

When Eris awoke again, it was because she heard a sound. There was someone beyond the iron door.

She ran, the wind swirling in her wake. She'd already decided what she'd grab. Pulling a laser rifle from the rack, she braced it at hip level.

The door began to open, and she sent a crimson beam of light through the gap. The beam moved in a diagonal line from bottom to top. The top half of the door clattered to the floor; the edge of the cut was molten red. The foe on the other side of the door would've been sliced in two in exactly the same fashion.

A sharp pain shot through her right wrist. A stark needle protruded from the skin. Pulling it out, Eris hurled it without even looking at her target. The attack was entrusted to her electronic brain and its sensors. It flew with a force that could penetrate iron, but D stopped it with his left hand.

"HoW dId YoU kNoW i WaS hErE?" Eris asked.

The question and its answer lay on the periphery of her electronic brain.

"There was the smell of gelled oil," a hoarse voice said. "You used a flamethrower. Can't say the exhaust system here did a perfect job of breaking down the color and scent of the smoke. Hey! If you're gonna attack, you'd better raise the muzzle before you pull the trigger. But this guy will put needles through both your eyes before you can do that."

"I pUt My fIeLd Up."

"There's something I'd like to ask you," said a steely voice.

Eris felt dizzy. The instant she heard his voice, something other than the mind of the Weapon Master became conscious of the handsome features of the young man before her.

"Was it you that killed the villagers?"

"YeS . . . i ThInK . . ."

"You mean you're not sure?"

"I cAn'T sAy FoR cErTaIn. PaRt Of My MeMoRy Is MiSsInG."

"Who caused you to go crazy?"

"A mAn In A vErMiLiOn RoBe. I tHoUgHt I wAs On My GuArD, bUt ThE nExT tHiNg I kNeW, hE wAs RiGhT bEsIdE mE. AnD hE wHiSpErEd To Me. ToLd Me I sHoUlD gO cRaZy."

"You remember that pretty well. Oh, that's right—you have an electronic brain, don't you?" said the hoarse voice.

"YoU dEsTrOyEd My NoRmAl BrAiN. On AcCoUnT oF ThAt, I rEtUrNeD tO mY sEnSeS. I dOn'T kNoW iF i ShOuLd ThAnK yOu Or TaKe My VeNgEaNcE oN yOu."

"What'll you do now?"

"FiNd ThE oNe WhO pUt Me UnDeR a SpElL aNd KiLl HiM."

As D stared at her quietly, he said, "The whisperer can do that to machines, too."

A time of silence flowed between the two of them.

The tension simply drained from Eris's body.

"YoU hAvE mY tHaNkS."

"For what?" the hoarse voice said, sounding rather proud of itself.

"The foe you used the flamethrower on—was she water?" D asked.

"ThAt'S rIgHt."

"She can appear anywhere there's water. Be careful."

And saying this, the Hunter turned around.

Eris watched without a word as his powerful but completely undefended back disappeared behind the iron door. If she'd fought him now, she'd have undoubtedly been slain—or so her electronic brain believed.

Going outside, D headed for the community center. The sun was still high.

"You seem bushed," D's left hand remarked with heavy sarcasm.

The Hunter was astride his cyborg horse.

"Humans live in the world of the day, Nobles in that of the night—and you're both, but neither. Wonder if you'll ever find a world that suits you. Oof!"

With his hand still balled into a fist, D rode forward.

About ten minutes later, the destroyed community center came into view—he'd reached the path through the fields where he'd had his battle with Eris. The wagon and car were parked by the ruins.

Halfway down the path, D looked back. He'd heard a faint engine sound coming from the west—from up high.

The form coming closer was that of a single-seater jet helicopter. Greed sat in an open seat like that of a go-kart. There was no windshield. His left hand gripped the flight stick, and his right held his laser rifle. His emotionless face was unsettling.

"That bastard—he's been possessed!"

At the same time his left hand spoke, D kicked his mount's flanks, spurring it into a leap. Without a sound, a deep crimson light shot down at him. A hole burned through the cyborg horse's neck, and it toppled onto one side. Earth and sand flew into the air.

A flash of white streaked from D's left hand toward the helicopter. Just before it got there, the helicopter climbed straight up. Blazing through the air, the rough wooden needle vanished.

Once it reached an altitude of at least three hundred feet, the helicopter started to circle. For all his strength, there wasn't much D could do at that range.

Blazing arrows rained down. Fire rose from the path. Flames engulfed a farmhouse.

D ran to the left, where he could see the village. Flaming arrows followed after him, getting closer and closer. The next one could prove deadly.

Without warning, the helicopter listed to one side. Its balance suddenly upset, it fell toward the center of town. Right after it vanished behind a row of houses, there was the dull thud of an impact, and then a few seconds later a pillar of flame arose, accompanied by black smoke.

Listening to the sounds of the destruction all the while, D walked toward the community center. He didn't so much as glance in the direction where Greed had gone down.

"You know, it wasn't Greed himself who was behind that attack. If he's lucky, he might've survived." Breaking off there, the hoarse voice then said, "Don't know if that would mean we've gained a foe or lost an ally. I really can't say."

D had already reached the community center. Matthew and Sue peered down at him from the driver's seat of their covered wagon. Sue held a motorized crossbow with both hands. Though it was said even a child could use one, having the eight-pound weapon score a direct hit on a helicopter at an altitude of three hundred feet was more than most young girls could do. Undoubtedly, her hit was the result of being incredibly desperate, mentally and physically.

The instant her eyes met D's, Sue dropped the weapon at her feet and slumped to the ground.

"How's that for a girl of fourteen? Seems humans can fight like mad even for someone else's life."

Naturally, D said nothing to that mocking remark from his left hand.

III

The two children hadn't gone into the community center. D had chosen a far more secure location for their hideout— the interior of Count Braujou's vehicle. This was one reason D had kept the vehicle even after the count's demise. Of course, only a Noble could use one of the Nobility's cars, but when D touched his left hand to the vehicle's door and whispered, the door opened easily and allowed the children to enter.

"Sue! Sue!" Matthew cried out as he shook his sister wildly, but restraining him, D put his left hand against the girl's face. Matthew watched in amazement as the lifeblood returned to her waxy skin and her eyelids opened.

"How'd you get out of the car?" D inquired after a short time. He'd instructed the computer that controlled the vehicle not to let the two of them out under any circumstances.

"I don't know. We were looking out the window and saw you were in danger. I figured we had to do something to help you. Remembering that we had a crossbow in our wagon, I shouted at the car to let me out. I said it over and over—and then, the door actually opened."

D put his hand on the girl's head, saying, "You saved me—thank you."

The girl's face colored with a rosy flush.

"You're just like her, you know."

"Huh?"

"Your mother. We fought together once. Your face looks just like hers did then."

Glittering beads welled up in the girl's eyes. Before they could roll down her cheeks, D turned his gaze to the road and said, "Let's go."

"Okay."

Matthew's face had stiffened. Dark shadows altered his features— shades of embarrassment and anger. He heard a voice in his ear say, "Go back to the car. And another thing—that crossbow's heavy. Next time, help her hold it."

When Matthew turned to look, D had already started walking off toward another cyborg horse.

A few minutes later, the group started forward, headed for the highway. Sue and Matthew were inside the car.

"You lured out the person who slaughtered the villagers to see whether or not Valcua's seven were behind it. By making it look like you stashed those two in the community center, you got to meet that girl—that's all well and good, but there's something that just doesn't make sense to me," the voice from D's left hand said in all seriousness. "First of all, all the warriors except Greed went crazy. That looks like Curio's doing, but he wouldn't order them to go nuts. There was no real point in doing that. Telling 'em to kill you and the two kids—now, that'd be more like it. So if that's the case, who gave the order? And if it was the Weapon Master and the warriors who killed the whole village, what was the reason for the slaughter? Even if Curio and Lucienne were here, this doesn't seem like their style. At least, they don't act like homicidal maniacs. Which would mean—"

D gazed straight ahead without saying a word.

"—There's another assassin here besides them. D, you remember what Sigma told you? It said it was sending an assassin after you, too."

In Galleon Valley, in its last seconds with D, the antiproton computer had indeed told the Hunter that.

"Five of Valcua's underlings remain, but how many assassins could Sigma have sent? This is shaping up to be a hell of a trip!"

There was no reply to this, but presently D halted his steed before the chunks of stone that buried the road. Getting off his horse, he took the blasting charges Matthew had supplied from the front seat of the wagon and went over to the rocks. Making a light leap up to cling to the surface of one rock, he made two or three more bounds before disappearing on the far side of the pile. It took about two minutes for him to reach the top of the rock heap.

"You sure are one scary character," his left hand groaned, sounding deeply impressed. "You set what I calculate to be the perfect-size charge in exactly the spots I would've chosen."

D still had the cords for a number of charges coiled around his right arm.

Suddenly D turned around. Countless figures were approaching from the direction of the village.

"Well, what do we have here?" the hoarse voice said with interest. "It's the villagers!"

There could be no question that these were the same people who'd lain in the houses and in the streets soaked in blood. Grins formed on faces stained with vermilion. The surging wave of the dead halted where the village road met the highway.

D leaped down in front of the foremost rank before they could take another step forward. Perhaps even the dead felt the unearthly aura that filled the young man, because the grins were wiped from every last face.

"What a handsome guy," a middle-aged man facing D said, nearly moaning. His voice was quite clear. "You wouldn't consider living in our village, would you?"

Each and every head nodded in unison at his suggestion.

"Your horse and your friends could live here, too. We'll even give you houses and fields."

Saying nothing, D peered at the man's face. The man's right eye was a gaping cavern of deep red, while his eyeball dangled down by his Adam's apple. All that connected the latter to the former was a whitish optic nerve.

"I see. The whole point was to make an army of the dead. Now I get why everyone was slaughtered."

The middle-aged man wore a perplexed look as he turned his eyes toward D's waist, where the hoarse voice had originated.

Forgetting about the voice, the man reached one hand toward D's shoulder, saying, "Come to the village."

The man thought a white light flashed by his nose, and then his right arm fell off at the elbow. With a vacant expression the man

first stared at his wound, and then toppled backward. A scream rang out. Not an act—a real one.

Could even the dead feel pain?

D jumped back.

"Come."

"Live in our village."

"Come back to our place."

Male and female, young and old alike held their arms out as if to embrace D as they rushed toward him. Ahead of them, fiery blossoms bloomed. Flames and shock waves threw villagers in all directions with a roar. D had backed away only after igniting the charges. Whether they were dead or not, this young man had no kind thoughts toward his foes.

Black smoke streaming behind them like ticker tape, the remaining villagers attacked. The Hunter's sword danced in the sunlight. Heads flew from the villagers as if they were jack-in-the-boxes. Out in the sun and without so much as a drop of blood being spilled, there was actually something invigorating about the scene.

The villagers had him vastly outnumbered. There was no way a single sword could stop a wave of more than a hundred villagers. But look! The instant the arc of D's blade touched the dead, their heads were sent flying mercilessly. The fallen bodies overlapped, building a rampart with their own corpses. As the others tried to climb over it, silvery flashes shot out, adding their freshly decapitated corpses to the pile. Unable to set foot in the zone carved out by D and his sword, the villagers met a new death.

From the tail end of the visibly shrinking throng of living dead, one figure dashed off toward the village. A scorching beam of red angled down from the sky above to pierce the figure at the waist. As the body thudded to the ground, a white puppy jumped out at his feet and made a beeline for the village.

Aided by the blistering red beams of light, the glittering sword mowed down the villagers.

Less than five minutes later, a jet helicopter touched down in the center of the vast expanse of corpses. Inside it, holding a laser rifle, was none other than Greed.

When his eyes met D's, the man frantically held out his left hand and said, "Don't get the wrong idea! The shock of the crash brought me around. See, I grabbed another helicopter to come save you."

"Who possessed you?"

"Some jerk in a red robe."

When Greed saw that D was approaching, his body stiffened, but the gorgeous young man paid no attention to this as he pressed his left hand against the man's brow. Something oddly cold sank into the warrior's brain. For a second, he felt like screaming, and then the sensation vanished.

Pulling his left hand away, D turned his back on Greed and walked toward the villager who'd fled. Apparently the examination had ended.

The fallen villager was a young man who seemed to be around twenty, give or take a bit. He didn't move at all.

"Is he dead?" Greed asked after following the Hunter, slouching forward a bit and looking down as he did so. "But I only shot him below the waist. He shouldn't have died from that—well, aside from the fact that he was already dead, that is."

"Are you certain he's from this village?" D asked.

"Yeah, the guy's named Egbert. Just a regular young fella."

"He was possessed."

The fact that only this average young man had tried to run made it clear that he wasn't like the other villagers.

"But why'd he die?" Greed inquired somewhat dubiously.

"He had a dog with him," D said. An almost imperceptible breeze tousled his long, black hair.

Even the slightest change in something truly exquisite could lead others to discover new beauty. Greed was in a state of rapture. The meaning of D's words dawned on him only after the Hunter had begun walking toward the village.

"Oh, so whatever possessed Greed hopped over to the dog? If we don't find it soon, it could move into someone else—but there aren't any more villagers, are there?"

The warrior was about to walk off to his helicopter, but he halted at D's voice.

"Stay here and watch over the kids."

Though the words resounded against Greed's eardrums, there was no longer any sign of their source.

"I just don't get that guy," Greed muttered pensively.

Entering the village by the back gate, D immediately put his left hand against the ground beneath the gates.

"You catch the scent?"

"Yep," the hoarse voice replied. "Take a right on that little lane up ahead—but who would've thought we could track whatever's possessing the dog by its scent? You've done me one better this time."

D became a gust of black wind that raced down a side road. Up ahead was a row of three enormous structures, apparently warehouses. The shutter on the first one was open.

"Be careful. There's the stink of oil and metal," his left hand warned him.

When they'd closed to about ten feet, something like a black whip shot out from behind the shutter to coil around D's right leg. His naked blade flashed out, cutting through the thing with ease, but just a second later, countless tentacles whipped out. There were easily hundreds of them, and they were made of steel. A dozen were left wriggling on the ground as he leaped back fifteen feet.

The Sacred Ancestor's Technology

CHAPTER 5

I

The warehouse's shutter exploded at the same time D touched back down to the ground. He saw something that, for all the world, looked like a mass of wriggling tentacles. Though there had to be a body somewhere, nothing was visible save the forest of wriggling arms, and aside from the ones that supported its weight, they reached out in every direction, glittering in the sunlight like the most disturbing mechanical creature imaginable.

"Seems like folks in this here village were making more than just regular weapons. But what set it in motion—that dog?"

As if in answer to the hoarse voice's query, a transparent bubble that appeared to be a cockpit rose from the center of the mass of tentacles. On seeing who sat in it, the Hunter's left hand let out a gasp.

"It's that preacher man!"

"What about the dog?" said D. Even with a machine of an indeterminate nature before him, the Hunter didn't seem at all unnerved.

"It's in the warehouse. Now, did that damn preacher find us and come out here on his own, or . . ."

Had the being that controlled the puppy's brain possessed Curio inside the warehouse? It seemed extremely unlikely that Curio would use such a device of his own volition.

The tentacles streamed forward.

As he backed away, D took in his surroundings with ungodly speed. This was the square in front of the warehouse. It also doubled as a testing area. Easily covering more than seven thousand square feet, the square had inspection equipment and tools scattered about, and nearby stood a well.

D and the tentacled entity faced off in the center of the square.

"Is this his doing—or the dog's?"

As if taking that murmured remark by the hoarse voice as a cue, the tentacles attacked. A naked blade mowed through them. The severed arms promptly regrew from the stumps. Apparently the engineers in this village had dreamed up a method for making metal regenerate.

"There's no end to this," D's left hand muttered in a disgusted tone.

At that instant, the tentacles turned in the Hunter's direction en masse. With the sound of compressed air being discharged, they flew by either side of D like spears. The Hunter cut down the ones that would've hit him.

For a split second, a gap opened in front of D where the tentacles should've been. Entering that space, D swung his left hand. Fresh tentacles flew at his body, three of which were sliced off while two more pierced his abdomen and the right side of his chest. As D dropped to one knee, the tentacles engulfed him, but their movements quickly grew chaotic and they began to move toward the right.

Within the cockpit, Curio was in his death throes. White needles jutted from his chest and throat. D's aim had been true. But what kind of strength did it take to put mere wooden needles through bulletproof glass that was both heat and shock resistant, and also have them nail their target? What kind of precision did that require?

Using the sword he had stuck in the ground like a cane, D got up again. There wasn't a hint of pain in his bloodless countenance.

Now that Curio had been slain, the tentacles would begin to run amok. If nothing were done, the device would probably get out of the village and cause endless slaughter and destruction. It had to be destroyed now.

D pulled out the tentacle that was in his chest. Bright blood struck the ground. Removing the one from his abdomen as well, the Hunter was taking his first step toward the mass of tentacles that was now a good thirty feet away when a voice called out, "WaIt!"

When D turned to look, a pitch-black globe was drawing closer without a sound, and then it came to a stop. From the top of it, Eris gazed at D's handsome features.

"LeAvE tHiS tO mE," Eris said softly. Her eyes were trained on the tentacles, but they soon returned to D. "I'm ThE WeApOn MaStEr. TaKiNg OuT wEaPoNs ThAt RuN aMoK iS mY jOb."

The Hunter said nothing.

"NiCe MeEtInG yOu. I'lL nEvEr FoRgEt YoU. ThOsE aRe My TrUe FeElInGs, NoT jUsT mY eLeCtRoNiC bRaIn TaLkInG."

Her voice had the same mechanical coldness as always, but it changed unexpectedly as she said, "Goodbye, D."

Her hair fluttered. A faint fragrance mixed with the breeze, and then disappeared.

D watched as the sphere raced toward the tentacles. All of them changed direction in unison. They opened to meet Eris. It called to mind some carnivorous plant, bizarre and brutal. The sphere plowed into them without hesitation. And the tentacles closed around their delicious prey.

"Oh, no—jump for it!"

Before the hoarse voice had spoken, about six feet of darkness had formed in the center of the tentacles and sphere. It instantly spread, extending its domain to include the entire form of both machines.

"That's a gizmo for creating a small black hole," the hoarse voice said. "The woman had it planted inside herself somewhere. Seems that was her secret weapon."

The darkness had consumed most of the sphere, but a pale visage remained above it. Eris was facing them. A second later, she was sucked into the hole in space.

"She was smiling, wasn't she?" the hoarse voice said shortly after the darkness had swallowed Eris and vanished. "And her perfume—"

The voice halted there. D hadn't stopped it. It held its own tongue.

The faint fragrance was something the girl had put on as she was preparing to meet her end. For whom had she worn it? Only D and the breeze had smelled it.

Saying nothing, D faced the spot where the darkness had disappeared. A portion of the ground had been carved out in a circle—the place where part of the darkness's circumference had encroached on the earth. At the edge of it, there gaped a hole, square and black. It was lined with stones on all sides. That was what remained of the well, since the part above ground had been consumed. And it was filled to the brim with water.

"A well, eh? You know, I don't follow this," the hoarse voice said in a solemn tone.

They knew that Curio hadn't appeared in the village alone. The water witch, Lucienne, was with him. And she could suddenly appear anywhere there was water. D hadn't seen the final instant when Curio had disappeared. Had the preacher escaped?

In any case, there was no point in remaining in the village any longer. D spun around and started walking back down the road that had taken him there.

The wind blew. All it carried was the scent of sunlight and grass and trees. There wasn't a whiff of the sweet fragrance that had graced the young woman's skin.

Thirty minutes later, hundreds of tons of rock had been effortlessly blown away, and D and the two vehicles started on their way. Greed saw them off.

As he was leaving, D asked the man, "Won't you come with us?"

Staring at him in surprise, Greed said, "You inviting someone along—now there's something! It sure is an honor. But I'm gonna stay here. See, there are a few folks who were out of town, and they'll be coming back. Somebody's gotta explain what happened here to 'em. They might decide to rebuild the village from scratch, or if they move on to another area they'll probably need some protection. Anyhow, seems like you took my vengeance for me. Thanks."

"That was—" D started to say, and then he realized he didn't know the girl's name. "It was the Weapon Master's doing."

"What?"

Knitting his brow with a vacant expression, Greed didn't even nod an acknowledgment as D got on his horse. The Hunter didn't look back after that.

"So long!"

Up in the driver's seat, Sue waved in response to Greed's words. The covered wagon and the figure of beauty slowly began to advance. After watching them until they'd disappeared down the highway, Greed walked back toward town. The sunlight had finally begun to exhibit the composure of afternoon.

The next two days of their trip were more peaceful than D had expected.

His left hand remarked, "Things are going too well. It gives me the creeps."

While D didn't reply, he did at least don a thin smile.

On the other hand, Sue and Matthew were overjoyed—well, not exactly. Inside the count's car, Sue's condition had grown worse. It was clear that the weird atmosphere of the Noble's vehicle had a negative influence on her feeble form. Fortunately, D had laid his left hand on her, and she'd quickly recovered. Still, her original frailty was unchanged, and she was forced to spend most of her time inside their wagon.

That was also the reason Matthew grew even darker and more ill tempered. Though their problems with their father had made things hard for them, under their mother the siblings had done a wonderful job of running the farm. And then along came these weird people with an old, old story—about how they would protect the three of them from something that was preordained five thousand years ago. Their journey up until now had proven that what they said was no lie. However, it seemed as if in exchange for getting the Hunter to look after him and Sue, their mother had died, and now Sue was wheezing and panting for breath. While Matthew knew it wasn't D's fault, his thoughts always came back to the same place: *If only these guys had never come at all . . .*

In the world that lay along that line of thinking, his mother was still fine, the farm was getting bigger, and Sue would be getting married in no time. Only it would be to a young guy far less attractive than Matthew, not to mention a good deal weaker and stupider. For a while, the two of them would leave the farm to enjoy married life, but the affection-starved Sue would come back to his mother and him. And the most important point in all of this: Sue's husband would possess almost no manly drive, never once bedding her.

These thoughts were Matthew's alone, and he could never speak of them to anyone. The harder they made his heart beat, the more dark anger he felt toward the trio he considered the source of their misfortunes, and now he'd begun festering inside. The decisive moment was when he'd noticed Sue admiring D. The count had been reduced to dust, and Duchess Miranda hadn't returned after going into Galleon Valley with D. Now they had no one but D on whom to rely. However, Matthew's perspective had become one of, "If only D weren't here." If he were to defend Sue on his own, surely she'd rethink her opinion of her brother and come to depend on him.

There was a very good reason why he could entertain such a startling misconception. As strange as it seemed, since the trip began, the siblings hadn't seen even one of the deadly battles D and the others had fought against the assassins. And since the inhuman nature of this conflict hadn't sunk in, the Dyalhis children didn't have a real sense of how terrifying their foes were. When they were taken from Marthias and carried off to Galleon Valley, no harm had been done to them. All of this could contribute to believing that they'd somehow manage even if D wasn't around. That was the conclusion Matthew reached when he decided to defend his sister alone. He was intoxicated by the thought of being more than just her big brother.

"We'll reach the fortress in another hour," D said to Matthew.

The boy made up his mind. Looking straight at the Hunter, he said, "Would it be a problem if we didn't go there?"

"What do you mean by that?" D asked in return.

Matthew already realized the mistake he'd made. This had nothing to do with whether you were male or female. Such beauty! As Matthew gazed, his brain became trapped in a wondrous fog and his heart began to hammer wildly. He could feel the very blood flowing through his veins. But stronger than anything was the impact of the eerie aura gusting at him. It made Matthew's blood freeze, yet his mind still melted into a daze from D's good looks.

"It's Sue—I wanna defend her. All by myself."

It was a miracle he even managed to say that much.

"I have to protect the two of you," D said. His tone was extremely soft. "That was the contract. Only the person who made it can nullify it. And she's dead."

The boy was speechless.

"But if that's what you want to do, so be it."

From the Hunter's left hand there was a cry of "Hey!"—but D squeezed it into a fist and stared off to the west. Burning the edge of a barren, rocky mountain, the sun was about to set.

"It'll be the Nobles' time soon," D said.

The remark wasn't meant to threaten Matthew. He was merely stating a fact.

Matthew shuddered. Fear of the night ran through Frontier people to the very marrow of their bones.

"I'll part company with you here. If you keep going straight, the fortress will come into view. You can turn back, camp out, or do whatever you like. I'll be back for you at dawn tomorrow." Giving a toss of his chin behind them, he continued, "I modified the car's doors so they'll follow your commands. I'll leave it with you. Use it however you like."

"We don't want the damn thing. Take it with you."

D was already in front of the covered wagon. The car silently followed behind.

"Oh, damn you!" Matthew shouted, pulling on the reins and halting the cyborg horses. He was rather desperate.

As D melted into the waves of the rapidly deepening twilight, the boy shouted at his back, "We're never gonna have to count on you again. Don't bother coming back tomorrow!"

His cries were promptly swallowed by the darkness.

II

"Things have taken a strange turn. Or should I say an intriguing turn?" a voice murmured from the air.

An invisible balloon with a light-bending coating floated a thousand feet above the ground—and in the gondola beneath it, the missionary Courbet was peering into a kind of periscope. Behind him were two of his compatriots—it was the preacher Curio and Callas the Diva.

Curio had survived. When Eris's deadly device created a small black hole, the preacher had narrowly managed to bring the tentacled tank to the well. Lucienne was concealed there, and she had aided him in his escape. However, his wounds were dire, and he lay in a bed to one side of the gondola. His throat and chest had been pierced by two of D's needles, but the strength of the bulletproof glass had prevented them from finishing him off.

Not even looking at him, Courbet said, "It would appear that the Dyalhis siblings have been abandoned by D. Or perhaps I should say they abandoned him? Well, it doesn't matter which it is. At any rate, I was worried that we were going to have a problem if they holed up in the fortress, but now a perfect opportunity has presented itself."

Courbet gave a low snort. His eyes burned with malice. He still remembered the blow he'd taken from D in the village of Marthias. Now he was hell bent for vengeance.

"They come all this way only to part company with D?" Callas said, her eyes seemingly filled with dreams as she gazed into thin air. "Not even they could be that stupid. This is some kind of trap to draw us out, right?"

"It might be. But if it were me who was an hour away from taking refuge in the fortress, I'd find that a hundred times safer than setting some weird little trap. My take on it is that they had a fight and went their separate ways."

"So, what now?"

"Our job is to dispose of the siblings. Lucienne is on the ground and has probably already captured them by now. Callas, you'll accompany me to the surface."

"Three of us to deal with two children? Isn't that overkill?"

"Lucienne will dispose of the children. Our job is to provide a little insurance."

"How so?"

"By going after D and slaying him."

For a second, the impact of this darkened Callas's lovely features, but the unholy diva soon shook it off, saying, "With pleasure. I'll most definitely accompany you."

She gave him an elegant nod. Then, she shot a quick glance over at Curio.

"Leave him be," Courbet said curtly. Not a hint of his former reverence toward the preacher remained. "Now he's worthless. He's just waiting to die; there's no point in relying on him. We'll head D off."

Thirty minutes later, the two of them entered the escape hatch and closed the door. When the sound of the door locking rang out,

Curio opened his eyes. A golden glow filled his sockets, the light swallowing his eyeballs. Getting to his feet, he looked all around as if he couldn't decide what to do.

The very existence of the central Frontier had been forgotten, and D silently advanced on his horse through a desolate landscape where the wind seemed to dine on death, and it alone was on the prowl for a meal. On either side of the road stretched dull red plains and rocky crags, and occasionally on the crest of a hill or at the foot of a mountain the apparent remains of ancient structures could be found. Lost travelers would ask where they were, and on learning this was the central Frontier, they would invariably cock their head to one side and ask if there was any such place.

It was said that the central Frontier had been wiped from human memory due to its land being nibbled away on all sides by the northern, southern, eastern, and western sectors. Topographically speaking, that was correct, but people liked another story better. They said that brutal battles had been fought here specifically to expunge the place from the memories of every living being. Over the millennia, this attempt had proved successful. Now, no one but those called elders knew of the central Frontier's existence.

Twilight had given way to a darkness that grew even thicker and heavier, as if to mire those who traveled through it. After D walked another ten paces or so, a bizarre event occurred. To either side of the road, where not so much as a single blade of grass grew, there were suddenly tiny, but brilliant, points of light. They were the flames of candles set in bronze dishes, and the rows of lights burning to either side of D were held up in the air by white marble pedestals. When the dozens, nay, hundreds of candles to either side of it appeared, the highway had started giving off a hard ring—the hooves of the cyborg steed were clomping against a marble road. And up ahead in the distance—in what had been a barren wasteland—there suddenly appeared the colossal shape of what was apparently a building.

†

"Is that the fortress?" a low voice asked. It was far closer to the building than D, in a thick forest that hadn't been there previously. The marble road ran through it.

"When was this place built? What was the purpose of this fortress?"

The first voice belonged to Courbet, while the second was that of Callas. Both of them were concealed behind a colossal tree of a variety they didn't recognize. Judging from its trunk, it seemed to have been there since ancient times.

"It's said that, fearing the wrath of Grand Duke Valcua, those three Nobles constructed it."

"What a foolish thing to do. Our lord Valcua could blow something like that away with a single breath."

It was rare for this lovely woman to compliment anyone, even if it was Valcua in this case. Surprise showed in Courbet's eyes as he stared at Callas, saying, "I wouldn't necessarily say that. The fortress incorporates the Sacred Ancestor's technology."

"Dear me!"

Though the science of the Nobility had peaked five millennia earlier, there was another type of super-advanced technology, the Sacred Ancestor's technology, which used physical laws not even the Nobility could comprehend. No one save the Sacred Ancestor understood the fundamental principles, but he permitted the Nobility, who generally understood how to use it, to incorporate his technology.

"But the Sacred Ancestor's technology was sealed away at one point, and everything that made use of it was destroyed."

Callas gave Courbet a pointed look. The missionary averted his gaze. For an instant the murderous malice that choked his brain was gone, transformed into something that was difficult to believe: grief.

"It's believed that was when the decline of the Nobility, as a race, began. Among the Nobles, many felt with the Sacred Ancestor's technology they might've staved off that decline for another ten thousand years, and they suspected that perhaps the Sacred Ancestor was trying to hasten the Nobility's deterioration."

"And what did the Sacred Ancestor do?" Callas asked intently. While they served a Noble and possessed incredible abilities, Courbet and Callas were not Nobles themselves, and they were not completely familiar with Nobility history.

"Not a blessed thing. He's not the sort of little man who needs to respond to every complaint. Also, there was no one to confront him directly. But as for what I think—hmm, I'd have to say the Sacred Ancestor chose destruction."

"And you mean to tell me our lord Valcua did nothing?"

"That's the problem!" Courbet said, his expression displaying his confusion. "When the Sacred Ancestor's technology was locked away, the great Valcua was still hale and hearty here on Earth. He should have been foremost among the protesters. Word has it you could count on both hands the number of Nobles who complained to the Sacred Ancestor . . . and it's said that our lord Valcua actually went to the Capital for an audience with the Sacred Ancestor."

Callas's lovely features were filled with more interest and curiosity than ever before.

"And?" she asked in a parched voice.

"And nothing. Less than an hour after they met, Valcua left the Sacred Ancestor's manse, returning to the Frontier that same day. To this very day, no one knows what they discussed. But I've heard that our lord Valcua—who was already terribly cruel to begin with—then went truly mad."

"Would that be around the time he had the fetuses ripped from the bellies of every pregnant woman on the Frontier and then torn to pieces? Ah, that is so like him," the diva said with a light, seductive laugh.

Courbet stared at her with a faintly disturbed expression, saying, "That fortress makes use of the Sacred Ancestor's technology. It's said to be the only use the Sacred Ancestor had no complaint about. Valcua himself says so."

"Now that you mention it—we were wiped out before this fortress was built, weren't we? Wiped out by Valcua's own hand."

Actually, the fortress had been constructed after the tragedy with Valcua had played out, as the whole purpose of the fortress was to guard against his vengeance should he come back. That point seemed to utterly elude the minds of the pair.

"At any rate, it won't do to have them get inside the fortress. Fortunately, D and the children have parted company. This is the perfect opportunity to accomplish our goal!" Looking back in the darkness at the fine, pale beauty of the diva, Courbet told her, "D will be coming soon. Give him a song."

He brought his hands up to his ears and put in earplugs.

Nodding, Callas opened her mouth without any hesitation. What came out was like a breeze that carried both the melody and the words. From the way her song behaved, it might've been more accurate to call it a fog, for it traveled through the entire forest, permeating the place. In no time, she shut her mouth and touched Courbet on the shoulder.

"Good enough," Courbet said with a nod, pulling a lumpy object from a pocket on his robe and setting it on the ground. "I've already told you what to do, right? Get going."

Bowing its little head, it dashed off down the highway with a speed that startled even Callas. It looked like a little human, complete with arms and legs.

III

D halted his steed.

Fifteen feet or so ahead on the marble road, a kind of midget ran out of the forest on the left-hand side and stopped right in the middle of the road. Less than eight inches tall, he was dressed in a long robe and trousers, and on his head he wore a brimless, boxlike hat.

"You're D, aren't you?" the midget said in an ear-piercingly shrill voice as he looked up at the Hunter. "I'm the missionary Courbet. We met once in the village of Marthias. Do you remember me?"

"Where's the real one?" D asked the midget—the fake Courbet.

"Don't talk nonsense. I am Courbet," the midget shouted, his already narrow eyes rising menacingly. "And I've come here to slay you. You'd best prepare to meet your maker."

The Hunter said nothing.

"Forget going to the fortress and fight me here. I'll crush the life from you now."

As he said this, he staggered and let out a groan. A stark needle had pierced him between the eyes, poking out through the scruff of his neck. But given his size, it seemed more like a thick stake.

Without a backward glance at the midget, who'd fallen so easily, D turned his gaze toward the forest on the other side of the road, where the figure had emerged. It was a look that could shake even stone.

There was a flash of light at his back. He'd drawn his sword. He remained just like that, motionless. His blade hung in the air.

From behind a tree, Courbet and Callas continued staring at the gorgeous young man. Courbet was shaken. In the village of Marthias, he'd taken a blow from D's sword. The pain of that, however, was child's play compared to the ghastliness of the unearthly aura that radiated in their direction from the young man. Courbet had been through hell more than once slaying many of Valcua's foes, including Nobles, but now he was so scared he was about to faint. Although he'd escaped by a hair's breadth—his power working its magic to manipulate a small hot-air balloon up in the air with great difficulty as he fled—the pain and high fever that had him screaming that night in a disgraceful fashion were due more than anything to his nightmares of a gorgeous young man staring him down with sword in hand. And now the Hunter turned that same gaze in his direction. The unearthly aura that radiated from every inch of the young man passed through a tree trunk so large it would take two men to get their arms around it. Courbet's blood froze, leaving the missionary utterly paralyzed.

"He's so . . . so fearsome," Callas said, and on the inside Courbet was violently nodding his agreement.

They heard birds chirping—not just one or two. There were hundreds or perhaps even thousands of them, all crying out in unison. All the sleeping birds had been awakened by D's unearthly aura. The trees rocked as if blown by a storm, and there was a terrific beating of wings as countless forms took to the air. Courbet and Callas could only look up awestruck, as the night sky became the stage for an enormous flock of wildfowl.

"A beautiful . . . monster," Callas moaned as if approaching climax.

Just then, a keen sensation split the night air. The birds fell noisily from the sky. At the peak of their maddened dance, they'd all been rendered unconscious with a word from D. Simultaneously, the pair in the forest let out cries of terror from the very depths of their hearts—hardly appropriate for two assassins.

D leaped from his steed's back.

"Run for it, Callas!" Courbet shouted, and he was about to run himself when above him there came one, two, three deadly bounds—and D crashed down through the tree branches with his sword held high before bringing the blade whizzing down into the missionary's head. Or so it appeared for a second, but the blade changed direction and severed the black band that had wrapped around D's chest. A vine. The vines clinging to the trunks of the stand of trees had wrapped around D's sword to stay his hand.

Watching Courbet and Callas flee, D swung his sword once again. All the vines were cut in two, and D went after the pair of assassins. But vines coiled around his waist and shoulders like serpents.

"Leave 'em to me," his left hand said.

Several of the vines restricting his right arm were seized in his left hand, instantly bursting into flame. Once more D's sword flashed out, slicing away the rest of the vines, and he advanced.

A succession of explosions rang out. Fire welled up by the roots of the trees surrounding D. It was the work of explosives set by Courbet and Callas.

To escape the tree falling toward his head, D kicked off the ground in a leap. Still hearing its rumbling thud as he touched back down,

D was engulfed by black shadows closing on the ground. This time there were three of them. If D hadn't slipped between the tree trunks with a kind of agility unthinkable even for a Noble, he would've been smashed flat.

The trees' accuracy in falling toward D was caused by something other than the force of the explosions: they had been commanded to aim at him.

Still slipping between the trees, D heard a faint song.

"She said her name was Callas, didn't she?" his left hand murmured with interest. "At this rate, those kids will be in danger, too."

To be honest, Matthew was bewildered to find himself in the forest that had suddenly sprung up around the highway. He'd parted ways with D half out of spite. But after entering the wasteland where he intended to camp, the world had undergone a transformation in less than thirty minutes.

"What's going on, Matt?" Sue asked after leaving the wagon, unable to conceal her fear at the change in their environment.

Both of them were down on the ground now. Matthew was just lighting the chemical fuel.

"I don't know. That jerk D's probably pulling something."

"Don't blame this on him!" Sue shouted, making Matthew stare at her. "I can't believe you got rid of D while I was asleep. What on earth were you thinking?"

"Don't get all hot under the collar. I told you not to worry. I'll keep you safe for sure."

"And how are you supposed to do that all alone, Matt? That great big count and Ms. Miranda were both taken out! The people after us are that tough; what good will you be against them? You've gotta wake up and face the facts!"

Matthew found Sue's shouts to be terrifyingly logical. There was no point in arguing it. At a time like this, his only resort was to adopt an illogical approach.

"Is that any way to talk to me, you little idiot? In all these years, have I ever once failed to keep you safe? That time in town when ten punks were giving you trouble, or when the two-headed dog attacked the farm, I always protected you. Show a little gratitude! Have some faith in me!"

"This time it's different, Matt!" Sue exclaimed, her body shaking. "The person after us is a Greater Noble who's come back after five thousand years. Face the facts. For starters, Matt, for someone who talks as big as you do, you couldn't even save Mom, could you?"

"Shut up!"

Sue saw her brother's hand swing suddenly. There was a dull impact on her left cheek that left her senses reeling. The next thing she knew, she was lying on the ground. Her back felt cold.

Matthew's face was right in front of her. His expression made him look like a completely different person. It chilled her all over.

"Matthew—get off of me! You're so heavy."

Though she sensed something bad was about to happen, she tried to hide it behind a smile. She moved her hand to try and push him away, but he pinned her wrists against the ground.

"I'm gonna protect you," he said. The voice that came out of her brother's mouth was the same as always.

"Okay. I get it already! You can get off me now. You weigh a ton, you know. A ton!"

Suddenly her lips were sealed. Her whole body trembled. More than from fear, she shook with horror. She couldn't believe what was happening.

"Matthew . . ."

Struggling wildly, she shouted at him to stop. Her left hand came free—but as soon as she lifted it, her left breast was squeezed.

"Stop it!" she screamed. "Have you lost your mind?"

With her free hand she grabbed Matthew's hair and jerked it to one side. At the same time, she twisted her body. Stunned, Matthew toppled over.

Getting up, Sue ran to the road. Someone might pass by. Most importantly, that was the road D was taking.

"Sue, wait! Sue!" a voice that resembled that of her older brother called out. But it wasn't her brother. It was another being entirely.

Between the trees she could see the marble road. Wiping her sweat off, Sue put her strength into her legs.

Suddenly, an upside-down female face appeared before her.

Her scream caught in her throat. She was positive the woman had appeared from her own forehead.

Executing an easy flip, the woman who landed in front of Sue didn't have a face the girl recognized.

"Who . . . who are you?" the girl asked, tongue tied. Although she didn't know the woman's name, she knew what she was.

"I am Lucienne," the lovely woman with one eye said. The white dress she wore displayed every line of her body. It was soaked with water. No, actually it was—

"Your sweat!" Lucienne said, spreading her arms. "Water is my world, my path, my gateway. As long as there's water around, you can never escape me."

Smirking and laughing disturbingly, she said, "Welcome to my world!"

Her pale hand reached out and grabbed Sue's right wrist. It felt just like water.

The girl tried to jump away, but her legs wouldn't move.

"Oh, doesn't that feel good?" Lucienne said, and as she spoke she dissolved.

She transformed into a mass of water in human form. Starting with Sue's wrist, the mass enveloped her entire body. Though Sue struggled desperately to break through the liquid membrane, her fingers merely sank into it, vainly clawing at the fluid. She gasped for breath. And inhaled. Water flowed in through her mouth and nostrils. She coughed. And as she did so, more water entered. Sue was fated to drown right there, on the ground. Suddenly, there was darkness before her eyes.

Help me! She intended to say the words aloud, but she couldn't speak. *Save me, Mom . . . D . . .*

Unexpectedly, the water in her stomach and lungs reversed direction. As she heard the feverish hiss of steam, Sue fell backward. But powerful arms caught her.

"Matt?" she cried out before coughing. Water vapor stroked Sue's face.

In his right hand, Matthew gripped a burning log from their campfire. The instant he'd seen that watery membrane engulfing Sue, he'd figured out exactly what was happening and shoved the fire into the liquid—into Lucienne's body!

The water pulled away from Sue and spread over the ground, swiftly taking on the form of Lucienne. Steam rose from her back.

"I wanted to take care of you separately," Lucienne said, letting her expression fade before her lips twisted into a fresh smirk. "But I shall kill the two of you together now. A crude flame like that won't work against me again."

"Shut up, you freak!" Matthew yelled, taking a step forward and thrusting his torch out before him.

Lucienne's right hand seized the blazing tip. There was a fierce explosion of steam, and the fire was extinguished.

Lucienne raised her right hand. It didn't have any fingers—undoubtedly they'd been reduced to the water vapor that drifted around. Lucienne then waved the same hand. Once again she had her fingers.

Matthew stood in front of Sue, shielding her. Sweat ran down his face.

"Such a lovely face," the water witch said, breaking into a grin.

Lamoa Fortress

CHAPTER 6

I

D had ducked down on the other side of the enormous tree.
A pale figure wafted into view—the fiendish diva Callas. On
hearing the song, even the stands of trees in this forest had turned
into D's enemies.

"Have you heard my song, O beauteous one?" Callas called out
to him. Even as she did so, the song flowed from her mouth. "Now
that things have gone this far, it's a matter of friends and foes. On
the course we're following, there's but one choice to be made: kill
or be killed. Please hear me out. I shall give you an easy death."

"I'll help you," said another figure, who appeared from behind a
stand of trees to take his place beside Callas. It was Courbet.

"Don't listen only to Callas's song," he continued, "but hear my
words, too. You're to carve out your own heart right here and now.
If you do that, our god will be most pleased. Aaaah . . ."

The missionary groaned and staggered at the end of this demand,
due to the dagger that had been planted in his back. Its hilt was set
with crimson jewels.

"What are you doing . . . Callas?"

"You have some nerve, trying to interfere with me," the singer
said coolly. "My song was going to gently rap on the door to the
hereafter, but then you told him to do something as revolting as

tearing out his own heart. I'll thank you to drop dead now."

And as she said this, the woman walked over to the reeling Courbet, pulled the dagger out of his back, and then drove it straight through his heart.

Ignoring Courbet as he fell limply to the ground, Callas laid one hand against her chest and took a deep breath. A wooden needle had just pierced the base of her throat. Staggering without making a sound, the diva saw the figure in black rising effortlessly from the tangle of fallen trees. She tried to shout something, but no voice came out.

"I can hear neither your song nor the missionary's words," said D.

"Why . . . why do this to me? I said . . . I would give you . . . an easy death . . ."

Reeling all the while, Callas watched in amazement as D drew closer without making a sound. A part of her was delighted.

A second later, D leaped to the right.

Flames were welling up in the forest. Napalm flames mowed through the stand of trees with their initial blast, then set to burning everything down to the core.

Even when Lucienne reached for him, Matthew didn't move. Her hand touched his face.

"You're wet," the water witch said. "I'll start with you."

But she made a sound like vomiting and doubled over. As her spine curved like a shrimp's, something resembling a log went through her stomach, piercing her through her back. It was a tremendously long and thick steel spear.

Clutching the spear with both hands, Lucienne raised her head. The expression that formed on her face said she saw something she shouldn't have seen.

"You . . . turned to dust . . ."

"For dust thou art, and unto dust shalt thou return," a voice called out beyond the shaft of the spear.

Matthew and Sue turned at the same time and shouted.

Illuminated by the flames to the sides of the highway was an enormous figure standing ten feet tall.

"Count Braujou!"

The giant who stood there was indeed Count Braujou. But how could he suddenly appear here when he'd been reduced to dust after his defeat by Curio in their battle at Marthias?

"Surprised?" the giant asked with a mocking grin. He seemed so amused he could barely stand it. "You're talking to a man who defeated Valcua. Did you think I'd die so easily from the spell of one of his worthless little underlings? So long as my dust and blood remain, I can be revived time and again. The dust returned to my car on its own, where it soaked in my stored blood. Do you understand now? Then you can die with an untroubled mind."

He pushed the spear. It penetrated Lucienne's body without meeting any resistance, but the water witch's hands clawed at the air as she bent backward.

"Going to turn into water to make your escape? You can't. You can't fight the energy my spear contains. This spear was meant to slay Valcua, and it's invested with the power of the Sacred Ancestor."

Lucienne's body fell apart. The stain that spread across the black soil was quickly absorbed. The count tossed a flaming lump on top of it. The flames spread out more than six feet in diameter, illuminating the trio. Sue thought she could hear horrific screams beneath the blazing flames, and she covered her ears.

"She's dead, isn't she?" Sue inquired.

"I don't know. That'll depend on the chemical fuel you provided," the count said, referring to the fiery lump he'd thrown.

"You've been with us all along, haven't you?" said Matthew.

"Yes."

When he smiled, it made a deep impression on Sue. Humans had made a Noble smile. And then something dawned on her.

"The reason Mr. D left was because he knew you were with us, wasn't it?"

Once again the enormous face broke into a grin, but the giant didn't reply.

Taking her brother's hand, Sue said, "Matt, let's go to the fortress."

Though she still harbored ill will toward her brother, she didn't show it. But she was planning to avoid being left alone with him tonight.

"Well, let's go to the fortress. Your beloved D should be waiting there on pins and needles," the count said, laying a gigantic hand on the girl's shoulder. It was incredibly soft and his touch was quite gentle, but Sue was in no position to notice.

"Wh-wh-what do you mean by that?" the girl sputtered.

"Dear me, you're turning red. Looks like I'm right on the mark. You must forgive me, but after spending three days with a girl your age, I can tell in a flash whether she likes a man or not."

"That's just . . . It's not like I . . ."

As Sue flushed crimson to her very ears, the count gazed at her with a mysterious look in his eyes. It was the way a father might look at his daughter.

"Ah, it's a wondrous thing. When it comes to love and infatuation, there's no difference between Nobles and humans, is there?"

Sue looked up at the count, her curiosity piqued by the way his tone rose at the end of that remark. Sue had a delicate temperament. She recalled how the song she'd sung without thinking had prompted the count to ask her to sing again.

"Do you have women like that?"

Sue wasn't asking about the count personally, but rather about the Nobility as a whole. However, a stunned sort of thoughtfulness spread across the count's face, and with a slight shrug he put the long spear over his shoulder and turned around.

"Shall we return to the wagon and get going? Since the road's here, the fortress should be back as well."

†

Plowing through the night air, the wagon and car raced along. Up in the driver's seat, the count lashed away with the whip, while the siblings sat inside the covered wagon.

To avoid looking at Matthew, Sue was gazing out a window at the expanse of marble road and the flames that illuminated it, sighing with heartfelt emotion.

For his part, Matthew said nothing to his sister and just lay on his bed. The count's reappearance and the sight of him in battle had left the boy dumbfounded. The black beast that had longed for his sister had vanished. But the count had said something awful. Sue knew it, too. That's why they couldn't talk about it. Even a third party like the count could see that his sister was in love with D. And Sue's reaction at the time had made her true feelings clear. Though it frightened him, Matthew had to acknowledge that the black beast that had vanished from his heart might rear its head again. And soon.

The shaking of the wagon began to slow.

Above the covered portion, the count's voice resounded as he said, "We've arrived. Come out."

Soon the wagon halted, and when the pair looked out over the driver's seat, they saw an enormous, towering structure surrounded by countless lights. Although it looked to be made of stone, its surface had the sheen of steel, and numerous corridors connected massive edifices that appeared to be one hundred fifty or two hundred feet high. Also visible were shrinelike buildings surrounded by columns, lights burning brightly in their windows. All these structures were enclosed by the ramparts that towered before the trio. Over one hundred feet high, the ramparts had a colossal gate carved into them, and between it and the group lay a wide moat that appeared to be quite deep. Its black waters reflected the lamplight.

It was so strangely beautiful it took Sue's breath away, but then she saw something that left her even more in need of breath.

By the edge of the moat in the spot where one would cross over to the gates, a young man astride a black horse was gazing at her. His features were so handsome as to leave a person dazed instead of merely trembling, and though he wasn't smiling in the least, Sue could feel something hot welling up in her heart and tears rolling down her cheeks.

Taking the reins in hand, the count guided the two vehicles over to D.

"I see we've kept you waiting," he said to the Hunter in black.

"Send out the bridge," D said. Though he'd been involved in deadly combat, he showed no hint of fatigue.

"There was quite a lot of noise, wasn't there?" the count said as he turned toward the gates.

"It came from the sky. Probably a dirigible."

"Hmm—we'll discuss that later. Open the gates!" the count said, raising his massive right arm.

The gates slowly opened to either side, and a long, black bridge stretched from the opening.

"You go first—no one would have a problem with that. Not even Miranda."

D advanced on his black steed onto the bridge. He didn't seem conscious of what the count had said. It was simply easiest to have whoever was closest go first—that's all there was to it. He didn't look back again as he rode across the long bridge, and watching him from behind, Sue thought he presented a terribly heartbreaking sight.

II

Thirty minutes had passed since the girl had settled in a luxurious room. Though they referred to this as a fortress, it was more like an extravagant palace, and she had to wonder how lavish the Noble palaces in the Capital could be. Sue tried to picture it, but she didn't have much luck.

Being separated from Matthew had allayed one of her fears, but only for the time being. Trying not to think about what they'd do next, Sue gazed out through the window. Her heart leaped in her chest. Just below, the Hunter stood at the edge of a pathway, his black garb swaying in the wind. Lights danced in the sconces on the wall to one side of him. Though there was apparently considerable wind, the tiny flames swayed but didn't go out, saving the figure in black from the darkness only to allow it to swallow him again.

What could that gorgeous man be thinking about? Sue thought as she slipped into a sweet fantasy. In it, he was thinking about her.

Another, far larger, form came over to D, shattering Sue's fantasy. It was the count.

Sue stepped away from the window—her mother hadn't raised her to eavesdrop on other people's conversations. Still, the pounding in her chest didn't subside. She thought she had a good understanding of her situation, yet she was happy to embrace these thoughts that made her heart grow feverish.

There's no difference between humans and Nobles, is there?

That remark sliced right through her.

"At any rate, there are no foes in the skies," the count said to D. "I've dispatched recon planes to check a sixty-mile radius. We'll have to assume they've already landed somewhere."

"Some assassins still remain," D replied.

The count nodded at this. Of the pair that attacked D, Courbet was probably finished, but the chances that Callas survived were quite high. Though she'd taken one of D's needles through the throat, she was still an assassin who'd earned a place as one of Valcua's seven. And they hadn't yet confirmed the death of the water witch, who'd been impaled by the count.

"But not even he can get into Lamoa Fortress. Sensors utilizing the very best of the Sacred Ancestor's technology monitor everything for six miles around the area, on the surface, in the air, and even underground, every second of the day. Not even a suspicious cloud of gas could slip by them."

"Do you mean to tell me Valcua never had anything to do with the Sacred Ancestor's technology?"

"Of course not. It was the Sacred Ancestor's technology that allowed us to maintain our way of life as the Nobility. And Grand Duke Valcua—the Ultimate Noble—was no exception. However, the instant the fruits of the technology he was given incurred the Sacred Ancestor's wrath, they were rendered inoperative. If he came back to life a hundred times, he'd still never be able to do anything against this fortress. What do you say to leaving the children here while the two of us go off to slay Valcua?"

"Fine," D said.

"Excellent!" the count exclaimed, his gigantic face beaming with delight.

Even a Greater Noble like him found this young man, who was so exquisite he made the moon seem dull by comparison, to be an awfully enigmatic being. Over the span of five millennia, the count had fought more than a few Hunters, easily dispatching all of them. Some of them had even been dhampirs. However, he would go so far as to describe this young man as some highly evolved freak of that species. First, there was his beauty. Next, there was the air that hung about him and frightened even the count—his unearthly aura, as it were. For a fleeting moment, he was gripped by a certain question. The count knew of only one person with an air anywhere near it. But that was impossible. To be honest, in the days that had passed since he first met D, this question and its dismissal had been replayed thousands, if not tens of thousands, of times.

The count gazed at D, who kept his eyes focused on the darkness. The Nobleman then rather uncharacteristically took a deep breath, firming his resolve.

"There's something I'd like to ask you."

D didn't move a muscle. He acted as if he didn't have the slightest bit of interest.

Regardless, the count said to him, "Are you the Sacred Ancestor's—"

The last word was drowned out by a warning klaxon.

Focusing on a point in the air, the count asked, "What is it?"

A machine's voice rang through his head, saying, "A flying object is approaching from the west. Altitude of fifty thousand feet, speed of one hundred twenty-five miles per hour. It's believed to be a dirigible."

"It'll get here in thirty minutes, then. Shoot it down!" he commanded. "I suppose that would be the assassins from the sky that you mentioned. Well, just watch. I'll take them down with one missile," he then told D with complete confidence.

But it seemed Count Braujou was too quick in making his assertion.

The missile was launched. It scored a direct hit. Far in the darkness, a flower of blue fire blossomed. The dirigible didn't come down, but rather kept closing at the same determined pace. Crimson beams of light ripped through the night sky to strike the airship—a mad dance of laser beams and particle beams. Not even blasts of energy that could penetrate three hundred feet of solid rock in an instant could impede the dirigible's advance.

Each and every successive tack he took proved ineffective, and despite the somber face the count wore as he stared at the monitors in the combat-operations center in the top floor of the fortress, his target was still ready to enter the fortress's air space.

"Given the circumstances, I'll have to board that ship," the count said, swinging the long spear he held.

But behind him, D said, "Let them do as they like."

Not knowing the Hunter had arrived, the Nobleman spun around.

"The opposition is using the Sacred Ancestor's technology too," D continued. "Instead of keeping up these useless attacks, it would be better to finish them off inside."

"You intend to let the enemy enter this fortress? If I were to put the barriers up, no one could ever get in!"

"And in return, we'd have a hard time getting out. If you let things continue this way, Valcua himself might step in. You can't expose those two kids to unnecessary danger."

"You have a point there," the count conceded, folding his arms and nodding his head. "The interior of the fortress is fully prepared to meet any attack. There's no need to rely on any machines. I'll run every last one of them through with my spear."

D's eyes ran across the figures that surrounded them. They were all colossal androids.

"The enemy should come after us, as well. I think I'll give them a taste of their own medicine."

Sharp fangs poked from Braujou's grinning lips. He was truly a Noble.

On reaching the center of the fortress's property, the dirigible rapidly began to shrink as its gas was let out. Losing its shape, the three-hundred-foot dirigible resembled a weird, flying creature as it became a mess of wrinkles and slowly came down from the sky.

"What silly bastards—imagine letting all the air out to make your descent. As soon as I find them, I shall strike them dead."

The remains of the dirigible were in front of a shrine—barely touching the great staircase as it lay on the ground—and on verifying its arrival, the count headed to the operations center with long spear in hand. As he walked down the corridor toward the elevator, the count realized that D wasn't in the operations center.

"Our opponent's probably that preacher man," the Hunter's left hand said, its voice flowing in the wind.

D was moving down a long corridor. Though to all appearances it was made of stone, the floor raced along at considerable speed.

If someone wished to go in a different direction, he could get on a strip running that way at an intersection in the corridors.

"That guy can even get computers to follow his sermons. That'd turn a human into an assassin with a single word. Plus, we have cause for concern that he's got a Sigma terminal in him. If things keep going this way, he could take over the whole fortress without spilling a drop of blood. Next thing you know, everybody around you could be the enemy. You're all set with your earplugs, right?"

The plugs in D's ears had apparently proved effective against Callas's song and Courbet's words. They'd probably work against Curio's sermons as well. However, Curio was possessed by Sigma's "terminal." A pair of earplugs might not do much against something with the power to raise the dead.

"If it splits from Curio, we'll be facing two foes. Hmph! That sure doesn't sound like fun."

D didn't reply.

A dozen minutes had already passed since he'd left the combat-operations center. Where was he headed?

After another five minutes or so, his destination became clear. The moving corridor halted in front of a massive doorway. Though the surface of the doors had the smooth sheen of obsidian, the wall around them was carved to depict bizarre creatures and worlds, which only served to emphasize the inorganic nature of the doorway and the weirdness of whatever lay beyond it.

"What are you doing?" Count Braujou inquired, his voice falling from the ceiling. "That's the heart of the fortress. It's the room for the antiproton computer. Not even you can get in there."

"Then open it for me," D replied curtly.

"Regretfully, that's not something I can do alone. The three of us who constructed this fortress must use three keys simultaneously; otherwise, those doors won't open. Gaskell has been destroyed, and Miranda's whereabouts are unknown. I'm afraid I can't do anything for you."

"You're completely useless," the Hunter's left hand cursed.

"Did you say something?"

Without answering the count, D stepped forward.

"Don't!" Braujou shouted, his tone laced with obvious fear.

His words were overlaid with the synthesized voice of a machine that said, "Three keys are required to pass through this gate. Please present them. If you advance without presenting them, you will be deemed an intruder and eliminated."

Undoubtedly there were already unseen weapons taking aim at D.

A cry of surprise rang out. D had moved in front of the doors without incident.

"Those defensive systems incorporate the Sacred Ancestor's technology. It's impossible to shut them down. D, who in the world are you?"

Of course, there was no reply.

D put his left hand against the surface of the doors.

The eyes of the unseen count were focused on the black-garbed, beautiful figure.

Ten seconds . . .

Twenty seconds . . .

"W-what in the world?" the Greater Noble exclaimed in unmistakable astonishment.

Look. The huge doors safeguarded by the power of the Sacred Ancestor had begun to swing open to either side without a sound.

III

Shoulders squared, Count Braujou advanced down the spacious corridor. Waves of anger swept across his face. Not only had the dirigible been allowed to invade the fortress's air space, but its crew had also snuck into the structure—even though sensors near the landing point and android sentries testified to seeing no one at all. On checking their memory banks, he'd found data on the trespasser. An intruder in a long, vermilion robe had descended alone from the dirigible when it invaded their air space. On one side of the square, a flight belt with an invisibility device had also been discovered.

The way things were going, it was quite possible every machine in the fortress might be turned against them. The fortress made use of the very best technology, but its greatest strength now posed the biggest threat to those it was intended to protect.

Up ahead in the deserted corridor, a turn came into view. From the left side a figure stepped out—one of the android sentries. Its chest and each arm were equipped with heat cannons. While it verified the count's identity, a light on its chest blinked for a second, but apparently the check revealed nothing out of the ordinary and the sentry passed by the Nobleman's side.

Several seconds later, every inch of the count was subjected to a six-hundred-thousand-degree shower. Without time to cry out, the count was reduced to ash that spread across the floor.

Behind him, the same android sentry he'd passed lowered the heat cannons on both arms. Had it heard one of Curio's sermons, been possessed by Sigma's terminal, or both? Its electronic brain already under the enemy's sway, the android had reduced the Greater Noble to ash with mind-boggling ease.

Once its chest sensors had confirmed the count's destruction, the android quietly changed direction. Up ahead of it stood a tremendous figure. The sentry's enslaved electronic brain gave rise to a faint pulse of surprise. Faster than it could trigger its heat cannons, it found its chest pierced by a long spear, and sparks shot from the machine in its death throes.

"What a waste," the count muttered. The android he'd incinerated had been a carbon copy of him, covered in artificial skin, with inner workings that duplicated his internal organs. Even if the security android's sensors had scanned the inside of the body, it couldn't have told the difference between the count and one of its fellow androids. The waste to which the count referred was the enormous cost involved in developing such androids.

Staring intently at the android sentry that now lay on the ground with black smoke pouring out, the count brought one hand to his chin and arched his heavy eyebrows.

"For every one you find, there could be a hundred more. How far has the contamination spread? It looks like D had the right idea."

A chime sounded. It echoed in Sue's ear like the peals of a golden bell.

Going over to the door, she asked, "Who is it?"

Sue knew nothing of the deadly conflict beyond her door.

"It's me," came the reply in Count Braujou's voice.

Undoing the lock, Sue opened the door. The huge count ducked his head to enter.

"There's been a bit of trouble," he said. "I'm sorry, but would you please come with me? I'll transfer you to D's location."

"Oh?" Sue exclaimed. Her expression was one of joy rather than terror.

As the giant looked at her rather intently, a smile came to his lips. "We must leave right away."

"Okay."

First the count and then Sue stepped through the doorway. Matthew was waiting outside.

"Both of you, stay together. Come with me."

D was standing in a white light. Both hands were busily pounding the surface of a white, crystal-like device that jutted from the floor. The device was a control panel, and its controls also resembled crystals—probably due to the tastes of its designer.

D had already been working on the panel for more than thirty minutes. There was no sign of a computer before him. All that filled this room of unknown vastness was countless lights—a collection of glowing points. All told, there must've been more than a trillion of them. The glowing points were visible, but if someone were to measure their speed, she would've found them to be traveling in excess of two hundred miles per second. Here was a substance faster than light.

The closer an object came to the speed of light, the more its mass increased, becoming nearly infinite as it approached the speed of light. It was for this reason that objects didn't exceed the speed of light, but the transmission medium this antiproton computer currently used was similar to tachyons, with their negative mass.

"Its computational speeds are even faster than Sigma's. As a result, it should be able to give itself the order to self-destruct before it could be told to deny access, destroy, or eliminate anything. That Sigma sure is a tricky one. The protection is nearly perfect. Can't tachyons break through it?" the left hand said, its tone hard.

"There are two terminals sent by Sigma," D said. "One is in another location."

"Hmm."

"The other is close by."

"I see—what?" D's nonchalant tone left the hoarse voice badly rattled. "W-where is it?"

"Right there," D said, looking over his shoulder.

The entrance was out there somewhere among the lights. In the spot where he thought it'd been, there stood a gigantic figure.

"That's the count."

"Did you let him in?" D inquired without turning all the way around. Both his hands played busily across the crystals.

"What do you want?"

"What are you doing?" asked the count.

"Searching for the invaders. I found one of them."

"Really?"

"Sigma has come after this computer, in a way that didn't require any keys to get in."

Two wills intent on dealing death barreled forward. The count's long spear pierced D through the back and out again through the chest, but then the Hunter suddenly vanished, and the Nobleman realized it'd only been an afterimage. D charged in for a backhanded slash of his blade—cutting the count open from the crotch to just below the right nipple with a single stroke.

Tinged by blue sparks and electromagnetic waves, the giant collapsed. His whole body shuddered in a death rattle most unbecoming a machine. A split second before the light faded from his eyes, a blinding sphere appeared at the edge of the electromagnetic waves, bouncing off the floor and walls repeatedly before disappearing.

D turned around.

The long spear was sticking out of the control panel.

"Can you fix it?" the Hunter asked.

"I don't know—but I'll give it a shot. Hurry up and get going."

Now that the androids that looked like the count were under the enemy's control, D and Braujou should have been worried about Sue and Matthew. As simple country folk, the siblings wouldn't have suspected their rescuer was an impostor.

Grabbing the long spear and pulling it out in a single, fluid motion, D stuck out his left hand. There was a gleam of white light, and then the Hunter's left hand flew toward the control panel as if it possessed a will of its own. Now it would be the one to challenge Sigma.

After going outside, D immediately shut his eyes. He seemed to be focusing his consciousness. In less than a second, his eyes opened again and he said, "Put me through to Sue and Matthew's rooms."

Immediately a reply rang out in his brain.

"They're not in."

"Where are they?"

"That's not clear."

"Someone took them out of there—find out who."

"It was Count Braujou."

Without warning, a powerful voice interrupted. It was imbued with such strength that it probably would've seared the average human brain.

"I most certainly did not take them anywhere!"

Nothing from the Hunter.

"I don't think it's Curio. He'd probably kill them right away. D, did you suspect as much when you wanted to let the crew of the dirigible inside?"

"How many androids are wearing your face?"

"Five—one of which has been destroyed."

"Make that two, including the one I got. Destroy the other three as soon as you find them."

"That's such a waste."

"There's a good chance our foe is possessing Curio. If it weren't him, there's no way all your sensors could be fooled. Do you have any sensors that won't fall under his spell?"

The count fell into silence.

"In that case, we'll have to make some. Where's the workshop?"

"I'll guide you there. Just follow my voice."

The stone floor began to carry D off at an incredible speed.

At just about that time, Sue and Matthew were in a strange and imposing place. The seemingly endless space was filled with weapons and other armaments both large and small. Laser guns, particle cannons, dimensional-vortex generators, gravity-field controllers, antiproton grenades, atomic-powered tanks, single-seater jet helicopters—each and every weapon was fully charged and loaded for combat. Here they waited, ready to go into battle with the press of a single button.

The siblings had realized this count was a fake, because when he led them there, it wasn't D that awaited them, but rather a man in a long, vermilion robe who looked half-dead.

"I'm called Curio," he said to the frozen pair by way of introduction, and then he appended a strange remark. "At least, I was. At present, this body serves Sigma."

"Are you one of Valcua's . . . ," Matthew asked, pointing a trembling finger at Curio.

"That's correct. But you two are most fortunate. My new master has no interest in your lives. Rather, it seeks D."

"D? What do you mean by that?" Sue asked, leaning forward in spite of herself. Though Matthew threw her a harsh look, Sue didn't notice.

"You don't know anything about it? Ah, I suppose you wouldn't. Any man who wasted time talking about his own problems wouldn't be cut out for hunting the Nobility. That's part of what makes him such a problem."

"If you don't want anything from us, let us go!" Matthew shouted.

"I can't do that. I have a use for you . . . and now I'll put you to it. Miss, you'll get to see D. I hope you appreciate that."

On seeing herself reflected in the cloudy, dead eyes of the one in the hooded robe, Sue felt a coldness rising from her feet and filling her body.

Virtual Assassin

CHAPTER 7

I

S ue instinctively tried to escape, but Curio's hand caught hold of her elbow. She was numbed to her very brain.

Seeing his younger sister buckle at the knees and fall, Matthew went crazy. He dove head first at Curio's waist. The robed figure was effortlessly bowled over. Carried by his momentum, Matthew went another five or six steps before he could stop himself.

Curio lay on the floor. Matthew went pale. When he'd struck the preacher, he hadn't felt any signs of life from Curio.

"That's just an empty shell, Matt," Sue's voice remarked. For some reason, Matthew didn't turn and look. "Now I've taken his place."

"Sue?"

"He died some time ago from D's needles, you see. But if I enter him again, he'll come back to life. Until then, I'll just store him here."

Matthew turned and looked.

Sue was on her feet. His sister was as bright, frail, and brave as always. However, there was something different about her.

"Well, I'm off, Matt," Sue said with a respectful bow.

"W-where are you going?" her brother stammered.

"To see the man I love. But you must've known that."

"Don't!"

Sue was going to see D. Matthew jumped toward her. It was the only thing he could think to do.

"See you, Matt. Just wait here like a good boy. God, how my body burns!"

Matthew heard a vile stream of verbal abuse. He didn't even realize it was coming from him. Shouting at Sue to stop, he wrapped his arms around her. Sue turned in his arms—but he didn't have time to think before a fierce blow exploded against his right jaw, sending him flying. By the time his shoulder hit the floor, he was already unconscious.

Giving her sprawled-out older brother a look of surpassing cruelty, Sue grinned.

"I'll tell you all about it later. You'll get to hear how the little sister you want to bed dallied with the man she loves."

"Okay, the repairs are complete—well, not really, but there's no more time. Here we go!"

Up on the control panel, the disembodied left hand made a fist. What's more, the hand then struck the fist. In terms of physics, the action bordered on impossibility.

"Oh!" it exclaimed in surprise. "Sigma, you sly bastard! Sent another terminal after us, did you? Damn! I was so busy with the repairs I couldn't respond. Watch yourself, D. Sigma, now you have to deal with me!"

At that very moment, a tremendous electrical blast struck the left hand, blowing it off the panel. Falling to the floor, the hand gave off black smoke.

"Son of a bitch!" the left hand cursed, standing on its fingers and starting back toward the controls.

It was a surreal sight . . . although a severed hand that could curse was in itself rather surreal.

†

Nearby, the ground was shaking. Something massive was approaching. She thought about greeting it with a song, but neither her body nor her throat would respond. The rumbling of the ground soon halted, and she sensed something enormous peering down at her.

Someone called out her name.

"Callas."

Her closed eyelids gradually began to open.

"That's the voice of . . . ," she began. Her voice was hoarse, but at least she could speak. "Valcua, milord!"

"Indeed. It is I, Valcua," the voice said. "But I am not alone. Seurat is here as well."

"That's so . . ."

Something touched her brow. She thought it might be a hand. However, it was simply part of a bottomless abyss.

"Rest now," the voice said gently. "Is that Courbet over there? Hmm. He's burned to a cinder, but it was the wound to his back that proved fatal. That was your doing, wasn't it?"

The diva said nothing.

"Have you fallen for D, for his beauty? Don't try to hide it. It's perfectly understandable."

His tone could be described as tranquil; there was even a certain kindness to it. And yet, Callas couldn't stem the fear and anxiety welling up in her heart.

"I have an interest in him as well," the voice continued. "For an ordinary Hunter, he's far too strong. He may prove to be the toughest opponent I've ever battled. However, he's ultimately nothing but a filthy half-breed. I will triumph in the end."

Something thick and incredibly dense wrapped around Callas's body, nearly suffocating her. She knew what it was: Valcua's mind.

"You'll have to die for the time being, Callas and Courbet," the voice of the Ultimate Noble informed them. "But you will live again, as new assassins for Valcua. In the meantime, I'll teach those inside the fortress to fear me."

Darkness flooded Callas's brain.

Not fifteen minutes after D had entered the workshop, he came out again. It didn't seem conceivable he'd assembled a sensor that wouldn't obey Curio's commands in such a short time. D saw a small figure coming down the corridor.

"D! D!" Sue cried, moving faster now. She clung to the Hunter for all she was worth. "I was so scared. I ran away. But my brother is still down there!"

"Who took you?"

"The count. He—he was possessed!"

"How did you escape?"

"I looked for an opportunity. I pretended I'd fainted, and the count and Curio both left."

"What about your brother?"

"They put us in separate rooms. I wonder if they're going to hurt him now because I ran off," Sue said, tears glistening in her eyes.

"Where was this?"

"In this underground . . . ," Sue began, but then she averted her face. Pink tinged her cheeks. "I can't say it. Please, come with me."

"You should stay here."

"I don't want to. Besides, what if the count comes around again— or what if whatever was possessing him jumped over to someone else?"

"Then stick close to me."

Sue's face was aglow with joy. Clinging to the Hunter's left arm, she replied, "I sure will!"

After saying this, she looked down and smiled. It was the sort of smirk that showed just how evil a human being could be.

Putting Sue on his back, D ran down the corridor.

"This is it," Sue told him when they came to a blue door.

D pushed against it. It opened easily.

A single glance made it clear this was a changing room. Metal baskets rested in cubbyholes in the walls. D's nose caught the scent of fragrant herbs—clearly the air here had aphrodisiacs mixed into it. That might've had something to do with why Sue wouldn't say where she had been earlier.

"Over there," Sue said, pointing straight ahead.

Set in the marble wall was a bronze door. Nobles often elected to use metal with a nice patina.

D opened the door. He didn't set Sue down. The fragrance became thick; that of the changing room couldn't begin to compare.

"My brother should be in here," Sue said, her voice like that of a full-grown woman.

II

The purpose of this room flashed into D's brain. A glance at the fortress blueprints he'd borrowed from the count had allowed him to memorize the layout completely.

An ordinary person would've called this a bathroom. However, the person it was intended for was no ordinary being. On the marble floor rested a bathtub filled to the rim with green liquid. In consideration of those who would be using this place, there were no mirrors.

Swaying clouds of steam swirled around D, grew more substantial, and began to take on human form. Then beautiful women were standing there, stark naked and alluring. If D's left hand had been present, it might've snidely remarked, *So, this is how ol' Braujou likes 'em?*

The liquid in the tub also bubbled mysteriously, kneading itself like dough to form the ample breasts, thighs, and face of a gorgeous woman. In light of the Nobility's aversion to water, the fluid was not bath water, but rather some sort of gelatinous substance with the ability to take on different shapes. Here, in this one room in the fortress, Count Braujou undoubtedly had enjoyed his privileges as one of the stronghold's creators.

Pale arms entwined D's neck, waist, and shoulders, while thighs wrapped around him—the steam women. D stood there without saying a word.

Oh, they'll wring you out like a sponge! his left hand probably would've said.

But a heartbeat later, the pale women moved away from D, returning to the steam from whence they'd come.

On D's back, the dazed Sue could be heard murmuring, "You know . . . I think I understand. You're so beautiful they were embarrassed to be around you. What a man . . ."

"Where's Matthew?"

As D asked this, Sue's arm wrapped around his neck. Sensuous and tinged with a faint red, it most definitely wasn't the arm of a fourteen-year-old girl.

"What do I care about him?" Sue said right by D's ear, a seductive female ring to her voice. "Right now, he's trembling in the armory. But enough about him. What do you think of me?"

Pale legs wrapped around D's torso. The legs of a grown woman.

"This bathroom has the most wonderful effect! It can turn anyone, from a little girl to a hundred-year-old crone, into the type of woman the user has entered as his preference. So right now, I'm the kind of woman Count Braujou fancies. But how about you, D?"

D didn't move.

"It seems I'm not your cup of tea. That's unfortunate, D. Now I'll have to go about getting you to love me in another way: through you."

A faint spasm passed through D's neck. Sigma's fiendish product had transferred over to him.

Sliding off the Hunter's back, Sue's body fell to the floor.

Staggering over to the wall, D used one hand to support himself. A long sigh escaped his lips, followed by a second, then a third, but by the fifth his breathing had returned to normal.

Matthew widened his eyes.

The count had stood by the door glaring at him, and he'd remained in exactly that pose as he toppled forward like a felled tree. A sound louder than he could have imagined shook the air, but the floor didn't tremble in the least.

At that moment, part of the fortress's sensors and several dozen of the androids became inoperative, only to spring back to life a few seconds later.

Getting up, Matthew looked at his other foe—Curio. After confirming that the man wasn't moving at all, the boy approached with trepidation. The man he rolled over had death indelibly stamped on his ashen face.

As Matthew edged closer to the doorway with the same fearful steps, the count's body became a mountain on the move. Leaving a scream in his wake, the boy dashed toward the door, but it didn't open, and unable to find the switch, Matthew could do nothing but turn and watch as the giant slowly rose.

In the heart of the fortress, a deadly battle was taking place unbeknownst to anyone.

"Well played, Sigma," the left hand said to its distant opponent, its tone equal parts shock and admiration. From the wrist to the fingertips, it was charred black. "That's some pretty tough protection you've got. But you've used too much power against me. We're nearly finished—what's this?"

Reading the lines of letters and numbers scrolling on the control panel, the left hand clucked its tongue.

"You've gotta be pretty beat, too. On top of that, you're ready to send another terminal at us?"

Lights flashed above the charred form. The luminous points around it were in their death throes. Sigma's attack hadn't ended with the left hand.

Shapeless and colorless, with nothing to betray their presence, Sigma's terminals could take possession of both people and machines, even bringing the dead back to life. If their numbers increased any more, it would clearly be more than D's hand could manage.

With the limp form of Sue over one shoulder, D was leaving the bathroom when Count Braujou and a group of androids came by.

"Suddenly, all the sensors and androids were back to normal. That was your doing, I take it. Where's Sigma's pawn?"

D touched his right forefinger to his temple.

The count knitted his brow, and then a stunned look spread over his face as he leveled his long spear at D.

"In your head? You wouldn't!"

"Your sensors are back online, aren't they?"

It took the count a few seconds to understand what the Hunter meant by that.

"He's dead, then?"

On seeing D nod slightly, the count said, "You let that thing possess you so you could destroy it in a battle of wills? D, what in the world are you?"

"Where's Matthew?" D asked.

"In the underground armory. He's with one of the androids disguised as me. It should be bringing him here soon. What happened to the girl?"

"She grew up a little too fast."

The count looked blank, but shaking his head, he said, "Take her to the hospital. There's a skilled physician there."

Following the count as he led the way, D put his right hand into his coat pocket and touched the exposed circuitry of the sensor he'd put together in fifteen minutes. The first possessed person the device had revealed was Sue. Of course, the Hunter had only played along with her to allow Sigma's terminal to transfer over to himself, where he could dispose of it. Though it would've been possible to render Sue unconscious, a problem would have arisen if he hadn't gotten the entity to leave her. The question remained of whether the advances Sue had made while transformed into a grown woman were entirely due to the will of the entity possessing her.

Now on the back of one of the androids, Sue had started breathing serenely. Perhaps the girl was fortunate to be oblivious to the fact that as D looked at her, his eyes didn't show even a flicker of emotion.

From the other end of the corridor, another Count Braujou appeared with Matthew.

It was at that moment that the lights went out. Warning klaxons resounded, and throughout the fortress a mechanical voice announced, "We are under attack from all sides. Range: five hundred yards. All personnel to battle stations. I repeat: we are under attack from all sides. All personnel to battle stations."

III

Their foe appeared suddenly—quite suddenly. By the time the fortress's three-dimensional radar confirmed their presence, ranks of soldiers in camouflage were already at the moat, working to construct the bridges that would be necessary to cross the water. An instant before the barrier was set up a dimensional-vortex missile launched from afar went into the fortress, sucking some of its storehouses into another dimension, but the barrier negated all other attacks. The warning D and the others heard came between that first shot and the rest.

Sue and Matthew got into an ultra-high-speed elevator with Braujou, with the impatient count telling D he would go on ahead to the operations center before the doors closed, leaving the Hunter behind. He was left with the faux-count android that had accompanied Matthew. Despite the fact that Braujou himself had constructed it, he couldn't stand to have a copy of himself around, and he'd kicked the machine out of the elevator.

The android count stared at D, who approached without saying a word. Their eyes met.

D sensed something. He made a great leap to the right, while the long spear that came whistling down on the spot he had occupied struck with sufficient force to crack the stone floor.

D had his sword at the ready.

"So, you've been possessed?" he said indifferently. It didn't seem to matter a whit to this young man whether he was right or not.

"You're very perceptive," the count replied, breaking into a grin. "While I was with Matthew, I became possessed. You'll have to match steel with me, D!"

"Are you one of Sigma's terminals?"

"Yes."

D found nothing surprising about this third terminal—the "new" foe his left hand had identified. For this young man, foes existed to be slain—that's all there was to it.

The "count" closed the distance between them—the possessed android had already discovered it was useless to try to play games with D. The spear thrusted repeatedly. Anyone could've seen its attacks weren't lacking in power. If D had tried to parry one, his sword would have been broken or knocked out of his hands. But before the Hunter could do anything, he'd have to contend with the swiftness of those repeated jabs.

The android count made thirty thrusts a second, and D dodged or blocked them all. The Hunter's parries were intense. Though it stood twelve feet away, the sentry couldn't come any closer. Both its hands were numb—they'd lost some of their functionality. It made one more jab using all its deadly skill—but though it possessed the utmost speed and precision, its attacks followed a certain pattern.

Batting away the long spear with terrific force, D kicked off the ground. He became a black shooting star flying toward the giant's chest. His blade bit deep.

When one of this young man's strokes landed, it didn't matter if his foe were human, Noble, or android. His sword had pierced a vital point—the section of the chest where the electronic brain was housed. Electromagnetic waves flew in all directions, tingeing D's exquisite countenance blue.

For an instant, the world shook violently, and from above the heads of the pair a vast amount of stony rubble and other building materials rained down.

The barrier had vanished. One of the missiles had scored a direct hit on the same floor where D was doing battle.

"I did it!" the blackened hand exclaimed atop the half-melted crystals. "You see that, Sigma? You're finished, so kiss your ass goodbye!"

The left hand made a fist and bounced up into the air, but around it the points of light were rapidly fading.

"Damn, did we get taken out, too? Well, we'll be back online in two seconds. Hang on, D!"

It was during those two seconds that the missile exploded.

When D managed to extract himself from the mountain of rubble, there was no sign of the faux count anywhere. That it was pinned under the wreckage seemed the least plausible scenario.

Two seconds later, the barrier was up again, but during that time the enemy, in flying gear, had crossed the moat and gotten about thirty men into the fortress. Lasers, missiles, and particle-cannon fire greeted them. Before the might of a defensive system that incorporated the Sacred Ancestor's technology, the enemy soldiers were slain one after another, and all of them were gunned down within an hour. The corpses of each and every enemy soldier were delivered to Count Braujou in the operations center. Taking one look at them, the count arched his eyebrows and snatched up a lifeless body.

"What's this?"

It was a dead tree branch less than a foot and a half in length.

The android count staggered aimlessly down the corridor. It had been given a backup electronic brain that supported the one damaged by D's blow, and this brain was allowing it to move its legs. However, its foe's attack had been sharp and precise. The shock had damaged the backup brain, and the android ultimately toppled in an empty stretch of corridor.

It was waiting for a death from which there would be no waking, but just then an incredibly large and wicked presence spread out above it.

"Hmm. One of Sigma's terminals, are you?" the voice said.

The speaker made no attempt to touch it.

"In that case, you should be able to possess people. Do you still have enough strength to transfer?"

Was this a friend or a foe? The possessed android couldn't decide, but for some reason it didn't feel like fighting. The being sapped even its electronic will.

"Seurat, put out your hand."

The android watched as an enormous hand stretched out by its face. It was about as large as the possessed android's own. But it couldn't possibly belong to the source of the voice. It knew that much. No matter how large the hand might have been, it still belonged to a living creature from this world. However, the source of the voice was not—he was something else entirely.

Using considerable strength, the faux count brought its right hand up to the outstretched one. As always, the final transfer was far from dramatic.

"Good enough," it heard a voice say once it was inside the persona of Seurat.

†

"Who are you supposed to be?" the count called out to the gigantic figure up ahead.

Halting, the shadowy form turned and looked.

"Dear me," the Nobleman said in spite of himself.

With a frame about the same size as the count's, the figure wore the blue shirt and black vest that were considered standard warrior attire, and stuck through the belt that girded his waist was a weapon—a longsword. The man's gloves and slacks were also black.

"Who are you?"

"Seurat is the name," the giant replied, putting his feet together and making a slight bow. His eyes never left the count.

"You're one of Valcua's seven, aren't you?"

Braujou could recall hearing the name before.

"That is correct. And you would be Count Braujou. Just the man I was looking for. I slipped in here during that missile explosion, but I have no idea where the children in question are. Kindly tell me where I might find them."

"Hmph! And if I refuse?"

"Then you'll leave me no choice. I'll resort to my sword."

The blade glistened in the giant's right hand. But when had he drawn it?

He was the last of Valcua's seven—Seurat. Now he stood against a Greater Noble.

Outside, the battle still raged. But where was D?

END

Postscript

What I remember about *Tyrant's Stars* is where I wrote it. Actually, I'd completely forgotten until I was asked to pen this postscript, and I was surprised when I looked at the postscript to the Japanese edition and saw it there. Where should I write it but Istanbul in Turkey?

Even on a sightseeing excursion overseas, I write manuscripts. You finish seeing the sights, have dinner, take a shower, and then relax . . . but I just can't take it easy like that. On a trip overseas for ten days to two weeks, I'll write anywhere from one hundred fifty to three hundred pages. Even in Japan, I'll write anywhere. On the platform for a train out to the airport, in the train, in a taxi—although the wildest of all had to be the time when a deadline coincided with the final showing of a movie I wanted to see and I was actually writing at the theater. I'm not talking about sitting on a sofa in the lobby between shows. I mean in my seat, while the movie was playing. Fortunately it was a movie I'd seen before, so I knew which parts I wanted to see and which parts didn't really matter. During the latter, I wrote by the light of the screen. Of course, that wasn't bright enough. Since I couldn't see the lines on the paper, I went by instinct. Just trying to get in the general area, you could say. When I checked what I'd written later, everything pretty much lined up, which was beyond strange and downright comedic! Even I had a good laugh that time.

That's how I am, so when I go overseas it's no different. While the bus is headed toward our destination, I write like mad . . . I only steal peeks at the scenery. But still it stays with me as a series of memories. Later, when I compare them to the recollections of my traveling companions, they overlap for the most part. Said companions then give me an odd look for a while, as if they were scrutinizing an alien disguised as a human being. Even I think it's kind of a shame after going to all the trouble of visiting a foreign country.

On a plane though, with just sky and clouds around me, nothing beats writing. The blinds get drawn and everyone goes to sleep. But since I do my work while other people sleep, my pen just keeps going.

While we're on the subject, I have this particular habit of always doing something while I write. On the way to New York, this inconvenienced those around me, but that discussion will have to wait until the next volume.

Hideyuki Kikuchi
August 19, 2010
while watching *Horror Hotel*

And now, a preview of the next book in the
Vampire Hunter D series

VAMPIRE HUNTER D

VOLUME 17

TYRANT'S STARS PARTS THREE AND FOUR

Written by
Hideyuki Kikuchi

Illustrations by
Yoshitaka Amano

English translation by
Kevin Leahy

Coming in Fall 2011
from Dark Horse Books and Digital Manga Publishing

The Offensive

I

It was quiet.

The fighting outside didn't reach the interior of the fortress at all. The Sacred Ancestor's technology had become a barrier that repelled every last one of the enemy's attacks. Seen from a distance, the fortress must've appeared to be wrapped in a ball of blue light. This was due to the ceaseless bombardment of lithium atom rounds and proton missiles. However, the fortress's antiaircraft weapons were shooting down these inbound birds of death one after another, while laser and particle cannons seared enemy troops in rapid succession. Anyone could see the soundness of the fortress hadn't diminished an iota.

The door on the elevator to the operations center opened and a dashing man in black appeared. The androids that focused their electronic eyes on him halted for a moment. He was so exquisite, even their electronic brains were briefly left inoperative.

Glancing around the operations center, which seemed shrouded in a bluish twilight, D asked, "Where's the count?"

"He's not here," one of the androids replied. "It really wasn't in his nature to watch the fighting from afar. So he said he was going to join the action."

"Do you know his location?" D asked.

A vast diagram in glowing lines appeared in the space before him: schematics of the fortress. A single red point glowed on them.

"He's in the second armory," the android told the Hunter.

From his fighting pose, his strength was evident.

Taking a glance at Seurat in his figure-eight stance, the count smiled and said, "Oh, you're good."

It was a warrior's nature to burn with a longing for battle when he encountered a formidable opponent. Going from a middle position to a low one, Braujou lowered the head of his spear. It was an invitation.

Seurat accepted it. Taking a step forward, he swung his sword at the right side of the count's neck with all his might.

I'm faster, the count thought.

His spear was ready to deflect the edge of his foe's blade—but it met only air. He saw Seurat so close their noses were nearly touching. The assassin's face was devoid of character, like a machine with eyes and a nose.

Steel bit into the nape of his neck. It ripped through the count's skin and innards like they were water, only stopping when it hit his spine.

"Wish I could let that heal," Seurat said, oddly enough, as he pulled his longsword back out.

Before the count fell, his foe pierced him through the heart.

The enemy assault seemed endless. A fresh volley of missiles exploded against the barrier, their light sliding across it like blue ripples.

"A hole has been made in sector three of the barrier!"

"Energy patch complete. Repairs took six nanoseconds. It's believed the aerial projectile was a worm hole."

Turning his back on the mechanical voice's softly spoken account, D exited the operations center. Taking the electromagnetic elevator both vertically and horizontally, he headed toward the infirmary, where Sue was.

The elevator wasn't a box, but rather a condensed, subdimensional version of the electromagnetic waves that ran through the center of an electromagnetic coil. Ignoring the law of inertia in instantaneous movements horizontally or vertically, the person inside didn't feel any kind of shock at all. For a door, there was merely an elliptical opening.

Without warning, D ordered, "Take me back to the floor we just passed."

His destination was verbally relayed to the mother computer. "Understood."

As it gave this reply, an opening appeared in the center of the greenish glow.

A savage lust for killing blustered in. Anyone but D would've covered their face and curled into a ball.

When D stepped out, a gigantic black figure that might've been mistaken for the count was standing about thirty feet down the hall. At his feet lay the actual count.

The gigantic figure noticed D, too. Not bothering to sheathe the longsword he carried, he asked, "You're D, aren't you?"

Perhaps he didn't expect an answer, because he immediately continued, "I'm . . . Seurat. One of Valcua's seven. I just slew this one."

He turned his eyes to the count, who lay at his feet, and then returned them to D.

D saw the giant's right hand move to bat down all three of the wooden needles the Hunter had hurled.

"Just what I'd expect . . . from D," Seurat said, the young man in black reflected in his narrow eyes. "No mercy for his foes . . . is what I'd heard . . . But to take it to such a level . . . It makes me . . . burn for battle now."

A cracking sound came from his right hand as he adjusted his grip on the hilt of his sword. He still didn't understand D.

While he was adjusting his grip, D kicked off the floor, and by the time Seurat reflexively leaped back, raising his sword, the Hunter was above him, bringing his sword down fast—and splitting the giant's head open to the bridge of his nose. D twisted his body in midair to avoid a lightning-fast thrust, something only the Hunter could do.

As he landed, another slash came at his head. With only the tips of his toes making contact with the floor, D made a bound to the right as he hurled a rough wooden needle. Aimed right between Seurat's eyes, the needle disappeared the very instant it seemed to pierce the giant, just like D's slash of a second earlier.

Seurat charged forward, his sword splitting D's left shoulder open. Bright blood went flying. It seemed to possess a will of its own as it slapped against the face of the still-pouncing Seurat, blinding him.

A black cyclone zipped to the chest of the stock-still assassin, sinking into him. The Hunter's blade ran through his heart. At least that was the intent, but the giant leaped back beyond the weapon's tip, and the elevator to his rear opened. The blade of the sword disappeared.

As he wiped away the blood that covered his eyes, Seurat started to leap for the elevator, but then he stopped dead in his tracks. The huge figure that stepped forward blocked his way. Even on realizing that it was Count Braujou, with long spear in hand, Seurat didn't look surprised.

"That other one was a well-made android. Are you the original?"

"Rest assured," the count replied, smiling ferociously. "Though its innards might look just like mine, it won't turn to dust when it's destroyed. But you'll be the one who falls now."

Though he made a beautiful bound to avoid a horizontal swipe of the long spear, Seurat still found himself in an unprecedented predicament. Behind him an amazingly eerie aura closed in—D.

"D, this fellow wounded you and remains unharmed. What is he?" the Nobleman inquired, but perhaps he realized the Hunter might not reply, for he continued, "Are you one of Valcua's seven?"

"My name is Seurat," the giant replied.

"How polite of you to say so. And because you've made such a favorable impression on me, I'll now send you to your reward!"

As the Nobleman took a fighting stance with his long spear, Seurat was the focus of a deadly determination. D and Count Braujou—against these two, even this fiend who'd used some bizarre power to keep the android count from landing a single blow and who'd made D's blade disappear seemed unlikely to escape unscathed. Nor were these the kind of men who'd be foolish enough to take turns fighting him one on one. Still, Seurat's face was free of emotion as he took a figure-eight stance with his longsword.

"Well—" the count said, and then the air changed.

It was the kind of phenomenon that occurred when someone who had no place in this world appeared.

"But that's—" the count began, his words sounding like a death rattle.

There was an incredible being present now. The overwhelming presence seemed to wrap around the count's bones and crush them, leaving him reeling. The air he inhaled in a desperate breath burned in his chest like acid.

And while all this was happening, a tone that was cool and unspeakably soft yet equally powerful said, "So, you've come, Valcua?"

"We meet again, eh?" came the reply, in a voice that was quiet but still had the angry ring of thunder to it. "I gave you a warning before you entered the village of Marthias. Do you remember?"

There was no reply. D was merely staring at a single point in space.

"Good enough. You're just a small fry, but an interesting small fry. I believe I'll grant you an audience. Right now, I'm in the fortress's reactor. Get here within a minute's time. If not, the fortress will be reduced to a fireball before another minute has passed. Braujou, I leave your fate in that man's hands."

"There's nothing I'd like better," the count said in a tone brimming with confidence. On hearing D's voice, he'd been freed from the spell of the Ultimate Noble.

The air eddied. Valcua's presence had departed. There was no sign of Seurat, either.

Looking at D, the count heaved a sigh. "I'll be a laughingstock till the end of my days, but may I ask you to do this?"

Before turning around, D gave a faint nod.

Watching the figure in black as he was swallowed by the elevator's door, the count let out another sigh.

"Seurat, was it? It looks like I'll have to analyze his power."

The Nobleman's nerves were far from calm.

Who was that man, and who was the overpowering "Ultimate Noble" who wouldn't show himself?

Before a huge door, D halted. On the other side of this fifteen-foot-thick entry of ultradense steel, the reactor that gave life to this fortress burned with the intense energy released when protons came into contact with antiprotons.

"I'm inside. Thirty seconds left—you don't have much time. I feel it only fair to warn you that anyone whose DNA hasn't been encoded into the Sacred Ancestor's technology won't even be able to touch the door. Keep that in mind as you make your attempt."

Already the computer had drawn a bead on D with a dimensional-vortex cannon.

D stepped forward.

"Ready to die?" Valcua's voice sneered.

Purple light fell from the ceiling straight down on D. The instant D's form rose from it the light faded, becoming a single beam that penetrated the center of the door. Slowly the door opened down the middle, allowing D to enter.

"Oh, my—not bad for a small fry!" Valcua said, his voice containing relatively little surprise.

This in itself was worthy of admiration. A person with his DNA encoded into the Sacred Ancestor's technology—that was tantamount to saying someone came from the Sacred Ancestor's bloodline. Valcua wasn't surprised by this. And he himself had made it inside.

"But you're too late. It's already three seconds in. The reactor will collapse in fifty-seven seconds. Neither Braujou nor Miranda can press the switch to stop it. Only the Sacred Ancestor could start or stop a meltdown."

As D turned without a moment's pause toward the reactor, he heard a sweet female voice say, "Collapse in fifty-one seconds. Fifty seconds . . ."

II

Who had selected that lovely female voice to inform them of impending death and destruction? Despite the pronouncements by the angel of death, D didn't seem at all afraid as he walked with great strides to the front of the reactor.

"What happened to your left hand?" Valcua's voice inquired mockingly. He'd said he was inside the reactor, but there was no sign of him.

Though the reactor was regulated from a control room, there were also controls inside the reactor itself for use in an emergency. The reason D chose the latter was simple: the reactor was closer.

"When those three who didn't know their place planned this citadel to escape my wrath, they needed the aid of the Sacred Ancestor to design this reactor. First came the reactor, and then the fortress was constructed around it. It is, quite literally, the source of life here. D, can you prevent it from becoming the cause of death?"

As the Ultimate Noble sought an answer to this, D didn't appear to look for him, but rather stood directly before the reactor.

The woman's voice counted out forty-six seconds.

Countless silvery grains rose up on all sides. In the blink of an eye they covered D's body, and then disappeared in another blink. They had been drawn into D's flesh.

At almost the same time, a green object appeared before D's eyes. Although the slim and graceful woman's hand was glowing green, it seemed somehow pale and white.

"Dear me," Valcua exclaimed, and this time he couldn't hide the hint of admiration in his voice.

D took hold of it with his right hand.

The female voice counted off, "Two seconds. One second."

Nothing changed, except for the female voice ceasing its count. The fires of hell that only those of the Sacred Ancestor's bloodline could control had been splendidly kept in check.

Looking up toward the ceiling as if nothing had transpired, D said, "Come out."

It wasn't a challenge. It was a command. A mere Hunter was ordering the Ultimate Noble to show himself.

In a tone that didn't hide his surprise, Valcua said, "So, you have the blood of the Sacred Ancestor in you?"

However, he soon retracted this, saying with absolute arrogance, "No, a drudge like you couldn't be one of his descendants. I don't know what kind of device you might have or where you might've acquired it, but this farce has gone on long enough. Die!"

D blocked the streak of light that plummeted straight down at him with his sword. The sparks burned D's shadow onto the floor. Bounding to either side without a sound, the pair switched places, a fierce will to kill binding them together.

D saw the Ultimate Noble for the first time. Quite similar to the Hunter in height and build, Valcua wore a golden cape. Given the hard, gleaming flecks that covered its surface, the garment seemed to be woven from some sort of metallic fiber. Beneath the cape, his torso and limbs were wrapped in lumpy pieces of bluish-green armor. His weapon was the golden light he gripped with his right hand. It wasn't metal, but rather seemed to be an ionlike substance that had undergone additional chemical treatment.

Not bothering to change stance, Valcua called out, "D!"

His voice emerged from a screen of gold. His forelock hung down to his chin, concealing his eyes, nose, and mouth, while the rest of his hair reached his waist.

"Nicely blocked. I imagine that is the proper response. Who are you, sir?"

D's toes inched forward.

"My goodness—you send a chill down the spine of the great Valcua and make my blood run cold. Who knew there was such a man in the world besides him and myself? It would be a shame to kill you. D, will you not join forces with me? Of course, in order to do that, the traitor and the two children would need to be dealt with first. Oh!"

Valcua raised his right hand. His sword of light sent a stream of gleaming particles at D, and the Hunter held his blade up straight to parry them. The light was slashed down the middle.

There was no change at all to the sword D held upright, and from his present position he leaped over Valcua. There was a clang, and sparks went flying. The blade of D's sword had been blocked over Valcua's head.

Roughly three feet in diameter, the perfectly circular shield had the same golden glow as the Ultimate Noble's sword of light. His foe hadn't kept it concealed. Valcua must've had the power to create it from thin air.

Light challenged light. There was no hesitation in D's attack. Striking with breathless speed, D's sword was dodged, parried, and countered with glowing thrusts as Valcua backed away.

As D parried one of these attacks, there came a momentary opening. The shield pushed forward. As if driven by the force of the wind, D leaped back. The glowing blade pursued him. When D deflected it, it broke off at an angle, flying up to sink into the reactor's outer walls.

Before D had even landed, a red light winked on in the room.

"Damage extends to the third layer of shielding," a mechanical voice informed them. "Repair systems operational. Level-five damage verified. Level-five damage verified. "

"Repairs are urgently needed. Repairs are urgently needed."

"It looks as if not even the Sacred Ancestor's technology could guard against the Sacred Ancestor's destructive power," Valcua said, his golden face upturned a little. There was bitterness mixed in his voice. "As this destruction wasn't at my bidding, there's nothing I can do about it. I suppose I should leave before I'm caught up in the consequences. D, won't you come with me?"

Even after their deadly battle, did Valcua still intend to win D over?

The outline of his form became indistinct and he was transformed into a gaseous mass that resembled gold and black oil paints swirled together. Once the air had assimilated it, D sheathed his sword and started walking toward the door.

"At present, repairs are under way. Repairs are under way. The damage has not been contained. The damage has not been contained."

"A dimensional fusing is required. Development of the technology is under way."

The stern voices of the machines came from behind the Hunter. They sounded frantic.

D was just coming out the door when he met a familiar face. Moving down the hall was his charred left hand.

"You're late," D said.

"What are you talking about? I finally silenced Sigma. Just look at the shape I'm in!"

"Did you destroy Sigma?"

"I can't say that for sure," it replied, its tone dropping. "At the very least, I left 'im so he won't be able to ever send another terminal at us. But as for whether or not his main form has been shut down—"

"The reactor's been damaged," D said.

"What?"

"The damage was done by one of the Sacred Ancestor's weapons. I need your help."

"You intend to get even more work out of me? You're absolutely heartless, like some kind of beautiful demon."

Even as it cursed him, it made mention of his beauty. D had that effect on everyone.

Leaving his left hand, D walked toward the elevator. Seen from behind, he was an exquisite sight befitting the stillness in the hall.

Even now, inside and out, a horrible battle to the death that burned everything down to its very atoms was growing even more intense. Within the fortress, klaxons had resounded for several minutes. The security computers that hadn't noticed Valcua's entry had awakened from the sleeplike spell that had been over them during D's pitched battle.

Even in the fortress's infirmary, security had its eyes and swords ready to strike down any intruders. Although this facility was intended in part for the trio of Nobles who'd constructed the fortress, there were also a number of sickrooms for any humans who served them. Behind a door protected by android sentries were Sue and Matthew.

Less than two minutes after D's fierce battle with Valcua, another android was walking past the infirmary. Once it came to the door, it suddenly turned and headed straight for the children's room.

"Halt," the sentries said, raising the particle cannons mounted on their arms, but that did nothing to stop its advance. Blue and white lights focused on the intruder, becoming blinding, cracked streaks that clung to every inch of it. The android shuddered, tumbling forward before the memory banks of its control unit were destroyed. Still lying as it had fallen, it reached out with its right hand and touched the foot of the sentry in front of it.

A heartbeat later the android it touched turned toward another sentry and subjected it to the same attack. Ignoring its compatriot as it too fell forward, the sentry drew a bead on the circuits for accessing the sick room with its particle cannon.

Matthew was gazing at the face of the slumbering Sue. Ever since he'd been brought back by the same android count that had led him into a trap before returning to its senses, Sue had been asleep. He'd heard she'd been possessed by part of something sent to defeat D. Apparently she'd lost consciousness as a result of that thing leaving her, but as the boy intently watched her sleeping face, something dangerous stirred in his heart.

Ever since she was a child, he'd found Sue's face to be endearing as she slumbered, and he would wait until she fell asleep before watching her for ages solely by the light of the moon. Even after they got separate bedrooms, he never tired of sneaking in under cover of night to gaze at her. In those days, they were still on the farm, and their mother was with them. But now that he was free of the bonds of that mundane existence, was the face of his soundly sleeping sister so lovely it stirred desire in him?

When he'd learned that his sister had fallen for a man, it bothered Matthew so much it nearly drove him crazy. And when Count Braujou pointed out that the man in question was D, the boy really did lose his mind. He'd attacked Sue, and as a result he'd only driven her further away. What little remained of his reason scolded him, telling him that her reaction was only natural, but now that the two of them were alone again he was finding it hard to restrain the manly urges bubbling up inside him.

Grabbing Sue's blanket, he pulled it all the way down to her belly. She was wearing pajamas. Matthew's face looked even stranger than Sue's had when she was possessed.

Unbuttoning her pajamas, he opened the front of them. Sue didn't move a muscle, which only emboldened Matthew. The flesh beneath the fabric revealed a pair of sizable swells that seemed fitting for someone her age, if not somewhat large given her fragile appearance.

Matthew's Adam's apple bobbed madly. Bringing his face closer to the pale pink tip of her breast, he took a breath as if he could stand it no longer, and then took his sister's nipple in his mouth. Sue's body twitched a little. After lightly sucking on her breast, Matthew directed his obsession to her lovely mouth. As her rosy lips continued to draw thread-thin breaths, the boy licked his own lips and brought them closer.

The door abruptly opened just as their lips were about to come together. It was an android sentry.

"What do you want?"

"The enemy is approaching. Please come with me."

The android came closer.

"Where are we going? What's the count doing? And what about D?"

"Both of them are fighting a defensive action. I will deliver the two of you to a safe area."

"But—"

The instant his field of view was filled by the pale blue light that shot from the sentry's right side, Matthew wondered if heaven wasn't punishing him.

III

In the operations center, D, who'd paid a call on the infirmary, informed Count Braujou that the two children were missing.

"They're gone?" the giant said to the three-dimensional holographic image of D, giving him an intense look as he took a swipe with his long spear. Three androids were sent flying, only to collapse and burst into flames.

"The sentries have been felled? What the hell have the security computers been doing? Rest assured—no matter how they got in here, so long as the barrier is up, they can't get out of the fortress."

"If they could get in, they can also get out," D said softly. "So long as Valcua is here, the barrier means nothing. I'm heading out."

"Very well, I'll go with you."

The Nobleman had intended to go out and join the fighting all along, but after the computer notified him of D's battle with Seurat, he'd gone to the operations center with hopes dashed. In his heart, his wicked Noble blood ran hot.

When the count got down to the combat exit, D was already astride a white steed. They hadn't summoned a single android soldier. The two of them pushed their way into the thick of the enemy troops, who were like a swarm of bees. Neither of them found it strange.

"Take these," the count said, throwing the Hunter something that looked like a pair of goggles.

"They're an information terminal. An SRPV surveillance drone has already been dispatched. It should locate the children within two minutes' time. When it does, I'll cut a path through the enemy. You'll have to rescue them, D."

Of course, there was no reply to this.

D put the goggles on. They fit well—to be more precise, their weight was negligible and they didn't seem bulky. There was no change to visibility with them on, either.

"Give them commands verbally. We'll soon—"

That was as far as the count got before glowing green lines made a topographical map that filled his field of view. Four luminous points were on the move.

"Expand those points."

Instantly, they took on the form of three humans and an android. Seurat and the android were carrying Sue and Matthew draped across their shoulders.

"The forest to the west," the count said, and then the fugitives halted.

A cyborg horse twice the normal size was tethered to the trunk of a colossal tree.

"On horseback, he'll make for the highway to the west and keep going all the way to Valcua's domain—he must intend to head north. Let's give chase!"

The count was also astride an enormous horse. Behind him was his car.

"It looks like the night will be at an end soon," he remarked in an unusual tone that made it sound like he was making excuses.

He then turned to D and asked, "What happened to your left hand?"

It was missing from the wrist down.

"It's on the job," D responded.

Whether repairs to the reactor were going well or not was unknown.

"Well then, let's go!"

At the same time the count gave a pull to the reins of the gigantic steed, the doors opened. From there they went straight through the central courtyard where a black dirt road stretched toward the distant gates.

First went D, followed by the count and the car. Thirty feet away, the main gates opened. The words "Barrier removal" danced across their goggles. At the same time, crimson streaks of light flew all around the pair. Struck by them, a portion of the ramparts instantly evaporated.

They crossed the bridge. About a thousand yards ahead, the enemy forces pressed forward. In front of them a titanic pillar of flame went up. The fireball that swelled from it swallowed all their foes in a fifty-yard radius. It was the work of a miniature missile launched from the fortress.

The air was still searing hot as D and his mount bounded forward. The reins were wrapped around his left forearm, while his right hand merely rested on them. As the white steed galloped like it was possessed, the enemy troops closed on it. From the horse's back, a stark flash of light mowed through them, and they fell. Severed heads and torsos promptly changed into dead branches. Valcua's magic was gone.

Enemies with rifles at the ready were mowed down by a blue light. The blistering particle beam of seven hundred thousand degrees was fired from a cannon mounted on the roof of the count's vehicle, and it evaporated not only the soldiers, but also trees and earth.

However, ahead of the pair the enemy milled in a thick black swarm, firing beams and missiles at them. The count's car was hit by the shots, and the count himself received wounds all over his body from flames and shrapnel.

Can we catch up? he wondered.

In addition, the count's internal clock was telling him dawn was nigh. As the enemy soldiers piled up, not seeming to have dwindled in numbers at all, the first doubts crept into the count's mind.

Will we make it in time?

Just then, the air suddenly froze. Shouts and shrieks from the enemy—in fact, all sounds—were completely silenced. Even the wind died out.

"What was that?" the astonished count said in spite of himself. He was asking D. Why did he think D knew the reason for this sudden silence?

D gave an abrupt kick to the flanks of his steed.

For some reason the count forgot to try to stop him, and he was unable to even follow D, but rather watched the young man's fate unfurl.

"What's this?" Braujou cried out, and rightly so.

In front of the galloping D, the soldiers that fell beneath his horse's hooves were suddenly transformed into dead branches. D dashed right through an army of thousands, if not tens of thousands, leaving nothing but trampled tree limbs strewn in his wake. The magical might of Valcua—the Ultimate Noble—had been broken!

"What in the world is this fellow?" the count groaned, finally giving his horse a crack of the reins.

After racing down the highway for about twenty minutes, Seurat heard the beating of iron-shod hooves ringing out behind him. The android carried Sue and Matthew on the back of the giant's steed.

Turning around, Seurat was expressionless as he said, "I underestimated them. No doubt only the man known as D could've smashed through those military forces to give chase. Grand duke, what would you have me do?"

He posed this question to empty space.

A grave answer came in return.

"Just keep going. I've taken measures."

"Yes, milord!" Seurat responded, feeling a chill run down his back.

Only three hundred feet to go. D's cyborg horse was rapidly closing on the enormous steed up ahead.

Riding another three hundred feet behind him, the count's eyes widened as he said, "Such speed! I'm glad it's not me he's after—well, actually he is after me, isn't he? At any rate, I'm glad it's not me today."

He watched as the black figure of D dwindled at an astounding rate. A second later, the count gasped. D had sunk without warning. And not just him, but the gigantic horse ahead of him as well. The ground had collapsed. And the black chasm was headed straight for him.

"This is bad!"

The Nobleman jerked the reins to make a sudden stop, but his body went flying through the air. In midair, the count saw his cyborg horse trip and the car behind it slam into the beast.

A section of road twenty feet wide and four hundred and fifty feet long had given way. It wasn't an explosion or an earthquake. The molecular structure of the ground had been altered, leaving it in an extremely weakened condition.

Were these the "measures" Valcua had taken?

As the ground swallowed him up, D took the reins in his teeth. Using the strength of his two arms and his mouth to control his cyborg horse, he demonstrated a skill that could only be described as wondrous. Though his steed sank up to the Hunter's knees into ground that now resembled pumice, it went no deeper. Skillfully working its four legs, the horse moved relentlessly, as if seeking solid footing.

No longer sinking but still not rising, D watched as Seurat, the giant steed he rode, and the siblings were swallowed by the colossal cavern that opened in the ground.

A sound became audible. A splash. Obviously there was a river running deep underground.

The earth and sand suddenly began to subside much more quickly. The water had begun to wash them away.

Seurat and the others were swallowed by the darkness.

It took about ten seconds for D to hit the water. Cyborg horses could swim across rivers where it was too deep for people to stand. However, the current here trumped that ability.

As he was swept away, mount and all, D focused his gaze behind him and ahead of him. He couldn't see Seurat, his gigantic horse, or the Dyalhis siblings. All that flowed through the massive underground cavern was black water. The cavern must've been at least thirty feet high.

Unexpectedly, the Hunter's horse sank. Something had dragged it underwater. And D went right with it.

The Nobility—and others with vampire blood—were known to have problems with water. Of particular note was their inability to cross running water. When completely immersed, a dhampir lost almost all of his Noble strength, leaving him with only the power of a normal human being at his disposal.

Even underwater D's eyesight was perfect. Leaving the saddle of his cyborg horse, he drew his sword.

The woman who appeared from behind the white steed had a long, white robe streaming out behind her like the garb of the celestial maidens. It was the water witch, Lucienne. Although this sorceress had been evaporated by the flames from a torch, she'd apparently survived by fleeing underground.

"So nice of you to come into my country, D!" she said, her voice as sensuous as ever.

However, the right side of her face was melted and her lips were half gone, leaving teeth and gums exposed. Scorched by fire on the ground above, it appeared she hadn't been healed even after returning to the font of her life.

"You may be invincible on dry land, but you can't defeat me here. Eventually I'll tear Count Braujou and Duchess Miranda to bits in my world, too. But you shall be the first."

A white piece of fabric closed on D. Lucienne had pulled it from her clothing. No doubt her raiment was composed of many such pieces stitched together.

D swung his sword. The fabric wasn't cut. It wrapped gently around the blade, robbing it of its cutting edge.

Lucienne laughed seductively. Her clothing had already broken down into a number of strips that lingered around her naked form as if loath to leave her. Her pale female physique had retained its perfect beauty, and even half-melted, her face had lost none of its former loveliness, giving this sorceress an allure beyond compare.

Her right hand pointed at D. Cloth flowed over and latched onto his shoulder, upper arm, and wrist, winding around D from the right shoulder down to the waist. His sword arm was restricted. Another strip wrapped around his throat like a pale arm.

Bubbles rose from D's mouth. His air had run out.